WINGS OF WAX

APOLLO PAPAFRANGOU

OLIVE LEAF

EDITIONS

To Sean,

Enjoy the ascent
on new found wings!

Apollo Robbins

5/2⅔/17

For my father and all the family in Greece.

To Katie for a heart's worth of adventure and plenty true luck!

ONE

ANGELO KOUTOUVALIS HAS long anticipated this day, this most difficult moment, and now it seems doubtful he'll survive it. He wields his pencil like a harpoon, but the page falls victim to a sudden tremor in his hand. White-hot tendrils of pain squeeze deep in his chest. A dim pulsing behind his eyes warns of further agony, and there are comets in his vision, auras of a massive headache brewing. He drops his pencil and draws a deep breath, exhaling slowly then inhaling again. He repeats the process until he feels reasonably certain that death isn't inevitable, at least not in the next five minutes or so.

The sketch is good, of that he is fairly certain, and he's as ready as ever to deliver it. Only a matter of walking to her table and laying it down. He scrutinizes the pencil strokes for a flaw which isn't there, just wanting to buy more time and gather his courage. The image seems a near photographic rendering of the young woman sitting nearby. He has captured every detail, from the way her bangs fall across her forehead (always combed to the left) to the pale freckles along her nose to the ornate patterning of her scarf. At last, there doesn't seem to be anything left to add.

He glances out the window, where pigeons gather on a telephone wire as if in conference. Then he's on his feet, the page dampening against his palm, the floor of the coffee shop expanding as he steps forward, the birds all seeming to watch him now. When he reaches her table, doing his best to appear casual rather than creepy, remembering to smile as if approaching her is the most natural thing, he's overcome by their sudden proximity; he's now so close he catches the scent of her perfume.

"Hi." The greeting comes out more as a gasp, and the woman doesn't lift her eyes from her phone. Angelo scans the table for inspiration, sighting a newspaper beside the woman's coffee mug. "G-g-g..." He pauses to calm his stutter, but the woman still hasn't noticed him. "Gas prices," Angelo blurts. "Up again I see?"

Really? Fossil fuels, you fuckwad? Is that the best you can do?

"Sorry?" the woman says, looking up from her text messages.

The trails in Angelo's vision have worsened into blind spots now, and he just points dumbly at the newspaper. If, as his father has told him, confidence is at the core of the Greek soul, why can't he summon any?

"Oh," the woman says. "Go ahead. I'm not reading it."

"No."

"Excuse me?"

Angelo swallows. This would all be so much easier were he a Greek native and this woman a tourist from some gloomy northern European country, Angelo able to bat his eyes and woo her with only a few choice phrases in English: "Hello, mademoiselle, do you like Greece?" or "Would you like to go for a drink and a dance?" Instead, he says, just above a whisper, "Mind if I sit down?"

The woman cocks her head, frowning. "I don't know you."

"I'm Angelo."

The woman glances around as if worried she may be the target of some prank, but upon giving Angelo another careful size-up, she offers her hand. "Sarah."

"Nice to meet you. But you didn't answer my question."

Sarah just blinks. "Which was?"

"If I can sit down."

"I'm not sure that's a good idea, Angelo."

Angelo's shoulders sag, and he nearly drops the sketch. He's about to scurry away, but something— perhaps the headache still threatening to break—holds him. "Really, Sarah, I'm harmless."

"I believe you, but..." Sarah glances around. "It isn't like there's a shortage of empty tables."

Angelo spreads his free palm. "You look like an interesting person and..."

Sarah smirks. "That's your best line? You must be harmless. Go ahead, sit. I'm leaving in a minute, anyway."

Angelo pulls up a chair. "So, I see you here a lot."

The woman raises an eyebrow. "I've never noticed you."

Angelo's cheeks go hot as he stammers a reply. "I-I work across the street. At the bird store. I come in every morning before my shift. And you're always here."

"Great. You're my stalker. At least you introduced yourself before bludgeoning me."

"I've been working on this," Angelo continues, resisting every urge to flee while revealing his sketch. "Thought you might like it."

Sarah takes the paper, and Angelo leans forward in anticipation as a slight pang in his stomach joins the mounting pulse in his head.

"This is great," Sarah says at last. "But really weird. I mean I'm flattered on the one hand. It looks exactly like me. But on the other hand, I'm more than a little freaked that you've been sitting in some corner watching me. It's creepy."

The room spins, and Angelo feels both hot and cold as if struck by the flu. Other patrons are observing now, their expressions distorted in the growing blind spots of his vision, leering like the Gorgons of ancient myth. This was a monumental misstep that still may prove fatal after all. Idiotic to think himself capable of maneuvering like his father, the ultimate fisherman, the king *kamaki*, who reeled in countless women at the end of his line.

"I'm sorry," Angelo says at last. "I didn't mean..."

"This guy bothering you, babe?"

A balloon-muscled man in an Affliction T-shirt appears, his oversize mitt caressing Sarah's shoulder. Angelo gets up, snatches his drawing, and, trying not to slink, heads for the door.

No sooner is he outside than the headache finally breaks. He makes for the crosswalk, the bird store due to open in five, but the agony halts him at the curb. Passing pedestrians become shadows, shifting around him as he stands wincing against the throbbing pain. Holding his head in his hands, the coffee shop disaster seems a distant memory. Despite himself, he can't help but be reminded of all those stories buried within him, narratives he seems to have known since before words and speech. As the hurt peaks at the crown of his head, he thinks of Athena, sprung from the skull of Zeus clad in full armor and shield, ready for war. Angelo almost worries that he, too, might give cranial birth.

He thinks of the tube, the plastic reservoir in his skull that, when functioning properly, relieves his brain of pressure and the cerebral fluid that would otherwise improperly drain. If the headache stops, it's just a headache. But if it lingers after medicine and rest, it could be more. These headaches come often, but mostly after the work day not before. A doctor once called Angelo a ticking time bomb. There's no way to tell which headache will trigger the fuse. If and when the bomb does go off, and excess cerebral fluid threatens death, the only option is to deal with the aftermath: rush to the hospital and let the doctors take over. The worst is not knowing, suffering through this time of *maybe*, of *what if*, when he empathizes most with Yiayia, unable to quiet his concerns.

He thinks of the past, of hospitals and their white linoleum. Closing his eyes, he sees the surgeons standing over him as angels in white, with soft music in the background and their voices distorted like words under water. He feels the vertigo as if this vision is real, and he can see the mask lowering onto his face, feel it clamp over his nose and mouth to bring sweet chemical breath and impenetrable darkness.

When he opens his eyes a few moments later, the headache is subsiding. No missing work, no call for emergency this time.

* * *

His shift is almost at its end. Angelo sits on a sack of canary feed in a corner of the storage room, away from customers, away from his boss. Pricing items with a label gun, he tries to forget his blunder with Sarah but determines to try again with another girl. *Carmen*. He'll confess to her that she's the one he truly wants; no more lonely mornings in coffee shops sketching women unworthy of his art. It seems he and Carmen have shared a connection since that morning nearly six months ago when Angelo, putting forth a half-assed job-hunting effort, first entered the bird shop after seeing the *HELP WANTED* sign.

Angelo soon realizes the bird toy he's been holding is layered with price tags. While pulling off the extra stickers, he hears the door open, catches a whiff of lavender, and knows instantly that Carmen has entered. With this level of stress, the headache could return at any moment. He must do this now! As he watches Carmen walk to the sink—so pretty, even in her work clothes—he slowly gets to his feet. Flecks of birdseed sprinkle his hair and stick to his apron, the air heavy with scents of bleach and damp wood.

"Hey, Carmen. Do you maybe, want to grab a c-c-coffee? Later, I mean. Tonight?"

She smiles. "Sure, Greek."

"All right. See you later." Angelo turns to leave and nearly slams into a shelf before stumbling over a sack of newspapers.

"You okay?" Carmen asks.

"Yeah. It's just these headaches. They make me clumsy."

"Aren't you forgetting something?"

Angelo looks around: Carmen is pointing to her apron, and Angelo glances at his own. "Oh, yeah. Thanks."

Now in the main store, he walks through the labyrinth of cages. Birds vocalize in unison, a cacophony of chirps, twitters, and warbles, causing his eardrums to vibrate like tiny tuning forks. The shop isn't large, yet the cages seem to stretch on infinitely, a telescoping sensation. Finally he reaches the last one in front, near the register. Skipper, the macaw, sits on her perch scratching at a spot between her wings. She smiles with her eyes as Angelo opens her cage door.

"Hey, girl. Hey." Angelo leans into the cage, makes kissy noises.

"*Haaa-looow,*" Skipper replies.

Angelo grabs fistfuls of soiled newspaper and dumps them in the trash, recalling a time when he was intimidated by Skipper's size, by her blueness. To gaze at her beauty was to become entranced, which led to further scolding from Ms. Wheeler. Now, still bent close to the cage bottom, Angelo feels the familiar prick of talons as Skipper steps off her perch and onto his wrist. Reaching his shoulder, Skipper rubs her beak against his neck. Angelo leans close to the perch and lets the bird step back onto it. After re-papering the bottom of the cage, he hands the parrot a treat and closes the door, watching the great blue macaw devour a tiny red biscuit.

"Angelo, I thought I told you to take off!" squawks Ms. Wheeler, appearing behind the counter.

Angelo is startled, as if a vulture has dropped from the sky. "Just doing one last thing."

"I can't have many more days like this one from you, Angelo. You need to pick up the pace and focus. I don't know where your head is most of the time. And I'm beginning to doubt you're right for this job." Something in her tone suggests: or right at all.

"Sorry, Ms. Wheeler. I'll try harder."

* * *

She actually said yes!

Angelo strides for home, almost marveling that Carmen accepted his invitation. At twenty-four, Angelo has asked out only two women, Carmen being the second, but that's a two-for-two success rate. Maybe quality if not quantity.

As he walks, Angelo scans the modest buildings lining the North Oakland avenues. No matter how well he knows their facades by now, he smiles whenever he spots a structure with Grecian-style columns. It's been many years, but he remembers trekking through Athens as a small child. One afternoon he was led by his mother down a path near the shopping district of Plaka—the street clogged with traffic, air heavy with exhaust. In the middle of the busy sidewalk, amid an area cordoned off by a chain-link fence, workers were digging ancient treasures from the ground. Angelo had watched as pieces of pottery were unearthed. He seemed conscious, even then, of the layers of things; a former world still existing beneath the present.

Carmen had called him by that nickname, "The Greek..."

* * *

Then he was ten years old again, standing before his fifth grade class, his body still sweat-slick from P.E. period and the taunting. He directed attention to a cork board behind him plastered with photos, his finger pointing at two in particular. The first was a large snapshot of himself standing at sunset in front of the Parthenon, the light making it appear as though he was merging with the temple. The other picture was of the Supreme Court building in Washington, D.C., and Angelo indicated the similarities between the two. As he gave this oral report of his summer vacation in Greece, he felt all eyes on him. For a few moments, he was no longer the boy who couldn't catch the ball, or the kid who missed the game-winning basket. Instead, he was a junior ambassador to this country his class had been studying; someone who had been there and seen those ruins, someone who could lift it out of the textbook and maybe make it live. As he continued to speak, the tremble in his voice steadily dissipating, he felt a sense of pride that put him on par with his classmates. Apparently the shift was visible. Later, during lunch, some kids commented on his slightly taller appearance. And that was when the nickname was first presented: Justin Wakeland began calling him The Greek, and soon others took it up. Of course, a few boys used it disparagingly, saying things like, "Hey, Greek, does that mean you like it Greek-style?" Still, for the first time, Angelo felt grateful for all those years his parents had spent infusing him with ethnic identity.

But that afternoon, when he'd strutted through the front door with his chest puffed like a rooster's and announced that, from now on, his mother and father would address him as The Greek, he was surprised when they raised their eyebrows.

Tasso had said, "*Sovara*? Well, The Greek... Or can I call you Mr. Greek? You still have to take out the garbage. *Peege, re!*"

And Despina chimed in with, "Don't go around thinking you're superior to people."

But there wasn't much risk of that. Angelo went back to feeling himself again, until high school and another short period of studying ancient Greece. A week or two in World History class, but long enough for Angelo to reap the benefits as girls batted their eyes and commented on the resemblance between his face and those of the statues in the textbook photos. However, Angelo, when he had looked in the mirror, failed to recognize this. Then time was up on ancient Greece, the class moved on to another civilization, and Angelo felt like an artifact buried again...

* * *

But now he hears The Greek in his mind, spoken from Carmen's lips in a way that lends it new vibrancy, somehow cleansed of the mud it has recently gathered in the media; "Greek" currently seems synonymous with "corrupt, tax-evader," and "austerity."

He wonders, were he to share those old photos now, the snapshots of himself standing at the Parthenon, what reaction would they inspire? But maybe, thanks to Carmen, The Greek of old has returned.

TWO

ANGELO STEPS INSIDE the house then recoils, greeted by the severed head of Medusa. Hanging from the entryway ceiling, it grimaces at him with eyes rolled back, hair coiling in an explosion of venomous locks.

"You like it? I picked it up at Mr. Vondas's store this morning."

Angelo ducks past the sculpture and finds his mother at the dining room table, poised with a red pen over a stack of student essays. People have said she resembles Irene Pappas, the actress who played the widow in *Zorba the Greek*.

"It's vivid, Ma," he says. "But hanging in the doorway like that?"

Despina chuckles. "What do I know about art?"

Angelo glances over his shoulder. "Sometimes it's not the art, just the place."

"Speaking of places, how was the bird store today?"

Angelo shrugs. "It's a living, I guess."

"No headaches?"

Angelo frowns. "One, but it went away."

"Good. Don't you have your phone with you?"

"*Huh*?"

"*Toh kinitoh sou, re.*"

"I forgot to take it this morning. Why?"

"I was trying to call you earlier. Yiayia had an accident."

"Is she okay?"

"She's all right now, but this afternoon I took her shopping, and she fainted in the middle of Mr. Vondas's store. Lucky she didn't break her hip. Second time she's fallen this week. It's best she stays with us in the guest room for a while." Despina reaches to touch her son's chin. "Must have been a good day at work, your face is beaming."

Angelo shrugs again. *Don't tempt the gods.* "Caught a little sun I guess. I'm gonna jump in the shower."

Despina nods. "After, go spend a little time with Yiayia. And you should eat something. We're having *psaria kai horta* tonight."

In the bathroom, Angelo stands naked before the mirror, tracing a finger over the scars on his abdomen, ever surprised by the lack of sensation in those inch-long ravines compared to the sensitivity of the flesh between them. He remembers how self-conscious he'd been as a child, always too shy to take off his shirt at the public pool or after P.E., understanding from an early age that he was different.

The first time he'd slept with someone—sophomore year of college—he'd been afraid the girl might cringe at the sight of those scars. But she had enjoyed touching them, kissing them even, saying they provided contrast, texture. Closing his eyes now, he's able to conjure an image of Tracy—that first love back in college—beneath him.

She wore only her panties; he still wore jeans; her legs wrapped around his waist. She stroked his cheeks, ran her finger along the bridge of his nose, over the peak of his upper lip, across his jawline. And then she whispered, "Do you even know how wet you make me?"

That whisper—even if Angelo is at the moment only imagining it—is enough to get him hard. He walks to the toilet and recalls how he had lamely wanted to respond, "Well, I had an idea, but hearing you say it is pretty cool." Instead, he had just smiled bashfully, gazing into Tracy's eyes. She had been the first woman to comment on his ability to get the juices flowing, and he now wonders if it was because of something he was actually doing or if women just naturally become moist in intimate company. The enigma is such that he forgets, at least momentarily, about tending to his erection, but then he begins to stroke. The fantasy evolves, Tracy morphing into Carmen. Angelo sees her dark hair, pouty lips, smooth bronze skin; the tops of her breasts peeking out of her blouse when she leans over in her apron. He holds the image, relishing it, his dick hot and solid against his palm.

"Angelo?"

Before he can conceal himself, the bathroom door opens. Yiayia thrusts her head in.

"Hey!" Angelo bellows, struggling to yank up his jeans.

"What you doing?"

"Nothing! Don't you know how to knock?"

"Jesus, Angelaki. You don't have to scream!"

* * *

An abundance of food is arranged on the dining room table like an offering to the gods, far too large a meal for the three mortals seated around it. Angelo piles his plate, thinking about Yiayia's eating habits or lack thereof. Yiayia never eats. She may gnaw a piece of bread, savor an olive or two, nibble a bit of feta, but that's snacking, not eating. And each time she takes a bite and chews, chews, chews, the air grows tense. Angelo and his mother brace for the inevitable verdict that will curdle the dinner. And now that Yiayia is living with them, the curdling will come on a daily basis.

"The fish," Yiayia says, frowning at her fork. "It's a leetle bit dry. Who cooked it?"

And there it is. Angelo sips water, peering over the rim of his glass, eyes flicking between his mother and grandmother.

Yiayia continues to examine the bit of cod on the end of her fork as though it has impaled itself there to mock her. Then she smiles mischievously at Angelo. "Angelo eats fast. *Pes mou, agori.* Is it because you like the taste, or you are just very hungry?"

Despina heaves a sigh. "Jesus, Mother. I cooked the fish. Who else?"

Yiayia sets her fork down and stares glumly at the table. "I never say another word."

Yiayia has the unabashed ability to say exactly what she feels whenever she feels it; like the time she innocently asked a family friend if the architect responsible for their extravagant new home had gone to school; or the day she told an acquaintance his wife was nice enough, though not a woman Yiayia would choose for any son of hers. Most people assume she's being funny; though on some occasions when she does offend someone, she will usually dismiss them as being *xeni*, as in non-Greek (no matter if they actually are Greek) and therefore oversensitive.

If Angelo had such a power, he would enter a bar, go up to the first woman of interest, and say, "Y'know, how about we cut to the chase. I really just want to lay you down." He chuckles at the notion, and Yiayia glances up from her plate.

"What's so funny?"

"Nothing, Yiayia. You should be eating."

"Ah," says Yiayia. "You gon' get on my case, too?" She reluctantly forks another bit of fish. "Let me tell you, Angelaki. Your father make the best fish soup!"

Ever the fisherman, whether the man's appetite be for sex or seafood.

"We're making nice, now?" Despina asks. "Those are about the only kind words you have for him."

"Not true! I always talk good of Tasso. After all, he come to this country a man not knowing the language beyond a few words. Within short time he was speaking English and had his contractor's license. He want something, he go after it, make it happen. He has strong mind. Full of ingenuity. He has Greek mind. Ancient Greek mind. Brain like Aristotle, he has. Angelo has same brain, too. Anyway, Despina, you and Tasso were always more like brother and sister. It better that he's now back to Greece. He happier there."

Angelo considers how things have improved since his father left seven years ago: no more yelling, the house feeling twice as large.

"Angelo," Despina says, "I was thinking you should visit your father this summer. Go to Greece. The trip would be good for you."

How? "I don't know, Ma."

"Me neither," Yiayia cuts in. "That big trip for Angelaki all by himself. What he gonna do there, anyway?"

"See the rest of his family, of course," Despina replies.

"*Bah*! They can come here. Besides, I look on the news, all these riots for the economy and crook government in Greece."

"They're rioting against the big banks, Mother. Not against common folk."

"The media blows it out of proportion anyway," Angelo says. "People are protesting, not rioting, Yiayia. It's a sign of a healthy democracy when citizens take to the streets and make their voices heard."

"Well, anyway, you too young to fly by yourself."

"He's twenty-four," says Despina.

"*Bah.*"

Angelo pushes a wedge of fish around with his fork. He hasn't seen his father in seven years, and just the thought makes him shudder, though he's not sure why. "Maybe she's right, Ma."

"Angelo, I know you're anxious about flying, but think of what an achievement it would be to overcome those fears."

"You know," Yiayia says, addressing Angelo now, smiling her mischievous smile again. "In Greek, the word for 'achievement' and the word for 'Greek' is the same word."

"That's not true," Angelo says.

"It sure isn't," Despina agrees.

"Where you people learn to speak Greek?"

* * *

Angelo has slept in the same room since he was a child. The bed is larger, the TV a relatively recent addition, as are the desk and computer; but for the most part, the space remains the same. Where once there hung an Oakland Raiders pendant, a painting by Angelo's maternal grandfather—his *papou*—now occupies the wall above the bureau. It's an abstract depiction of three horses in mid-stride, their black bodies set against Aegean blue and bold magenta, like a sunset reflecting off the sea. Above the desk is another painting by Papou, a self-portrait he'd done in middle-age. The man was an artist—just like Angelo aspires to be—and yet Angelo's mother can't understand why Angelo has embarked on a similar pursuit. Perhaps she fears he's setting himself up for a life of struggle, as her father did.

Sitting at the desk now and erasing such questions from his mind, Angelo gazes up at the piece as he often does before working. He searches the man's intense expression, his eyes vivid yellow-green like a leopard's, for inspiration. If he stares long enough, Angelo will be overcome by an urge to draw. In the meantime, he enjoys gazing at the painting as though there is always something new to discover, some fresh glimpse into the man Papou had been.

Dimitri Lambros died before Angelo was born, but Angelo grew up hearing stories of his grandfather's journey from the island of Crete to the city of Chicago at age fifteen. Angelo especially enjoys the tales of Papou's experiences exploring Chicago's Greektown. Something about that neighborhood even now is intriguing, though Angelo has never been. He peers into the eyes of the portrait and almost sees the streets reflected in Papou's gaze: those avenues lined with storefronts bearing names in Greek; the cramped markets offering olives and cheeses and Cretan *paximathia*; the bakeries churning out fresh batches of *koulourakia* and *bougatsa*; and the coffee houses—best of all—those establishments perpetually fogged with cigarette smoke where men go to read newspapers and play cards and *tavli*, fondle their *komboloi* and run numbers. So much more than just sip *kafe*.

For Angelo, the Greektown of his grandfather's youth sounds like a place he might dream of discovering amid the bird shop's labyrinth; an exciting world beneath the present mundane. To him, it seems that is what ethnic enclaves have always been—communities operating below the mainstream, their cultural ties conjuring a sort of magical bond invisible to outsiders. They are places immune to loneliness, free of the desolation he so longs to escape, the desolation he feels now in his bedroom, even while his mother and Yiayia are just down the hall.

In the Bay Area, the Greek community has no definitive center, and Angelo considers that that may be why his father, despite his success, always felt so alone in America. Angelo feels it, too, despite being born here.

At last he takes out paper and pencil and begins to draw, gliding across the white space in light strands then darker strokes, hunching close to the pad, merging with it. It's not long before his surroundings disappear and the page alone remains.

Has an hour passed? Two? He can't recall when he began to experience these episodes—the timelessness—but they have long been a part of him, like the scars and the headaches that sometimes come after prolonged stretches of work. Angelo checks his cell phone: 8:15. He smiles up at Papou's portrait in gratitude for the muse. Then he considers calling his father, but Greece is ten hours ahead, which puts it at quarter past six in the morning. He wonders what the weather is like, if the spring has grown hot enough for swimming.

He thinks about his uncles and aunts: Aunt Voula's *garithes saganaki*. His stomach automatically growls. He thinks about his cousins. It's been so long since he's seen them; not since he was ten years old. As of the last update, Manolis's wife has given birth to twins. Yiorgo is almost through with his Army service in Athens, lucky that someone had pulled strings to get him stationed only two and a half hours from home. Panos, ever the wild one, had crashed Uncle Christo's company truck while speeding down a dirt road just outside the village. Luckily, he walked away with only bruises. And, according to Tasso, Angelo's female cousins have grown into beautiful young women.

But then an image of an airplane bursts in and with it a wave of claustrophobia. He takes a breath and thinks that, if he can get past that anxiety, there will still be the issue of actually seeing his father again. He checks the clock a second time. In an hour he will meet up with Carmen. It's a shame he won't converse with his father beforehand, glean some lingo from the man's vast lexicon of smooth talk. Tasso Koutouvalis had arrived in the U.S. not knowing much English, but before long he learned all the words American women seemed to love.

But Angelo will just have to make do himself. Even without the aid of his father, perhaps he can still call up The Greek.

He pads down the hall to the living room. His mother is on the couch perusing her grading log, Yiayia slumped in the lounge chair, bluish flickers from the TV reflecting off her face. He sits on the couch next to his mother, and Yiayia twists in her chair to smile at him.

"*Natoh* Angelaki *mas*." She points a knobby finger at the TV. "We watching the bald man. Mr. Know-It-All talk show. Dr. Bill."

"Dr. Phil, Yiayia."

"Whatever."

Despina says, "Angelo, keep an eye on Yiayia for a while, okay? I need to go out for some air."

Yiayia's eyes go big as chariot wheels. "For what you need air? Is plenty in here, and is dark outside. And is going to rain soon."

"I'll only be gone ten minutes, Mother. And Angelo will be here."

Yiayia struggles to stand. "Wait, Despina!"

"Ma!" Angelo cries. "I need to leave in an hour!"

But Despina is already out the door.

Angelo sighs. Yiayia hums.

She has always done it, though Angelo is more conscious of it now. It's a low, guttural sound like a small motor letting off a continuous rev, interspersed with a Greek mantra too garbled for Angelo to comprehend. He finds himself listening to Yiayia's engine instead of the TV. In time, Angelo is also humming, unable to resist. His eyes fix on Yiayia's hand, the arthritis-withered fingers knobby and thick like tree limbs, winding a tight circle against her thigh.

"Yiayia?"

"*Eh?*"

"What's that you're humming?"

"Who?"

"You. Is that a song?"

"I donno. Some ol' church hymn. I don't remember." Yiayia turns to the window. "Where's your mother? She should have stay home. I walk the street and don't see nobody at night. Is scary! When I first come to this country with your *papou*, there always people out in the evening. Dimitri stay home painting, but me? I go out with my sisters. Friday nights we drive to San Francisco, go listen *bouzoukia* music at the taverna. We never have problem. Now? Forget it. Stay home always, Angelo. After your classes, come straight home."

"I'm plenty old enough to take care of myself. I'm going out tonight, in fact."

"No you don't!"

"You remember how old I am, Yiayia?"

"Ten. Ten years, I say."

"You're off by fourteen."

Yiayia sucks her dentures. "Come on, *re*."

"It's true."

"Come on."

Angelo sighs. Resistance is futile. Growing up, Yiayia lived just a few blocks from his parents' house and was always around; sometimes picking him up from school or from a friend's place or presenting him with freshly ironed underwear when he arrived home. She never failed to have a candy bar set aside; always a Snickers—because they satisfy, as Angelo was known to quote. He would munch his chocolate while she lectured on the importance of keeping his bedroom clean—a must, given that one day he would desire a wife. No decent woman would marry a slob (not even a woman straight from Greece, properly village-trained in the art of caring for a man). She also told stories about Papou: "Oh, he would have love you, Angelaki mou. He always talk for wanting a boy, instead I give him two daughters, and they both come with green eyes, like him. A beautiful boy like you, Angelo? Dark hair, dark eyes? He would have jump for joy."

And tales of her childhood in Greece, like the one where she described huddling in the family home during a rain storm and watching in awe as a bolt of red lightning hit the steeple of the church where their father was a *papas* yet didn't leave a mark.

Angelo continues to study the woman, watching as she fidgets with the frilly edge of her pajama top. *Who wears black pajamas?* Apparently Yiayia does. Angelo smiles at the thought; the woman is eighty-six years old and still maintains an impeccable sense of style. Despina had said that when Yiayia fell that afternoon, she had been most upset that she had torn a hole in her stocking and dirtied her designer jacket. Sitting as she is now, a strand of gray falling across her face, shoulders hunched, spine frail under the papery skin at the base of her neck, Yiayia still looks fabulous.

A few years back, an Oakland-based photographer published a small book of "who's who" snapshots depicting local celebrities and notable characters in the community. To everyone's joy and surprise, Yiayia made the cut. She was photographed in her customary earth-tone garb: smart brown skirt and matching jacket topped off with an elegant 1920s-era hat. Cup of coffee in hand, a smoldering cigarette between her fingers. That's the image of her most prominent in Angelo's mind.

"When your mother say she be back, *re*?" Yiayia asks while taking another look out the window.

Angelo glances at his phone. His mother has been gone twenty minutes already. He needs to get going soon. "Tell me one of your stories," he says. "Occupy your mind with something else."

Yiayia waves him off. "This days my mind work slow. I can't switch from one thought to the next so fast."

"*Aw*, but you have a big Greek brain."

Yiayia grins impishly. "I just have big old brain now. *Ah*, life long and hard. I go from Greek goddess to now just another ancient Greek."

Angelo and Yiayia laugh, then Yiayia goes back to her humming and chanting, and Angelo checks his phone again. It's a twenty-minute walk to tonight's meeting spot, fifteen if he really pushes it. He squirms on the couch, knowing he's already lost valuable time. He closes his eyes, thinks of Carmen. *What will she be wearing? Something casual? Dressy*? Whatever she chooses, the outfit will accentuate her curves. How can she be single? And how could she have chosen him? And how could he not have already blabbered about it to everyone? Now we're talking, Bryce would say. "Angelo has a date. Forget sliding into home plate, he's just lucky to make the Little League squad at this point. Baby steps, Greek. Baby steps."

He should text Kevin or Bryce with the news. But, no. It's Thursday. Bryce almost never answers calls during the week, and for Kevin, Thursday's are "Family Home Evening." Angelo chuckles at the thought. *Only in America,* his father would say. *Only the whitebread people.*

Angelo wishes he had more Greek friends. Friends who could relate to evenings spent at home in the company of his Yiayia. Friends named Dimitri or Kosta or Alexandros. Greeks are always there for other Greeks, at least according to his father. And they were always there for Tasso. When he ran Olympus Electric, the majority of his clients were fellow Greeks, just like Spiro at the newsstand, Mr. Vondas the grocer, or Mr. Skourtis the diner owner. Angelo had had quite a few Greek playmates when he was younger; many were the sons and daughters of his father's customers, while others were kids he met at the Orthodox church. But the family had attended services with less frequency as Angelo grew older, and Tasso closed his business shortly before deciding to move back to his homeland.

"Yiayia?"

"Yes, *agori mou.*"

"Where in Greece is Mr. Vondas from again?"

"Lamia. Up north."

Angelo stares pensively into the foreground. "And he and my dad were good friends?"

"Yes."

"And he has kids?"

Yiayia cocks her head. "*Nai, re.* Why you ask so many question? Don't you remember going to their house to play when you were a boy?"

"Vaguely. Why did I lose touch with them?"

Yiayia sighs. "I don't know. People grow apart."

"But..."

"I'm very concern."

"About what?"

"Where is you mother? Something must have happen. And is going to rain."

"Don't worry, Yiayia."

But Yiayia goes from tracing invisible circles along her thigh to fiercely rubbing the flesh below her bottom lip. "Something did happen," she says. "Maybe somebody come up behind her and knock her on the head! Maybe one of the *mavri...*"

Angelo frowns. "Don't start with the racial stuff, Yiayia. Maybe she went to a store."

"This late? The stores are close."

Angelo checks his phone a third time. If his mother returns in the next ten minutes—nine minutes now—he can leave without being late.

The woman fingers her chin with increased vigor. "I have terrible feeling. I'm going to see if she coming."

Angelo, growing impatient now himself, sighs deeply. "Yiayia, just wait."

But his grandmother is up faster than he expects, marching to the dining room window. Angelo follows, sees her gaze fix on the street below.

"*Thaymou*," the woman utters. "*Se parakalo!* Please! Where are you?"

"Yiayia, everything is okay! You just need to calm down!"

But Yiayia is headed back to the living room. Angelo is impressed by her speed. She stumbles once, and his heart jumps when she nearly falls, but the woman catches herself and keeps on, peering out the other window. "*Pou eisai?* Oh, dear!"

Angelo takes a breath. Yiayia always does this when anyone is—in her opinion—out of sight for too long. There was Angelo's first day of college—college, not kindergarten—when he had taken longer than expected to arrive home from San Francisco, and Yiayia had walked all the way to the BART station to wait and make sure he hadn't been "knocked on the head." Or the morning she had called the house to remind Despina of something, and then rushed over in a panic after nobody had picked up (because they were all still asleep).

Five minutes until Angelo has to go. "Yiayia, come sit down. You'll hurt yourself."

"No! I have to go look for her! Is been too long!"

"Absolutely not! You'll fall on those stairs. Besides, she's a grown woman, for Godsakes!"

"I am going down those stairs!"

"*No!*"

"*Yes!*"

Angelo wants to laugh. Here he is arguing with an eighty-six year old woman who's acting like she's only six. Yiayia starts for the front door, but Angelo takes her arm. *Four minutes now.*

"Don't touch me!" Yiayia shrieks. She pulls loose.

Angelo is startled by her strength.

She's out the door before he can make another move. And then, just as Yiayia reaches the sidewalk, Despina appears, grocery bags in hand.

Angelo shakes his head, seeing his mother's surprise upon finding Yiayia at the bottom of the steps. Even from inside he can hear the confrontation:

"Mother! What the hell are you doing out on the sidewalk in the dark?"

"Nothing, Despina. I came to check the garbage to see if it had been put on the curb. I see a leetle worm, and tomorrow is garbage day."

"Today was garbage day! Get back in the house! Now!"

"You don't need scream, Despina! For heaven's name. You were gone such long time!"

"I went to the store, Mother! For some ice cream."

"*Pagoto*? *Eh*, did you get my favorite? The Rocky Road?"

Angelo comes down the steps. "I tried to stop her, Ma."

Yiayia looks over her shoulder. "*Ela*, Big Brain. Where you going?"

"Out."

"Now? But is late. First she go, now you. Everybody leaving me. And is going to rain."

"I'll be back, Yiayia."

"Where are you going, Angelo?" Despina asks.

Angelo checks his phone again. Thirty seconds to spare. "I'm meeting up with... a friend. Shouldn't be long."

"Okay," says Despina.

THREE

ANGELO QUICKENS HIS stride, hands jammed in his coat pockets. Despite the darkness and drizzle, birds huddle in the trees. Rare to spot them after sundown, but Angelo is conscious of a new awareness gained from working at the store. Mrs. Wheeler knows her birds, if not how to treat her employees, but that's not surprising, being a buzzard.

He often raises his head these days at the rustle of flapping wings and likewise follows the course of birds as they cruise from tree to tree or collect on telephone wires, continually lifting and then descending. They are never solitary, always among their kind: pigeons with pigeons, seagulls with seagulls, sparrows with sparrows. There are moments at the store when Angelo is struck by the strangeness of seeing birds behind bars. Then there are the babies housed in incubation chambers.

Angelo contemplates his own birth: two months premature, small enough to fit in the cup of his mother's hands. He'd spent the initial few weeks of his life in an incubation chamber hooked up to breathing tubes. When he yanked out the tubes, determined to breathe on his own, the nurses referred to him as the little miracle boy. And then, miraculously, he had been released from the chamber only to find greater confinement waiting: bars separating him from his flock, though he'd perhaps welded them himself.

But tonight feels different. With the tightness gone from his chest, it seems as though he's flying.

Eying a pair of birds barely visible on a branch, he wonders how he arrived at this point with Carmen. A miracle? Or has the "gift" with which Angelo's father had promised his son he would one day be bestowed finally revealed itself? He urges himself onward, spots her now through the coffee shop window. He enters, and she greets him with a smile.

"You look nice," Angelo says, taking a seat across the small table.

"Thank you."

"Hope you haven't been waiting long."

"No, it's fine."

"Can I get you something?"

"I've got a mocha on the way."

Angelo breathes deep. "I know this to be a pretty chill place. They're renowned for their mochas, actually. And I remember that's what you like."

"You're sweet."

"I try. So, how was it closing at work today?"

Carmen shrugs. "Ms. Wheeler's been in a mood lately. But, taking that into consideration, it went fairly smooth. I heard her squawk at you, though."

"I was helping her trim Jerry's claws, and I guess I wasn't moving fast enough."

"Don't sweat it, Greek." Carmen laughs. "Maybe it's just the change."

"What? Oh." Angelo feels his cheeks flush. "You always seem to understand."

Carmen's mocha arrives, and Angelo orders an iced tea. Things go quiet, Angelo watching Carmen stir the whipped cream into her drink then blow the froth a good while before taking a sip, her lips full and moist as they touch the rim of the cup. *Lucky cup.*

Maybe this isn't so hard after all, Angelo thinks. Pretty women usually leave him speechless, but evidently he can carry on a conversation if he just gets out of his own head.

"Really," he begins again, feeling some of his anxiety fade. "It's great having you there at work every day, making the time go by."

Carmen chuckles. "My gosh. Such the charmer. This is a side of you I haven't seen enough of. You're usually so quiet."

"People tell me I should come out of my shell."

Carmen considers. "I don't know if being quiet is necessarily a bad thing. At least not for you. I think it means you observe and notice details other people miss.

But it would be nice to hear more from you. We've been working together all this time, and I don't feel like I've even skimmed your surface yet."

Angelo frowns a little. How can it be that he has learned so much about her—birth date, parents' names, even the details of family conflicts—and yet he has remained such a mystery? Maybe he overestimated his candidness? The waiter brings his drink, and Angelo takes a gulp. "What do you want to know?"

"I think you mentioned before that you're in grad school. What are you studying?"

"I hope to be an artist," Angelo says, overcome with a sudden urge to get it all out, years one through twenty-four. "An illustrator."

Carmen tilts her head. "You mean, like, drawing cartoons?"

"Well, sort of."

"Good luck," Carmen says, the way someone might respond to a three-year-old who has just announced he can dress himself. "So," she continues, "what do your parents say about that? Are you close with them? Wait, your dad's in Greece, right?"

"Yeah."

"Tough times over there, *eh*?"

Angelo nods. "They'll get past it, though. Look how much Greece has endured through the years."

Carmen shrugs. "Gyros and democracy are the extent of my knowledge when it comes to Greece."

Angelo takes a breath. "I live with my mom... and grandma. At the moment. Financial reasons, of course." A long silence follows, and Angelo remembers why he's always been reluctant to divulge personal info. Finally, he adds, "But it's kind of a cultural thing, too. Greek families tend to be really close. And back in the old country, a lot of times sons and daughters live at home until they're married. That way, they can help out with expenses and give back a little of what their parents gave them."

"It's the same with a lot of Chicano families," Carmen agrees. "Old-country values. But we're not in the old-country, I say."

"Would you have trouble dating a guy who lives at home? I mean, it's not like I just sit around doing nothing. I have goals. And I do my own laundry."

Carmen leans in and takes his hands. "I had an idea this is where things were going when you asked me to coffee. I think you're a great guy, really. I'm just not attracted to you that way."

Angelo feels the blood drain from his face. His stomach drops, and he fights to stay upright in his chair. "No worries. Hey, that's how it goes."

Carmen squeezes his palms. "Oh, Angelo."

"No, it's fine. Really. I hope this won't make it awkward at work."

"It won't for me," Carmen says.

Angelo manages a smile. "Good."

He rises from the table, surprised that his legs support him.

Carmen asks, "Don't you want to finish your drink?"

"I have an early class tomorrow."

"Sure you're all right, Angelo?"

"Fine."

"Well, how about I walk you to your car?"

"I don't have a car."

"Oh. Did your mom drive you?"

* * *

Back home, he stands at the bathroom mirror. He touches his face, stretches the skin, checks for flaws, but his flesh holds barely a blemish. He continues to examine himself like a doctor, like the surgeons who had examined his head pre-surgery, preparing to make their incision. Where would he begin, were he to make a cut? Where does his insecurity lie? Is it hidden beneath the flesh of his forehead, the smooth olive skin above the brows thick and dark like streaks of charcoal? Is it buried behind his eyes, deep-set and dark?

In high school, he may not have been able to see what others saw in his face, but now he can admit that he looks much like his father as a young man. Why shouldn't he share the man's luck with ladies? Women flocked to Tasso Koutouvalis in winged migration.

In his room, Angelo lies on the bed holding an old photograph of two long-haired, well-dressed Greek men standing on a cobblestone harbor, their backs to the sea, flanked by Nordic-looking women. With great self-assurance they smile into the camera, heads held high, chests puffed. Angelo studies the photo, as he does most nights, until he is asleep, fitfully dreaming of that particular morning several years ago.

FOUR

ONE RAINY SATURDAY morning around his thirteenth birthday, Angelo accompanied his father out to the suburbs, their destination a diner called Democracy where Tasso Koutouvalis had installed new lighting. The owner, a man named Zacharia Skourtis, whom Angelo had never met, insisted they come enjoy a complimentary breakfast.

On the drive over, the pair said little, both content to enjoy the sounds of classic Stevie Wonder on the stereo as Angelo stole side-glances at his father. He paid particular attention to the man's posture behind the wheel—slightly slouched, steering with one hand, the other flicking a string of amber *komboloi*. He wondered what Dad was thinking, what great secrets his furrowed brow concealed, but Angelo couldn't find the words to ask him, unsure what he'd even do with such insights were they revealed. Those weekend excursions with his father had increased over the previous months. Angelo possessed a vague sense that they were meant, on some level, to help him transition into adolescence.

They arrived at Democracy Diner, an A-frame building of white-and-blue exterior. Upon entering, Angelo marveled at the custom bubblegum machine, its base a statue of Atlas holding up a world of multi-colored candies.

"Ah, you must be Angelo! Your father has spoken much about you. The girls better watch out, you're even more handsome than your *patehra*."

Angelo smiled, feeling his cheeks flush as he took the hand of Mr. Skourtis, a man around his father's age with eyes the color of Tasso's string of worry beads. "*Efharisto, kai heyro polee*," Angelo said.

"Ah, the boy speaks Greek! And with good accent. Bravo!"

Angelo looked to his father and experienced a rising sensation in his chest, as though his heart had sprung wings at the sight of the man's approving smile. The feeling was short-lived, however, as Tasso replied, "*Amai*! He speaks pretty well. Of course, it won't do him much good when trying to talk to American girls. He has some trouble with them. Nervous, I guess, though he is young still."

Angelo lowered his gaze, and when he looked up again, Mr. Skourtis regarded him as though he were a complete stranger.

"Trouble with the girls? With this guy as your father?" Mr. Skourtis asked. "Unbelievable."

Angelo felt heat at his cheeks a second time, again averting his eyes. His father and Mr. Skourtis conversed in Greek at a pace and fluency with which he couldn't keep up, and Angelo wandered back over to the bubblegum machine, eyeing his tiny reflection in each bright little ball.

Angelo and his father ate at the counter, Mr. Skourtis serving them plates of eggs over-easy, hash browns, Greek sausage, and toast with hunks of feta cheese. The men resumed the conversation in their mother tongue, and Angelo was content to focus on his breakfast. He eyed various knick-knacks: salt and pepper shaker statuettes of Zeus and Hera, napkin holders shaped like ancient ships. Framed pictures of the Parthenon hung on the wall behind the counter, and between them, Angelo spotted a sizable photograph of two men—in their late teens or early twenties, he guessed—standing at the edge of a cobblestone harbor, the ocean at their backs. They wore their hair curly and long and were clad in wide-collared, button-down shirts—open at the chest to expose their muscular torsos, identical gold chains encircling their necks—and pants that flared out at the ankles. The men were flanked by women, their forms just visible at the edges of the frame.

Angelo eyed the picture as he ate, unable to shift his attention. Something about their piercing gazes and broad-shouldered stances resonated with him to the degree that he found himself posing in the reflection of the chrome espresso machine, trying to mimic their supreme air of confidence. Then he heard his father's laughter and went red in the face yet again.

"*Ti kaneis ekei, re*?" Tasso asked, and then, "I see now. You like the picture, eh? Recognize those two?"

Angelo took another look at the photo, and suddenly it dawned on him; only surprising that he hadn't realized sooner that the men were none other than his own father and Zacharia Skourtis. "You guys look... cool," Angelo said. His father set his fork down and laid a hand on his shoulder.

"Summer of nineteen-seventy..."

"Nine," Mr. Skourtis finished for him.

Angelo's father snapped his fingers in apparent affirmation. "Yes, some time before you were born of course, Angelo. Those were the days. I was just twenty in that photo. Zacharia and I are from the same town, but there we were on the island of Spetses. You remember from the last trip, *eh*?"

Angelo almost reminded his father that it had been a mere three years since their most recent visit to Greece, but he just nodded instead.

From behind the counter, Mr. Skourtis refilled Tasso's coffee then Angelo's juice before leaning his hairy forearms against the Formica and adding, "Summer of nineteen-seventy-nine, the year your father and I established ourselves as the kings of the *kamakia*! Has he told you the stories?"

Angelo glanced from his father to the photograph then back to Mr. Skourtis before shaking his head.

Mr. Skourtis seemed to regard Angelo's father with some surprise, and then he said, "*Toh pethee einai* what, thirteen-years-old now? It's time he learns the truth."

Angelo, his heart rattling in his chest with the frenzy of a caged bird, sensed that that which had long been hanging in the air between him and his father would finally be revealed.

Tasso looked to Mr. Skourtis, who gestured a pushing motion with his open hands as though to give Angelo's father a final boost, and then Tasso leaned forward on his stool. "There was a group of us young guys," he said, "old friends from the *horyo*, and they looked to Mr. Skourtis as a leader, though I'm not sure why..."

"No, no," Mr. Skourtis chimed in, "they looked at you as leader, *yiati eisai polee manggas!*"

Tasso chuckled. "That's not quite how I remember it."

"Your father had the extra confidence," Mr. Skourtis said.

Tasso shrugged. "It's a typically Greek quality, but perhaps all the Koutouvalis men have more than the usual."

Angelo wanted to remind his father that the trait had apparently skipped a generation, but he kept quiet.

"Your father would walk down the street like this," Mr. Skourtis said, stepping out from behind the counter to demonstrate a square-shouldered strut, his arms held slightly away from his body. "Mr. Cool."

Tasso laughed. "Don't pay attention to this guy, Angelo. He is known to exaggerate. Anyhow, you must understand Greece was regaining a sense of freedom at that time, after years under military rule. The Greek girls were still very sheltered, but the towns were flooded with tourists from France, Germany, Finland, Norway, Denmark, Sweden. Blonde-haired, blue-eyed women everywhere..."

"And when your father saw one he liked," Mr. Skourtis began, "he went right for her. Just like a true *kamaki*! That is the Greek word for—"

"Harpoon," Angelo cuts in.

"*Bravo ta Ellenika sou!*" said Mr. Skourtis. "But also 'hustler' or 'flirt.' *Katalaves*?"

Angelo nodded again.

"As I said, Mr. Skourtis is good at spinning tales," Tasso said. "I didn't know much English then, but obviously I didn't know any German or Finnish or Danish or whatever. I would say to them 'Mademoiselle, you are beautiful. How do you enjoy Greece?' 'Would you like to go for a drink or dance?'"

Angelo looked to Mr. Skourtis, who nodded in confirmation of the story.

"Most of the time," Tasso said, "the women just ignored me."

"Ha!" exclaimed Mr. Skourtis. "As I recall, it was typical for your father to go with four women in one day!"

"That's not exactly—"

But Angelo, with eyes wide, cut in to ask, "To dance?"

Mr. Skourtis flashed a smirk. "*Ohee, re!* To... you know... to bed."

Angelo's eyes went even wider. He looked to his father, but the man only shook his head.

"No, I remember!" said Mr. Skourtis. "It was definitely four in one day, average."

Tasso smirked. "I think you have your past confused with my own. Understand, Angelo, things were different back then. In most parts of the world, including Greece, it was much more open. Sex was no big deal. I know you are growing up, and girls will start chasing you like they occasionally chased me. I want you to understand the power you have and use it wisely. But definitely use it when you are ready."

Angelo couldn't help but think of his Spider-Man comics. *With great power comes great responsibility.* "The gift of the *kamaki*?" he asked.

"Yes!" said Mr. Skourtis.

Tasso said, "Gone are the glory days of the *kamaki* in high numbers." He laughed then said, "But who knows? You may follow in Mr. Skourtis's footsteps and lead a new generation."

Angelo lowered his eyes. "I've never even kissed a girl."

Tasso just waved. "Nothing to be ashamed of. You have time. Now, finish your breakfast."

Later, back in the car on the way home, Angelo couldn't look at his father without picturing the man as a twenty-year-old lothario, despite Tasso's inexplicable efforts to downplay his past. It was a bit like discovering the man was a super-hero, and Angelo wondered when his own powers would reveal themselves. He supposed he could hold off investing in a suit and cape, at least until he sprouted his first few chest hairs—sure signs of the emergence of his inner-*kamaki*. He smiled to himself, sensing even then that that was a morning he would long remember.

FIVE

THE NEXT MORNING, Friday, Angelo rises an hour earlier than usual to get ready for class, allowing himself enough time to call his father before leaving to catch the train. It has been almost a month since they last spoke, but Angelo isn't sure what he wants to say. Or admit. Maybe it will be enough to just hear the man's voice, let Tasso deliver the news from afar while Angelo simply pictures the scene. Perhaps his father will reveal that he knows of a particularly beautiful young woman in the *horyo* eager to start a new life in the States. So eager that Tasso has already made arrangements for her and Angelo to get acquainted, her flight on Cupid Airways soon set to land. Angelo chuckles to himself while dialing the phone, thinking it can't hurt to dream.

"*Legetai?*"

"*Yiasou, Patehra.* It's me, Angelo."

Tasso laughs. "I don't have another son. At least not to my knowledge."

"What?"

"I'm kidding you, *re.* What a pleasant surprise to get your call. How's everything?"

"Good. For the most part. How's life in the *horyo?*"

"Same as always, *agori mou.* Beautiful, but quiet. Everyone's in good spirits and health. Missing you, of course."

"Doesn't sound too quiet, Dad. All that traffic in the background."

"I'm in Athens. I've been working a small job with my cousin the last few days. Lucky to find work at all. We're actually headed to a party. Somebody's Name Day."

Angelo presses the phone against his ear, struggles to catch the last word of each sentence. "Party? What about all the protests?"

Tasso chuckles into the receiver. "What about them? Old news. Stay clear of Syntagma Square, and you don't realize they're even occurring."

"Should I call back some other time?"

"*Ohee, re*. I can talk for a bit. *Pes mou*, what's new?"

Angelo has a feeling he should keep it at the surface but responds with, "I've been having more headaches lately."

"Sorry to hear."

"And I've been feeling more anxious, so I'm not sure what to do. Dad? You still there?"

"Yes, Angelo. How many times have I told you not to worry so much? About headaches, flying, and sometimes nothing."

"I know, Dad, but it's hard."

"It's not hard. You just don't try."

"I do, but..."

"You're going to drive yourself crazy, *re*."

His head swimming now, Angelo takes a breath. "I went out with this girl last night."

"That's another thing," Tasso cuts in. "Women will come if you just be yourself."

Angelo snorts. "So simple." Then regrets it. "Sorry, Dad."

"Sometimes the truth is simple. That's why we don't believe it."

Angelo sighs. Of course he'd been hoping for real advice. Or maybe a magic spell. "My powers haven't revealed themselves yet."

"What?"

"Powers, remember? Maybe you should teach me how to be a *kamaki*."

Tasso only laughs. "As I explained to you when you were still barely a teenager, no longer are young Greek women so sheltered that young Greek men have to resort to strutting around with their silk shirts unbuttoned to show off their hairy torsos and woo tourist women with a few choice English words."

"Such as, 'Mademoiselle, you are beautiful. How do you enjoy Greece?'"

Tasso laughs again. "Good memory, but why are you so convinced that I even was a real *kamaki* in my day? I told you years ago that Mr. Skourtis exaggerates."

"I still have a copy of that photo, Dad."

"We're almost at the house, Angelo. I should probably go."

"Okay. Love you, Dad."

"Love you, too, Angelo. We'll talk again soon. And remember, just be yourself."

* * *

Angelo shuffles into his figurative drawing course and plops down next to Lucy at a desk, with a frontal view of the model standing on a platform in the center of the room.

"Hey you," says Lucy.

"Hi," Angelo replies, unable to meet her gaze as he readies his sketch pad. "How's it going?"

"Pretty good," Lucy says while brushing back her hair. "I was out at this club last night. Sweaty people and loud music, not really my scene, but it was my friend Lisa's birthday..."

Angelo watches her mouth move, already worried about his reply, his heart thudding. And this triggered by a woman he isn't even interested in romantically. Heaven forbid the nude model steps down from the platform to share her own tale of late-night adventures.

"So, do you know what I mean?"

Angelo blinks. "*Huh*?"

Lucy chuckles. "Earth to Angelo. I asked if you ever get that urge? The one where your whole body is just yearning to create?"

Angelo clears his throat. "Oh. Yeah, all the time. For me it hits at the back of the throat like a thirst."

Lucy's brown eyes sparkle behind her ultra-modern tortoise-shell glasses. "You should totally write that down."

Angelo watches Lucy toy with her hair as its illuminated by a halo of sun, the light also shimmering off her glasses, and it's not the first time he's thought she's pretty. And smart. And funny. Just not his type. Though what does that mean? Not his type because she's available? Not his type because they truly share some common interests? Not his type because they're just friends? As if he can afford to be picky. But, whatever the reason, they're strictly platonic—so much so that Plato would be proud—and maybe that's for the best.

"What are you thinking about?" she asks.

"Art."

"Hush, hush!" Ms. Miller commands from the front of the room. "Let's begin, people."

Angelo adjusts himself in the desk, snagging his pencil. The model on the platform, a tall, thin redhead, drops her robe, and Angelo can't help but swallow. Subjects are not chosen for "ideal beauty." Over the course of the semester, the class had drawn a variety of figures, men and women, fat and thin, tall and short, young and old; each model presented—so says Ms. Miller—to provide contrasting and challenging sketching sessions. But this particular subject looks like someone who should spend a majority of her time in the nude.

Angelo starts at her feet, his gaze drifting up her long legs, past the sparsely-haired V-shape between them, past the slight pudge at her stomach with its small crescent birthmark, past the high, round breasts, the lightly-freckled shoulders, the delicate neck, to the thin but expressive lips, parted just a bit to reveal her perfect front teeth.

Angelo enjoys looking at her, though he thinks, *For god's sake, this is an art class!* And yet he wonders, glancing around the room, if other males feel this way, too—maybe also a few females. But their faces reveal nothing, eyes flicking from paper to model and back. Doubtful that Angelo is alone in his attraction to this nude woman, alone in his desire for her, yet he feels suddenly lonely. She becomes another woman out of reach, standing without clothes, but she is not naked for him. He remembers reading somewhere that the word naked once meant unprotected.

He sketches, willing away the feelings. Soon he's drawing at a feverish pace, imagining himself in the model's place. He considers what it might feel like to be on the platform, wonders if he—who so often shies from the gazes of others—could stand there for all to see. Ms. Miller walks by, peruses his sketch, and leans in to say, "Great job."

* * *

Graduate studies are done for the day, the sky dark by the time Angelo exits the BART station. He shoulders his pack and quickens his pace up the street. Families are seated in the windows of a Mexican restaurant: husbands in slacks and loafers, jeans and polo shirts; wives wearing subtle dresses or baggy sweatshirts with names of universities on the front; babies in strollers, toddlers in high-chairs, grade-schoolers with budding senses of cool who try to appear aloof from it all.

It's quite a walk to the comic book store, but a hike Angelo enjoys after hours hunched over a sketch pad. He can people-watch and let the air clear his head. Friends tend to rag on him, saying things like, "Why walk so much when you could drive?"

Especially Bryce, who has owned a vehicle since high school and rarely leaves his ride but for eating, working out, and sleeping. No matter how many times Angelo reminds people that he doesn't have a car— number one reason he has trouble getting laid, so says Bryce—they still ask. Sometimes Angelo goes so far as to mention how in Greece, at least in the small towns, lots of people don't have cars, and even those who do often walk. Bryce and the guys just give blank stares, while his cousin Jacob fires back with, "Well, in Athens everyone drives, and we're not in Greece anyway, *malaka*!"

Angelo jogs the final block to the comic book store, even though choosing a stack of issues is not a process to rush. The store is wedged between a Laser Copy and a Baskin Robbins, but there is no mistaking it for a franchise. The facade is marked by two Ionian-style columns made of plaster and painted with cracks. The name *PANTHEON NEWS & COMICS!* is printed on its blue awning in white letters, the yellow exclamation point shaped like a lightning bolt. In actuality, *PANTHEON* is more of a glorified newsstand than a true comic book shop. But Angelo likes the place due to its name and ambiance, not to mention the déjà vu feeling of being in the company of one of his father's former associates.

He enters, checking to see if Spiro is at the counter, then makes a stop at each comic display, flipping through issues, examining them as if they are documents holding long sought-after truths, golden pamphlets deserving of careful handling and heavy guarding. Alex Ross, Grant Morrison, even Chris Gage, a fellow Greek. Angelo knows all the writers and artists, follows them from title to title the way other people might track their favorite athletes. Books chosen, he steps to the register where Spiro Karras leans on the counter as he fondles his *komboloi*, the string of amber beads wrapped around his fingers like bandless rings.

"*Ela, fileh. Pos eisai, re?*" Spiro greets Angelo with a grin.

"*Kala, kai ehsee?*"

"*Mia hara.*"

Angelo is glad to practice his Greek with someone other than Yiayia. He's also tickled by the looks he and Spiro receive from customers who seem to wonder what they're prattling about. It reminds him again of the layers in things; the words spoken by him and Spiro create a world impenetrable by many, a pocket of connection below the surface of the everyday.

"How's Gus?" Angelo asks.

"He's working in San Francisco."

"Say hello to him for me," Angelo says, a bit worried about his syntax, though Spiro doesn't register a reaction. "I haven't seen in him a long time."

"You were only boys back then, but he still remembers you. I will give him your regards."

Angelo just nods, though he wants to say more, perhaps ask Spiro to arrange a reunion with Gus and other local Greeks from his childhood, but he doesn't.

"How's your father?"

"Doing well," Angelo replies. "Living the good life."

"The good life? In Greece? *Bah*."

Angelo feels offended somehow.

"Well," Spiro says, "when you talk to him, tell him the lights are giving me trouble." He points to the overhead lamps. "I want him to come back and re-do the job as soon as possible. Always knew he was a good-for-nothing jerk-off!"

Angelo raises his eyebrows, but Spiro only laughs. "Relax, friend. I'm just kidding."

* * *

Angelo enters a bar and finds a stool at the counter. He sets his bag of comics aside and smiles when the female bartender flips him a coaster.

"Whiskey and soda, please."

The bartender glances at Angelo's face but doesn't ask for I.D.—*is that a good or a bad thing?*—then fixes Angelo's drink. "New around here?"

"No. I was in last Friday."

"I usually remember faces."

Again Angelo wonders if that's good or bad. His father has a face that no one forgets; a face that Angelo's supposedly resembles. "It was Saturday, actually."

The bartender smiles. "That explains it. Cheers."

Angelo raises his glass in salute then takes a long pull off the drink, savoring the cold, crisp liquor on his tongue. To his right sits a man in white jacket and trousers heavily spattered with multi-hued paint. His face is leathery, deeply browned from the sun. At his left sits another man whose beard is flecked with the debris usually collected while crawling beneath houses. The man scoots his stool closer to a puffy-eyed woman running a stubby finger around the rim of her martini glass. He's rolling a small yellow knob between his index finger and thumb—like a tiny toothpaste cap. A wire-nut.

When he was a boy, Angelo would find drawers full of them in his father's work desk, hurl the multi-colored knobs at his GI Joes like missiles, connect wire upon wire to construct snakes. His father didn't mind as long as Angelo didn't lose them, and now Angelo supposes that they were a way to connect with the man on a different level, work with his hands in a way at once removed and connected to his father's.

The man catches Angelo gazing at him, and Angelo lifts his head to the TV screen showing an NBA game. He takes another swig of whiskey, thinks that perhaps that's why he comes to this particular bar, to be around men who do real work: shovel dirt, lay brick. Angelo places his hands on the counter. His fingers hold hardly a callous, barely a scar.

"They're dishing out quite an ass-whooping, *huh*?"

Angelo turns to see the man with the wire-nut pointing a finger at the TV. "I guess," Angelo replies. "I'm not much of a fan."

"Sports. 'The opiate of the masses.' Somebody said that once. Somebody much older and wiser than me. This a nice bar, *eh*?"

"I live close by, so..." Angelo lets his voice trail off, his gaze shying away.

"Nice bar for sure. Beer's always cold. Stool's always warm. I saw you eyein' these wire caps before. You in the business?"

"My dad was."

"Retired?"

"He... moved away."

"What do you do?"

Angelo's eyes flick away again, impatient, like the flutter of a fly. "I'm an art student."

"Art? Can a man make a living off of his art these days?"

Angelo has been dreading such a question. "Guess I'm trying to find out."

"Don't doddle your dick too long. A man's gotta bring home the bread. I don't care what these women say."

"Ernest, leave the poor kid alone," says the woman with the martini.

Ernest shrugs at her. "What? We're just talkin' here. And try nursin' that booze a little, huh, Marie? That's the last cocktail you're swindling out of me tonight." He turns back to Angelo with a wink. "Don't mind her. She's been planted on that stool since four this afternoon. Anyway, if you can make money off something you love, well, grab that opportunity by the balls and squeeze until you find a lump."

Angelo raises an eyebrow. "A lump?"

Ernest takes a swig of beer. "A lump sum, that is. No glamour in crawling under houses to rewire 'em, that's for sure. Bet your dad would echo those sentiments."

"You're probably right."

Ernest gives a nod then turns back to the woman beside him.

Angelo gazes into his glass. Maybe he will become a teacher like his mother. Not grad school, that's for sure. Being the subject of critiques is bad enough; he wouldn't want to spend his day dishing them out. *High school?* No way he is going to endure that experience twice! He downs his drink, orders another, then snags a cocktail napkin. On it he scrawls a muscled figure: half-man, half-horse; another centaur to add to his school assignment.

He sips his second drink then props his elbows on the bar. His stomach feels warm, thoughts growing a bit more optimistic as he stares at the light reflecting off the rim of his glass, watching it expand like a flame when his eyes go out of focus. Down the bar, the man still fiddles with the wire-nut, the woman sipping her martini. They're speaking but not looking at one-another. Further along, it's the same: people talking sans eye contact, their gazes instead fixed on the game. The TV screen casts their faces in ghost-blue.

"Want another one, babe?"

Angelo turns to the bartender. "Not quite yet. I'll take some pretzels, though."

The bartender pours the snacks into a small basket. Angelo reaches for a pretzel while fiddling with his phone. He doesn't want to let a good buzz pass without tipsy-dialing someone, so he rings Bryce.

"Ah, The Greek! How you?"

"I'm good, Bryce. Here at the watering hole. Want to join me?"

"I got a lady or three comin' in a couple hours. S'pose I could get out for a cold one, though."

"*Ladies*, huh? How about sharing the wealth?"

"No go, my friend. Unfortunately, these chicks only seem to be cravin' the chocolate persuasion, know what I mean? Maybe next time."

"Aren't you forgetting something?" asks Angelo, as if reminding a child to put his pants on before going outside. "You're white. And you know I don't even like saying that because it's not an ethnicity. Remind me, where are your people from?"

"I don't know."

"That's part of your problem."

"My mom grew up in Anaheim, how's that?"

"Not far back enough."

"Whatever, bro. Not everybody can be The Greek like you. Besides, you know how women are. Then again, maybe you don't. Anyway, they pay more attention to what a person got goin' on inside. And deep down I'm all brown."

Angelo laughs. "I thought you were black."

Bryce laughs, too. "See you in a few."

Angelo reaches into his bag and begins reading *Hercules*. When he eventually glances up from the comic, he doesn't need to check the time to know it has happened again: twenty minutes, a half hour, gone in a flash.

"Looks like you need another drink, babe," the bartender suggests.

"I'm waiting on a friend. Oh, here he is."

Bryce strides up to the bar, greets Angelo with a fist bump, then nods at the man with the wire-nut. "Mind movin' down one?"

"Sure thing."

"Ho, shit," Angelo says, addressing Bryce. "Did I detect a glint of gold in your mouth, sir? Please don't tell me..."

Bryce smiles wide, flashing a grin full of jeweled teeth. "You know it, son! Just got this grill last week. In today's world, it's like, are you shining or are you *shinin'*? I think your boy Socrates once said that."

"I doubt. Want a beer?"

"Fo' sho'. MGD is the brew for me."

Angelo shakes his head and laughs. "Excuse me, miss? A Heineken and an MGD for my slightly confused friend here."

"Thanks, Greek," says Bryce. "So, what's new?"

"Same old. School, work."

"I feel that. I quit my job at Home Depot over in Emeryville. Hours were killin' me."

Angelo takes a long hit off his beer. "You need an income to satisfy all those ladies in your life."

Bryce shifts on his stool, begins peeling the Miller label off his bottle, reminding Angelo of a song. "Got a few things in the works."

"So, where'd you meet these women who are coming through tonight?"

"Where I meet most my dates. BlackPeopleMeet dot com."

"I see."

Bryce laughs, shows his teeth again, the overheads glinting off the cubic zirconias set in the gold. "What you mean, 'I see'? Oughta give it a try your ownself. Maybe not that particular site, 'cause you an all right lookin' dude, just don't know if you got enough flavor for the sistahs."

Angelo snorts. "You're the expert."

"But really, my dude. Give the online thing a try. Hell, I'm sure they got like a site for Greek people. Lotta honeys online, man. We talkin' dime pieces. I'm tellin' ya." Bryce tilts his chin toward the comic bag. "Less time with cartoons, more time loggin' on for love. You bitch so much about not being able to find a girl."

Angelo slides the comics closer to his chest, shielding them from view. Bryce seems to catch the gesture and shakes his head.

"That's part of your problem right there, my man. Don't worry about what nobody got to say. You a Marvel fanboy? So what? Do you! Pump your chest out! Women like a dude with some swagger, know what I mean? An' stop puttin' the females on a pedestal."

Angelo almost snaps, "Who said I was?"

Bryce tilts his head to one side, shoots Angelo a smirk. "C'mon, bro. Be honest with yourself. It's Friday night. You up in this bar drinkin' alone. I don't see no honeys in sight. None under forty, at least. Hey, except those two, just walked in. There, her friend's headed for the bathroom. Go talk to the one sitting down."

Angelo spots a slender brunette up the counter, model pretty with colorful tattoos running the length of both arms. "Yeah, right."

Bryce clicks his tongue. "It's really not hard. I promise."

"I don't even know what I'd say."

"Doesn't matter, asshole! Just talk, keep your mouth moving. Compliment her on her ink."

Angelo slides off the stool, steps forward, then retreats: forward, back, forward, back, like some awkward mating waltz. "I can't do it," he mutters, planting himself on the stool again.

"Go over there!" Bryce hisses.

"I can't!" says Angelo, nearly in a panic now.

"All right. Whatever. But remember, man. Sooner or later, you gotta do you. I mean you're The Greek! Walk with some confidence, bro."

Angelo feels a sudden tingle in his chest and a tightness in his throat; the same sensations he experienced in high school when his friends got dates and he was passed over but he'd occasionally accompany them to the movies, watch them touch in the dark and wonder why it couldn't be him in his buddy's place. He gulps more beer and narrows his eyes at Bryce.

"Just do you, huh?" Angelo says. "Is that your deal? You just doing you with the gold teeth and the BlackPeopleMeet and all the slang?"

Bryce leans forward on his stool as shadows play across his face, rendering it suddenly sinister. His voice comes out low. "Hold up, now. This is me. Always been. You should know that. Lotta people may not approve of the way I talk and dress, but that's on them. Only person I need to be true to is number one. Respect that."

Angelo slumps his shoulders. "You're right. Sorry."

"No thing. Guess I shouldn't rag you about the ladies so much."

Angelo feels the tightness try to build in his throat again and downs more beer. "I don't want to be stuck in this shell, man."

"Hey, 'round our age, a lot of life seems to be about discovery, gettin' in where you fit in. Shit, don't you see that's why I come down on you so hard? You already got a solid background. I envy your position in a buncha ways, Greek."

"Those are some wise words, friend."

Bryce scoots off his stool. "C'mon, my dude. Let me buy another round, and then we'll hit the pool table."

Minutes later, Angelo leans in and thrusts his cue, the white ball exploding the pyramid, a solid orange ball dropping into a corner pocket.

"Nice break," says Bryce, working the chalk.

Angelo smiles, leaning in again for his next shot. He ricochets one ball off the next, sending the first into a pocket.

"Ho, two for two!" shouts Bryce.

"*Eh*," says Angelo. "Lucky streak."

"There you go again, dog. You gotta believe!"

On his third attempt, Angelo fails to bank anything, takes a swig off a fresh beer. "You're up."

"Lemme show you how it's done," Bryce says. He leans his butt on the edge of the pool table, the cue stick behind his back and, looking over his shoulder to aim his shot, sinks three stripes. "See? It's like sex. Gotta get your stroke down."

Angelo whistles. "Maybe that's your new calling. Pool shark."

Bryce jousts his stick and knocks in a fourth ball. "Naw. But I'm gonna have lots of time to practice while waiting to get shipped out."

"Shipped out? Family sending you back to Anaheim, home of your ancestors?"

Bryce sets his stick aside, runs his fingers over his blond buzz cut. His eyes go distant. "I enlisted in the Army."

Angelo cocks his head. "Seriously? You told anybody?"

"You and my mom."

"How'd she react?"

Bryce shrugs. "She's cool, I guess. Glad I'm doing something. I'm twenty-four, y'know."

"But the Army? What about going back to school?"

"Now? You already got a Bachelor's under your belt, Greek. I barely got a high school diploma. And how would I pay for it? I ain't got a support system like you. My family's not there for me that way."

Bryce kills his beer then things go quiet. Angelo takes another swig from his Heineken, lets his eyes go out of focus again, the green of the table blurring with the green of the bottle. He thinks of high school, sees Bryce eating lunch with the black kids; away from Angelo's table, away from everyone.

"What are you going to do with your car?" Angelo instantly regrets asking the question, wonders where it came from.

"Probably sell it. You want it, bro? Might do you good."

"No, thanks. When do you leave?"

Bryce picks up his cue, sinks another ball. "June."

"Damn. That's only two months."

"Yup."

Angelo wants to escape his thoughts, escape the tingle in his chest. He looks to the bar, searches for the man with the wire-nut, but he isn't there. Angelo thinks of the Army, all the stories he's heard: his father's tales of driving trucks for the Greek forces—M37s, whatever they were; his cousin Jacob's plan to try for the Air Force, and the hell Thio Yianni had given him in response. He even thinks of that old movie *Jarhead*. While there are far better cinematic depictions of war, that one scene where the recruits watch a graphic video of one of their buddies's girlfriend filmed in the act of cheating seems particularly haunting.

"So, you've already had your physical and stuff?"

"Passed, no problem." Bryce flexes a bicep. "Still in good shape from those years on the football team. And I quit smokin' weed. Just to be safe though, I downed a bunch of water and Red Bull right before my piss test."

"Smart, I guess, though I've heard it really doesn't work."

"Shit, ain't you happy for your bro?" Bryce asks before banking another shot.

"Yeah, it's just..."

Bryce gazes at the ceiling and fingers the stubble on his chin, resembling a Caucasian rapper pondering his next line. "Look, man. I know what you're thinkin'. It's not like I'm all gung-ho for this war shit. But they paying me a lot of money." Bryce jabs his stick and makes yet another shot.

"Shit," Angelo says.

"What now?"

"I think you won."

Bryce's gold grin returns. "Guess I did. My winning ways will rub off on you yet, Greek. Now, that next fly female you lay eyes on? Go get her!"

SIX

"BIRD LOOSE!"

There is a sound a small bird makes when flying free; a nearly inaudible whistle of wings slicing air. The finch zips past. Angelo, still grasping the food dish hooked to the back of the cage, whirls around to watch the bird land on one of the far shelves. It twitches its tail, pondering the ceiling with head cocked sideways, one tiny eye focused on the light fixtures. Then it takes off again.

Angelo bellows a second warning of "bird loose!" just in time to see Ms. Wheeler slam the front door. A few people who had been on the verge of entering gather at the window to stare while she waves her arms high above her head in an effort to prevent the bird from flying into the cat cage. Fortunately, the tabby is asleep, as usual. Angelo sprints into the storage room and fumbles around for the net. The next ten minutes are complete chaos as Angelo, armed with his snare, and Ms. Wheeler, equipped with a bag, leap about opposite ends of the space like kids playing Keep Away. The finch soars frantically back and forth while the entire shop echoes with sound—birds squawking and screeching as they witness one of their own teetering on the precipice of freedom.

"*Wuh-oh!*" exclaims Skipper, the Hyacinth Macaw.

Finally the finch lands on one of the cages to rest, the parrot within pecking defensively at the bars. Arm raised, Angelo leaps forward, brings the net down, flips it over, and scrunches the opening in his fist. He places the bird back inside its cage then shoots an over-the-shoulder glance at Ms. Wheeler, who regards him with a furrowed brow and a shake of her head.

Angelo spends the majority of the remaining day out in the back alley, under the sun, wearing an apron and bulky rubber gloves while he cleans shit-crusted cages. He disassembles the structures and sprays them with a high-powered hose. His mouth is sticky, and sweat trickles down the small of his back, making its way into his boxers. He's unsure whether or not this is punishment, Ms. Wheeler's forcing him to labor in the heat, but he doesn't mind. An occasional breeze carries scents from the Mediterranean Flavors restaurant, and there is something soothing about the repetitive tasks. Scrubbing at the bars of one cage with a Brillo pad soaked in diluted bleach, watching the metal emerge clean, he recalls the events of the previous night...

* * *

After leaving the bar, Angelo and Bryce ended up at a Thai restaurant where Angelo stared pensively down at the mint-green tablecloth while waiting for his meal and listening to his friend divulge more details about his Army plans, Bryce speaking at length of his expectations for boot camp. The more Bryce said, the more anxious Angelo became. He wanted to express how afraid he felt—for Bryce, for himself—and yet couldn't find his voice. It wasn't until he lay under his covers later that night, with the old photo of his father and Mr. Skourtis placed beneath the glow of his bedside lamp and the TV's low, droning barrage of advertisements—zero-calorie sodas, Nike "Just Do It," Rogaine for Men—filling his head like white noise that Angelo finally relaxed...

* * *

The last cage is clean, and Angelo sets it in the sun with the others. He scrutinizes the metal, makes sure no obvious gobs of shit remain, and recalls what Ms. Wheeler once said about microscopic mites that sometimes prey on the birds. You can't see them, but you can see what they leave behind: tiny white specks on the cage bars. He yawns and stretches. His hands feel clammy inside the gloves, but he can't take them off yet. He drags the buckets of diluted bleach aside to be dumped later down the toilet then lifts a pail of hot water, pours it into the drain, and goes for another.

* * *

Evening comes and Angelo sits in his dining room, contemplating the sunset beyond the window and wondering why the days, growing longer now that it's early spring, feel so brief. Is it the work schedule? Or has Angelo, at twenty-four, already reached an age at which people start speaking of time's rapid passing? Perhaps it's only the evening hour that makes things seem more dramatic. Since he was a kid, Angelo has always been bothered by the quiet transition between day and night, as if the forces controlling the sun's descent are pulling him down, as well. It's always the time when he most worries about his chronic headaches or some matter at grad school. It's the time when he has the most trouble transferring the images in his mind to the paper in front of him; the drawings come out all wrong until night finally falls and his hand corrects itself.

He turns away from the view and goes to a corner shelf holding an array of small abstract sculptures, many of them done by Papou. Among these are also a set of marble figurines. They are in various stages of decay: some missing heads or limbs, others with heads but no faces, their features erased by time. He picks one up—a woman in a robe—and feels the ridges etched into the woman's garment, the stone alternating smooth to rough against his thumb. According to Yiayia, one of her sisters smuggled the figurines into America after their discovery by a cousin who worked with archaeologists during an excavation in the Peloponnese. They had never had them appraised due to fears the information would be turned over to Greek officials, who might then demand their return.

He puts the figurine back then goes into his bedroom and logs on to one of the dating websites Bryce suggested, cycling through profiles of local women aged twenty to twenty-four. Bryce is correct: there is a good variety of women online. Angelo, however, finds they all have a certain look in their photos, a gaze that seems part come-hither stare and part too-proud-to-beg sneer. It could be, of course, that he is just projecting what he wants to see. He's most interested in the borders of the photos, after all; the way they make it appear as though the women are boxed in comic book panels, stars of their own series.

He revises his search, types *comic books* in the tag box, and the screen fills with new faces. Disappointing, though hardly surprising, that a majority of them are who most people would expect: eraser-faced women wearing thick glasses and too-eager smiles. Still, he knows better than to be entirely superficial. He clicks on SciFiCindy510 and decides he doesn't really dig the full-costume subculture. He tries another profile, then one more. Dissatisfied, he revises his search yet again. This time he types *Greek* into the box. More disappointment, as his efforts don't yield many Greek singles. Most results appear along the lines of:

I'm Stacy. I'm a sucker for all things hot and exotic!... Favorite food? That's easy: Mexican, Italian, Indian, and Greek.

Or, *I'm Rachel. That's R-Dog to all my sorority sisters! Hey, Kappas! Any Greek bros out there?*

Angelo is hopeful when he skims the profile of Goddess777: *Hi, boys, I'm Athena. I'm looking for my Greek god. Do you fit the description?*

But then Angelo checks "Athena's" ethnicity and sees Spanish and Irish listed; a hot combination for sure, just not what he has in mind.

Later, he sits around the dinner table with the usual suspects. Yiayia even takes bites tonight, albeit small ones. Angelo reaches for a bowl of tomato slices drizzled with olive oil and scoops a few onto his plate after making room beside the helping of *keftethes*.

"How was work?" Despina asks.

"Not too bad."

"For such a good artist, you sure don't paint a vivid picture."

Angelo shrugs. "A bird got loose, that was something."

"Oh, yeah?"

Angelo nods. "A finch. It flew all around the shop. Ms. Wheeler had to lock the doors, and we chased the thing a good while before I finally captured it. Funny though, it didn't seem like it really wanted to escape. At least not leave the store, I mean. Like taking a spin and stretching its wings was enough. It seemed relieved when I put it back."

Despina frowns. "You could tell with a bird that size? Finches, sparrows… the smaller varieties don't seem like they have much personality. Not like parrots, anyway."

"Maybe when you work with them so much it's different. You see things most people miss."

"*Hmm.*"

"Tomorrow we must go *steen eklesia,*" Yiayia announces.

"Oh, you'd like to go to church?"

"Yes. I want to light a candle for my sister before the service. Angelo comes, too. Father Stavropoulou ask about him many times."

Despina gestures at her son. "You up for it?"

Angelo takes another bite of food. *I'm an adult,* he thinks. *You people don't have to talk to me as if I'm equipped with a bib every time we sit down to dinner.* But it has been years since he was last in church, though hard to figure why. He used to be able to blame his lack of religious commitment on his father, the man who'd decided long ago that Holy Liturgies weren't for him and caravanned the family to services only on select occasions, namely Christmas and Easter. But Angelo has been his own man for some time now. *Maybe too much time has elapsed, and he's strayed too far to make up ground*? He doesn't want to go and be a stranger, not only among the other parishioners but also in front of God Himself. Angelo supposes this is silly. He recalls Father Stavropoulou often saying that God accepts all. He remembers the priest well: the man's thunderous voice, his beard ever-trimmed with uncanny precision, and the trademark wire-rim eyeglasses that always seemed to catch light flickering from candles or flowing through windows so it appeared his eyes were flaring with some otherworldly insight. The man was always smiling and approachable.

Angelo, in his younger days, had little trouble marching up and kissing the priest's giant hand as is the customary greeting upon conclusion of services. The man's calm demeanor always put Angelo at ease. And during the Greek Festivals conducted on church grounds every spring, Father never missed an opportunity to appear as guest chef during one of the cooking demonstrations, cracking jokes while wielding kitchen utensils.

So maybe it is worth giving a shot, Angelo thinks, staring now into his glass while Despina and Yiayia wait for a reply. "Ma, can you pass the *keftethes*?"

Despina reaches for the platter, but Yiayia grabs her arm.

"Forget meatballs, *re*. What about church?" Yiayia demands.

Angelo smiles. "Sure. I'll go."

"Good," Despina says. "Maybe you'll connect with some of your old Greek friends, and then you can get off my back about it somehow being my and your father's fault that you lost touch with them in the first place."

Angelo lowers his eyes. "I know it isn't your fault, it's just frustrating."

"How come it's so important now to be connected with other Greeks? If you do go to Greece, you'll be reminded that most of us can barely stand each other for long. We all want to be the big shot, and it's that mindset that partly got the country..."

"Ma."

"Okay, so what's wrong with the friends you already have?"

"Nothing. Other than there's not very many."

"Quality, Angelo, not..."

"I know. But, still, at a certain point, everyone wants to be around their own people."

* * *

Angelo sits in his room contemplating a blank computer screen. He's thinking about the dating website, knows it will take more than one or two tries to get it right, though he is hesitant to log back on. He doesn't want to become, or perhaps admit he already is, one of *those* guys: the type who spend Saturday nights in their boxer shorts, alone, sipping Mellow Yellow and skimming the profiles of legitimate ladies while watching DVD porn with the volume low.

He swings his chair away from the computer. He starts a sketch but trashes it, attempts a second one and ditches that, too. Finally, he picks up his phone. He doesn't have good reason for keeping Tracy's number in the index, but her name remains, beneath his father's—Tasso—and above Trevor's, one of Angelo's art school classmates. Even after all this time, her listing seems to warrant a pause when he scrolls through the contacts folder. A simple click of a button would solve the problem, yet he can't bring himself to do it. He'd tried once, shortly after they ended things for the final time, but then rationalized the reasons he might still need to get in touch with her. What about all the things she had borrowed that he'd eventually want back? He had finally breathed a sigh of relief upon finding Tracy's number still stored in the calls-dialed database.

He gazes at her name now and has to shake his head. At the very least, there is no porn currently playing on the tube, and he is wearing jeans over his Haynes briefs. He can feel his heart thudding as he calls.

"Hello?"

"Hey, Tracy. It's me. Angelo."

"Ah, The Greek! How goes it?"

Angelo swallows. At least she used his nickname. "I'm good. You?"

"I'm okay. Just staying busy, keeping it moving. How's school, all your art work?"

"Good. Great… Y'know, I called because I was looking for that book of mine."

"Book?"

"*The Elektra Saga.*"

"Oh. I think it's still around here somewhere. Want me to try and dig it out for you?"

"Yeah. *Er,* no. Never mind. Why don't you keep it?"

"Oh. Okay. Great."

Angelo gazes at Papou's painting, narrows his eyes until it appears the stallions are moving. Below the painting there was once a photo of him and Tracy dancing, Angelo leaning a bit awkwardly with one arm out-stretched, Tracy in mid-spin looking back at him over her shoulder, mouth pursed with a hint of naughtiness. It was from the night they first met. Bryce had taken the picture to document Angelo's appearance on the dance floor, a rarity well-worthy of capture. A day and a half later, he had called her; three days after that, they were on their first date. And then, three weeks later came the night when Tracy had first commented on Angelo's ability to get the good juices flowing. All so long ago.

"Hey. You still there?"

"Oh, sure. Sorry. I might have some of your stuff here, too."

"I don't think so, Angelo. I'm pretty sure I got all my things back from you."

"Yeah, well, if anything does come up missing, you might call here first because at one time a lot of your... y'know, clothes and maybe a few perfumes, even, were in my room."

"Ah, mister. You're so thoughtful."

Angelo feels that tightness in his chest, in his throat, and swallows to ease it, knowing there is still time to save himself. Yet he plows on. "Tracy, really, if you ever need anything, I'm here."

"Thank you. I really appreciate that, Angelo. But I should get off..."

"Remember our song, Tracy?"

"*Hmm*?"

"'Casanova,' that old eighties tune by Levert?"

"I wasn't aware..."

"You remember. It was playing that first night we met, and I asked you to dance."

Tracy sighs into the phone. "Yes, I remember."

"And do you remember the line I used?"

"The one about how you had this problem with your phone, an empty space in the contacts index that needed filling, and that my name and number would be just the right fix? Now that I could never forget. Corny!"

"It worked, didn't it? Earned me a smile from you and a few pats on the back from my friends."

"I suppose it did, but..."

"Bye, Tracy." He doesn't wait for her to echo a farewell before ending the call and erasing the number for what he is certain to be the last time.

SEVEN

ANGELO TRAVERSES A shabby stretch of Market Street where shadowy figures huddle in the doorways of smoke shops, liquor stores, and tacky little tourist-traps. Garish sweatsuits, 49ers and Giants caps with spray-painted logos, and oversized jeans made in child-labor countries are suspended from wire in the shop windows as if floating in space. With iron gates rolled shut in front of them, it appears that the clothing is being prevented from flying away. This Angelo wishes to see: jeans and T-shirts escaping with no one inside them, like the wayward pajamas in his favorite Dr. Seuss book from childhood.

He moves to the next corner. It suddenly seems that this neighborhood is one of clones, each block identical to the one preceding it—the same sequence of stores. The same mostly black and brown faces: empty gazes cast down on the pavement with its spider-web cracks and puddles of spilled liquor making tiny islands out of broken glass. The majority of people are headed in the opposite direction. *Are they fleeing from some danger just as I walk toward it?*

Angelo considers that perhaps he is still home in bed dreaming, never having tossed and turned until he finally left the house and boarded a BART train for San Francisco. A new scent haunts his nostrils, incongruously overpowering the musk of cheap weed, urine, and garbage from alleys and doorways. He lifts his head, breathes deep. Bacon and eggs. The aroma wafts from a tiny Chinese-American diner cramped between the T&A market and yet another smoke shop.

Then a barrage of sound: the wail of an oncoming siren, the blast of a car horn, someone's scream of, "Fuck you!" And then, perhaps in answer, someone else lets forth a strange parrot-like screech, *"Coo! Coo! Cooouuu!"*

Next to the T&A market is a strip club; Angelo wonders if the joke is intentional or simply obscene serendipity. The club glows pink neon, and he stares up at a giant photo of a buxom woman gazing down at him, her hands clutching her bare breasts, her heavy-lidded eyes beckoning.

Once inside, Angelo pays the cover fee and passes through a curtain to make his way along a corridor lined with mirrors. He tries to ignore his seemingly slinking reflection but can't; wonders why anyone would want to be reminded of their presence in here. He finds it interferes with the fantasy, if he has to see his own sad self and grow more conscious of the fact that his wad of dollar bills will soon be swallowed by a hungry G-string. The mirrors are grouped in threes, and after every third mirror is a dark side passage. He has a flash of Howard the Duck pushing a cart and chanting, "Towels, lotions… antibiotics."

"Well, hello there."

Angelo turns to see a dancer up the corridor. She's a shapely, blue-eyed brunette in feathered orange bra and panties, her well-sculpted legs rendered taut by spiked heels.

Angelo clears his throat. "H-h-hey."

The dancer lets forth bubbly laughter, and then, before Angelo realizes it, she is beside him.

"Now, that's better, isn't it?" she says. She indicates a mirror. "We make a striking couple, don't we?"

"S-sure."

The dancer giggles again. "I like you. You're a hottie."

Angelo manages a smirk. "And I'll p-pretend you don't say that to every other jerk who strolls in here."

"Well, I do have a real thing for Mediterranean men. What's your name, hottie?"

"Angelo," he says, absurdly pleased she has noticed.

"I'm Jeanine. Have you been here before, Angelo? Let me give you a tour…" Before he can dig in his heels, Jeanine is whisking him by the hand down one of the side passages. She looks over her shoulder and says, "So, lemme see. Are you Italian? Greek?"

"Greek."

"Oh, I love Greece. All the history! I'm studying ancient history in school, y'know?"

"Paying your way through college?"

"*Huh?*"

"Nothing."

She frowns slightly. "The ends can justify the means."

"Yeah, you're right. Sorry."

The passage seems to continually twist and turn. Eventually, Angelo finds himself in a small, dark room with only a narrow couch in one corner and a desk in the other, above which, mounted to the wall, is some sort of plastic contraption with a timer and a slot in which to slide bills. Jeanine eases him onto the couch and runs her fingers along the crotch of his jeans.

"Do you have your wallet, honey? I want to do a special dance for you."

"W-well..." Angelo manages to utter, trying his best to ignore his sudden hard-on.

"C'mon, baby, lemme see the cash. It'll make me so hot."

Guess it would. Angelo reaches into a pocket.

"Yeah, there you go. So, you're Greek, *huh*? I was there last summer, y'know. Had a blast. So where's your family? Athens?"

Jeanine is straddled atop Angelo's thighs now, her words coming rapid-fire. Angelo, slouched as he is, can't dig far enough into his pocket to reach his wallet.

"Some," he says, writhing about in effort to yank his money free. He notices that the woman has a piercing above her lip, a small diamond stud where a beauty mark might otherwise be, the stone shimmering in the sickly light. He becomes momentarily distracted by the shine, just long enough to ease his struggling for the wallet. Only then does it come free. The wallet's solidity, the feel of its worn leather in his palm, causes him to wonder for the first time just what in the hell he's doing here. Why, for god's sakes, is he sitting with an all-but-naked woman on his lap, comparing Greek travel stories on the verge of paying for—among other things—the opportunity to hear more about her jet-setting ways?

"Hang on a second!" he finally blurts. "I'm not holding like that." He manages a chuckle. "It's a down economy, remember? Just came in to see some of you ladies dance on stage. This is all off the itinerary."

Jeanine smiles. "Off the itinerary? Sounds like an adventure to me, babe. Let's see what you have here." In a flash Jeanine is clutching Angelo's wallet, leafing through the bills.

"Hey!" Angelo shouts. "Hold up, now!" He feels silly, light-headed, and curses his erection, the waste of blood that could instead be boosting his brain. He wonders what his father would do in this situation, imagines the man giving Jeanine "the look" until she becomes a puddle, practically paying for his company. Angelo's face, at the moment, can only form anxious expressions. He watches Jeanine's hands as she counts the money, and he can't speak nor move.

"Here we are," Janine says. She stuffs half of the money into a purse on the desktop, the other portion going into the plastic contraption, digital numbers on its face beginning to tally the minutes. Then, Jeanine flings her bra aside and begins grinding atop Angelo's lap, fingers running through his hair, her breasts pressed against his chest. He can see the incision scars just below her nipples, and despite it all, he's thinking about surgery—her operation elective; his a necessity; yet a subject on which they could relate. Perhaps, if they had crossed paths under another circumstance it would be something they could discuss.

"You can touch me, you know."

Angelo swallows, letting Jeanine guide his hands along her thighs. Then he begins groping unassisted.

"*Mmm*. That feels nice. So, what do you do?"

"I draw."

"You draw?"

Flashes of his date with Carmen, but Angelo erases them. "Yeah. I'm in art school. Graduate program."

"Cool. I can barely draw a stick figure. So, do you have a girlfriend?"

"No."

"Seriously?"

"Yeah. Tough times."

"Hard out here for a pimp, huh?"

"I don't know about that."

Jeanine giggles. "*Mmm.* You're cute."

Angelo decides that he doesn't want to talk anymore. He looks into Jeanine's eyes and wonders what she's thinking. The experience might be better if neither of them had to pretend. Maybe if she comes out and says she isn't enjoying any part of this, Angelo can relax and at least stop over-thinking things. But what if she *is* enjoying this or taking at least bit of pleasure in the fact that it's him and not some stereotypical dirty old man in a crusty raincoat?

It's a familiar dilemma, something he often ponders when around women working in service industries... of any kind. Are they smiling at him, or are they smiling only because it's their job? Is a glance just a glance, or is it something more? Or is he altogether invisible? He usually leans on the side of modesty, giving them the benefit of the doubt. This dancer, Jeanine, is most likely somewhere else entirely, maybe thinking about her trip to Greece. Or about fucking her boyfriend. Or about fucking her boyfriend in Greece.

He watches the plastic box. He's never seen one before. Then again, he's never been a frequenter of these places. The minutes count down as Jeanine continues to gyrate atop him, sliding her hands across his chest. Angelo realizes he isn't even erect anymore, having out-thought his hard-on. He curses himself, thinks of his father again. Instead of wondering if this woman is enjoying his company, the man would undoubtedly ask himself, why wouldn't she be?

"It's hungry for more money, babe."

"What?"

Jeanine giggles again. "The box. You have to pay again. We're almost out of time."

Angelo feels suddenly groggy, as if emerging from a dream. "I'm low on cash."

Jeanine gazes at him for a long moment, her lips parted, forming a small smile. "I want to do something special for you." She says nothing else, and before

Angelo can shift position, his pants are unzipped. "I just need a little more money."

"Hey!"

Jeanine slides a condom down Angelo's shaft. Her hand is warm, and she begins gently stroking him, Angelo breathing deep and holding it a long time. Without thinking, he snatches his wallet and hands the dancer another bill. Jeanine is bent close to him now, working her wrist, pushing her breasts in his face, their softness brushing his lips. He can smell her perfume, her hair, he can feel it against his cheek; her breath, too.

For an instant—despite himself—he considers that he could have stayed home and done what she is currently doing for him... for free. But he pushes the thought away and goes with it. Everything is silent. Then Angelo is startled to find that he is somehow watching all this happen, gazing down at himself and Jeanine from above.

There comes a long, steady beeping that Angelo at first believes is only in his head. Maybe the tube about to blow? But then he realizes it's coming from the goddamn box. Jeanine is suddenly on her feet, tinkering with the device, and Angelo is back on the couch, inhabiting his skin again.

"Did you finish yet?" Jeanine asks.

"No. It takes me a long time... sometimes."

"I noticed. Did you enjoy it anyway?"

"Of course."

"Well, you have to go. Sorry. They'll start looking for me now, making sure I'm where I'm supposed to be."

"Okay."

"We can try again in a little while."

"But I don't have any more money. Really."

Something flashes in Jeanine's eyes. "You don't have to pay me again. Just find me after my dance."

"Oh..." Angelo watches her leave then exits in a daze. He stands outside the door for a moment to collect himself and realizes that he still has the condom on. The latex clings to his flaccid dick beneath his shorts and jeans. He supposes that would make sense if he was planning to go for round two. *Was Jeanine actually serious about the no payment part?* He moves up the passage, back toward the main corridor then loses his way. He tries to retreat down the passage and nearly walks into a mirrored wall. Maybe not unnaturally he thinks of the fabled Labyrinth.

"Oh, babe. Are you lost?"

Angelo sees Jeanine smiling at him. "I think so."

"The stage is this way. Come watch me dance."

"No. Sorry. I mean I'd like to. Just need some air first."

She points him in the right direction. Angelo glances over his shoulder to see her disappear behind the stage curtain as he heads for the main doors. Outside, he stands at the curb and watches the traffic lights change: green, yellow, red, and back to green. Someone crosses the street, coming toward him: a ruddy-faced, balding man in warm-up pants with buttons along the sides. They're the kind NBA players wear over their uniforms and then rip off as they hit the court. As the man hurries past him, eyes averted, then enters the club, Angelo wonders if Jeanine will give him the same spiel.

The wind blows, and Angelo hunches against the chill. He thinks of Jeanine's body, of her touch, and can't help but question why she offered more. But what is he going to do? Go back and ask for her number? *Yeah, right!* He'd paid a dancer for her time, gotten his money's worth and maybe a bonus. Why try to make it into something bigger? Or meaningful.

EIGHT

"ELA, BIG BRAIN! Wake up, *re*."

Angelo opens his eyes. "Sorry. I was just resting, Yiayia."

"Don't tell me you sorries. Save it *yia ton Thayo*. Is to His house we going on this Sunday, and you have to be alert."

The car climbs toward the church, passing houses painted American-tasteful pastel colors and boasting immaculate lawns, bringing to mind Easter eggs and spring grass. This seems fitting since the last time Angelo attended services was Easter Sunday seven years prior, just before his father left for Greece. Yiayia had insisted they all go together, and Tasso had agreed, even though he was living apart from the family for close to a year by that time, holed up at some younger woman's place in the 'burbs. She was a busty redhead he had reeled in one afternoon at the supermarket as, supposedly, she had stood puzzled in the "ethnic" aisle, scanning a box of phyllo dough.

Back then Yiayia had said that a little religion was just what her daughter and soon-to-be-ex-son-in-law needed, not to mend their marriage but to cleanse themselves of all the hurt and anger that had been festering for so long. A pre-closure, of sorts, before their union was officially terminated. That morning seven years ago, after Tasso arrived from the suburbs via train, they'd all approached Despina's car like an unfamiliar rental, no one quite sure where they belonged. Tasso instinctively went for the driver's seat—he'd often driven when he and Angelo's mother were still together—nearly colliding with Despina as she approached the door. Tasso stepped back with a chuckle and a bow. Angelo imagined that the man had displayed similar grace as a *kamaki* after landing a big catch.

The watershed moment in Mr. Skourtis's restaurant, where Tasso revealed his secret identity as King Kamaki, seemed like it had occurred only days prior. But four years had passed since Angelo was thirteen. He climbed into the back of the sedan hoping Dad wouldn't ask how "the fishing" was coming along. Angelo's net had as of yet never been full.

Upon hearing the engine start, Angelo donned his headphones, but those crummy earbuds lacked the power to drown the stilted dialog emanating from up front.

"Your fingers are all red," Tasso stated from the passenger seat.

Despina glanced at her hand on the wheel. "I was up early doing the eggs this morning. Nothing redder than Greek Easter dye."

"Yeah. I tried to teach Amanda the traditions, but it's not the same..." Tasso let his voice fade. Despina's exhalation through her nose was audible even over the traffic. Angelo tried to crank his music, but it went no higher. The rare sight of his parents together provoked knots of tension in his chest. In two days, his father was due to permanently leave for Greece, and Angelo didn't know how to feel. He hadn't expected the sudden numbness, anyhow.

All fell quiet until Yiayia spoke up. "You know, I read in the paper yesterday an unbelievable story. A retired fire fighter-man was killed by a frozen block of the piss when it dropped from an airplane's broken toilet. Can you imagine? One minute sitting out in the yard, next minute giant piss chunk crack your skull."

No one responded, perhaps muted by disbelief. Angelo turned to the window as they curved into the parking lot. The Greek Orthodox Church sat atop a hill overlooking the San Francisco Bay; he contemplated its expansive view as Despina cut the engine. Tasso was out first, going around to the driver's side to get the door, but not before Despina opened it herself, brushing right past Tasso.

Angelo exited next, smoothing his slacks, adjusting his tie, all while trying to read his father's stoic expression. He couldn't tell if his parents were annoyed with one another or just maneuvering like strangers. He gave up struggling with the puzzle and instead helped Yiayia from her seat. One arm braced around her shoulder, the other hand grasping hers, with a gentle motion he lifted the woman to her feet. Lastly, he grabbed her cane.

"Here, Yiayia."

"*Efharisto*, my dear boy." Yiayia's silvery hair was beautifully swept back from her face, and around her head she wore a brown scarf fitted with a purple pin shaped like a poppy. "Smell the fresh air, eh, Angelaki? We stand on this mountain like is Olympus."

Angelo brushed lint off Yiayia's coat. "It's just a hill, Yiayia."

Yiayia made a face. "*Bah!*"

Angelo took Yiayia's arm and escorted her along the path, Despina and Tasso close behind as they went into the church's Narthex to cross themselves before bending to kiss the icons. Then Yiayia went to light one of the candles in memory of her sister. Finally, they entered the Nave, settling into a middle pew. The copper ceiling glowed in the candlelight, Angelo gazing up at the mural of a bearded, bronze-toned Jesus who stared down at him with life-like, melancholy eyes. Byzantine paintings had ever intrigued Angelo. The rich, dark colors and the somber faces never failed to capture his attention in a way similar to comic books.

Father Stavropoulou appeared at the altar, chanting in Greek too quickly for Angelo to comprehend. Clouds of incense hovered as an intoxicating mist. Angelo was lulled by the rhythm of the words as he fixated on his parents's posture down the pew. They'd ended up next to one another but seemed separated by an invisible divider. Angelo watched the muscles in his father's jaw flex. Meanwhile, his mother kept wringing her pigment-stained palms. Angelo couldn't help wishing the service was over, his father already on the plane.

At liturgy's end, Father Stavropoulou handed Angelo a piece of chocolate from the Easter baskets usually reserved for young children. "Hello, my boy. I still remember you as the tiniest of babies... I can tell you're worried about your mother and father. It's a shame they've separated, but it seems God has separate plans for them. I'm always here if you need to talk."

Angelo nodded. "Thank you, Father." He started up the aisle, arm-in-arm with Yiayia. His parents had almost reached the exit, though they walked far apart.

Angelo recalls this as the current services conclude and he enters the banquet room for coffee hour. Parishioners gather at round tables before a backdrop of an ornate mosaic depicting ancient charioteers. It is a sight to behold, this blending of antiquity and modernity. But Angelo takes it in from the sidelines. He stands apart from the crowd, having just returned from a bathroom stop. Already he has lost sight of Yiayia and Despina. Sound echoes through the space, a mish-mash of laughter and phrases in Greek and English. At a corner table sit a group of four—two young men, two young women, dark-haired and olive-skinned—whom Angelo estimates to be around his age. He watches them laugh and sip from Styrofoam cups. He imagines walking over and introducing himself but can't make his legs move. He looks away but is still unable to spot his mother and Yiayia amid the crowd.

"Hello there."

Angelo turns as Father Stavropoulou approaches with his palm extended in greeting.

"Hi, Father," Angelo says, taking the man's hand. "I enjoyed your sermon today."

"Thank you, Angelo. It's nice to see you back. It's been too long."

Angelo lowers his eyes. "I know."

"Do you have a car yet?"

"Not yet."

"When you do, it will be easier for you to join us on Sundays. You won't have to rely on your mother, *eh*?"

There seems something funny in that: car ownership making it easier to visit God. "That's true."

"I'm just kidding, Angelo. All on your own time."

Angelo's eyes find the young people's table again. "You know, Father, I've been interested in meeting more

Greeks my own age. I think it would be good for me to be more involved in the church and make new friends."

"Wonderful, Angelo. Our parish needs more young men like you. In fact, we're approaching festival season. Why don't you come by next Saturday? There will be some young folks working, putting booths together and such. They'd appreciate your help."

"Thanks, Father. That's a good idea." Angelo finds himself admiring the man's beard again.

"All right, now," Father Stavropoulou says, smiling. "Go on and get yourself some *loukoumades* before they disappear. Sister Legakis and her group from the Philoptochos made them."

Angelo smiles, too. "I will." He gives Father a final nod then heads toward the refreshment counter. Despina and Yiayia sit at a table closest to the *meze* offerings. They apparently heeded similar advice from Father Stavropoulou as a paper plate of honey-drenched *loukoumades* glistens between them. Angelo pulls up a chair and reaches for one of the fried dough balls, careful to not dribble syrup on his necktie.

"Bravo, Angelaki *mas*," Yiayia cheers. "*Fai! Fai!*"

"They're good, huh?" says Despina.

Angelo nods, savoring the warm, sugary burst of each chew. He watches Yiayia wave to Konstantina Mavromatis sitting with a group a few tables over. Then Yiayia points a knobby finger at him.

"Don't eat too many, *re!*" She says. "You don't want to have big American belly. You ever see a drawing of a big-belly person on side of ancient Greek vase? No way, José."

"Yeah, well, I don't know about ancient Greeks," Angelo says, "but there are plenty of plump modern ones."

Yiayia waves a dismissive palm. "Ancient, modern, *bah*! We all Greeks with the same small bellies. Look, here come Ms. Mavromatis. You remember? She used to babysit you."

A tiny woman with hunched shoulders, dark glasses, and an impeccable bouffant hairdo crowning her head like a red-tinged dandelion puff turns at the sound of her name and waves enthusiastically.

In a shrill voice, Yiayia responds, *"Ande, re* Konstantina! *Pos paei? Ola kala?"*

"Nai, mia hara eimaste!" The woman plants Angelo with grandmotherly kisses, then turns back to Yiayia. *"Eisaste etime?"*

Ready for what? Angelo wonders. But then Yiayia says she isn't ready, and Kostantina goes back to her own group.

Angelo slowly sips his coffee, and for a third time, his eyes find the corner table where the four young people are sitting. He wishes he was close enough to eavesdrop; hear them talk of their lives as Greeks and Americans and silently compare those stories to his own. The women have long, wavy black hair and curvy figures. He has never dated a Greek girl before but imagines it would feel different; maybe a greater potential for true connection. Eyes still fixed on the corner of the room, Angelo pops another *loukouma* into his mouth.

"I worry for your belly to get big, *re,"* Yiayia says.

"Leave him alone, Mother," Despina retorts. "For heaven's sakes. He's not even chubby."

Angelo rolls his eyes. "Plus, I am twenty-four."

"That's right. He's a grown man, besides."

Yiayia purses her lips, shooting her daughter a look. "Never mind this, Despina. I say what I say because what if there is a nice girl looking Angelo's way? He don't want to look like a *yoorooni* to her."

"Mother, that he resembles a pig is the last thing a woman would say about Angelo."

"Hey, c'mon! Can you guys stop?"

"Sorry, hon'."

Yiayia's face takes on its sly, elfish quality, her eyes narrowing, her pointy chin jutting out. "That remind me..."

"Reminds you of what?" asks Angelo.

But Yiayia leans past him, waving her hand in the direction of Konstantina Mavromatis's table. "Konstantina *mou! Eimaste etime!"*

Angelo cocks his head. "Wait, ready for what?"

Yiayia and Konstantina wink at one another, nodding conspiratorially like village women in days of old must have done while plotting against the occupying Turks. Angelo frowns as Konstantina rises from her chair and goes to the corner table, whispering something into the ear of one of the ladies. The young woman meets Angelo's gaze before he can look away, his cheeks flushing despite his nonchalant lean in the chair.

Konstantina steps aside and extends an arm as if to show the young woman the way or perhaps present her to a groom-in-waiting. Angelo realizes an instant too late that he has been cast as the husband-to-be. His heart pounds as he shoots Yiayia a glance. His grandmother refuses to meet his eyes, giggling into her napkin. How long has she been planning this? Angelo reaches for another *loukouma* in hopes that the sugar might override his anxiety but knocks over his water glass. The young woman comes nearer, and, close behind her, Konstantina giggles into her own napkin. How long have *they* been planning this? The young woman— Konstantina's granddaughter, perhaps—is even prettier up close.

"Angelo," Konstantina begins, "*afti einai e eggonee mou*, Mihaela."

So, Angelo was right. He stands on unsteady feet and offers a sweaty palm. "H-h-h..." Angelo clears his throat to halt his stutter. "*Heyro polee.*"

Mihaela takes his hand and smiles. "*Epesis.*"

Angelo retakes his seat while Konstantina and Mihaela pull chairs up to the table, Angelo kicking himself as he realizes he should have offered one of the women his own seat. A full minute passes in silence. Konstantina and Yiayia still nod conspiratorially at one another. Angelo wonders if it's possible that neither woman realizes how obvious they are being.

Angelo refills everyone's coffee cups and steals subtle glances at Mihaela. He makes a mental sketch of her, imagines what it would be like to transfer her image to paper, wonders if his pencil line could do justice to the symmetry of her face, the delicate slope of her neck. Just as long as he refrains from giving her the sketch, no matter how true to life it may be.

"So," Despina finally breaks the quiet. "Mihaela. That's a beautiful name."

The young woman smiles shyly. "Thank you."

"Now, I detect a touch of an accent. Did you grow up here or in Greece?"

"I was born in Patra and lived there until I was ten."

"Ah, the Peloponnese. Our family's from there. Well, actually, my father came from Crete. But the rest, including everyone on Angelo's father's side, is from a town in the Peloponnese."

Mihaela smiles again.

"And after you left Greece?"

"We moved to New York."

"Queens?"

"Of course."

Everyone laughs except Angelo, who is frustrated by the fact that he should be having this conversation with Mihaela.

"Yes, you see," Konstantina cuts in, "Mihaela only come to California last year to study. She live with me."

Angelo looks at Mihaela across the table, admiring the way a lock of hair falls across her face. It makes her appear less intimidating somehow, but he still can't will himself to speak. If only he had a plethora of witty stories at his disposal the way his father always seemed to. Angelo conjures a memory of Tasso at some dinner party: kicked back in his chair, wine glass in hand, working the room with comical tales of a village childhood spent in the company of quirky characters whom he brings to life via theatrical impressions.

Angelo averts his gaze, but Mihaela hasn't met his eyes since their introduction. He stares now at the wet spot on the tablecloth where the water spilled. So, he inherited his dad's looks. But had the rest of that gene pool been drained before Angelo could fully soak up the goods?

"What do you think of that, Angelo?"

"*Huh*?" Angelo glances up at his mother.

"Mihaela was just mentioning that she's at Cal studying civil engineering in the Master's program."

"Oh. Hey, that s-s-sounds great. Good luck with that," is all Angelo can muster. Really, he's thinking *Just great; not only is this woman pretty, but she also must be pretty damn smart to be taking on such a field at the grad level at Berkeley. She's out of my league.* Why have Yiayia and Konstantina gone to such lengths? Haven't they come to a similar conclusion about where Angelo stands in comparison to this woman? Above all else, it seems that she, rather than Angelo, is in possession of a truly big Greek brain, to which Yiayia will undoubtedly soon testify.

"Mihaela *mou*," Konstantina begins, "*einai* top of her class."

"Oh, Yiayia, please," Mihaela protests.

Angelo smiles, enjoying the way she speaks the word *yiayia*.

"What, Mihaela *mou*?" Konstantina says. "You should be proud to share this accomplishment."

"Yes, is true," Yiayia adds. "Never be shy to brog about you big Greek brain!"

Bingo, Angelo thinks.

"I think you mean brag, Mother."

"*Eh?*"

"Brag about her big Greek brain, not brog."

Yiayia waves her daughter off. "Brag, brog, is all Greek to me."

Everyone laughs, even Angelo this time.

"Anyway," Mihaela says, "I don't want it to seem that all I do is think about civil engineering." Now she does meet Angelo's eyes. "I do like to go out and have a good time with friends." She seems to hesitate, then adds, "And I collect comic books."

Angelo's eyes widen. "You do?"

"I really enjoy Alan Moore's work, *Promethea*."

"Really?"

"Here we go," Despina groans. "Aren't you both too old for those things?"

"A lot of comics target an adult audience, Ma," says Angelo.

"And we know what kind of pictures they're full of."

Angelo rolls his eyes. "That's not what I mean."

Despina winks. "So, Mihaela, despite my efforts to instill in him a sense of practicality, Angelo here is studying..."

But, frowning back at his mother, Angelo cuts in with, "I'm an art major, focusing on illustration."

"Cool," replies Mihaela. "What do you have planned for after graduation?"

"I'm not sure yet."

"*Ah.*"

"So, yeah. That's me."

The table goes silent once more. *There I go, dropping the ball as always.* But the harder Angelo tries not to withdraw into himself, the further he recedes.

Mihaela drums her fingers on the side of her coffee cup then leans back in her chair to gaze at the table where her friends wait. *Damn. The girl is bored already.* Angelo knows he's supposed to do something. Mihaela was brought to him with an apparent purpose. He makes a last attempt to pluck words out of the air like trying to net escaping birds. Instead, he impulsively plucks a *loukouma* from the plate. The treats are lukewarm now, though that hardly matters. Angelo is thankful for the distraction. But then he catches Yiayia's attention. *Big mistake.* Something strikes in her eyes; a lightning flash that is there and then gone, just long enough to do damage.

"Angelo," the woman begins.

"Mother, please," Despina interjects, she, too, sensing the coming storm.

But Yiayia barrels on. "*Ti sou eipa preen, re? Meen fas tous ahlous loukoumades!*"

Angelo swallows, feeling the color drain from his face as the pastry slides down his throat. He wonders why she bothers speaking in Greek. It's not as though her remarks will be lost in translation among this crowd.

Mihaela chuckles, perhaps thinking it is all in good fun, and Yiayia zeroes in on her.

"*Koukla mou,*" she says. "You have such nice figure. How you keep this? It must be that you don't eat many sweets, eh?"

"Well, I do have a weakness for a good piece of *karthopita*, but..."

"But you don't eat many, yes?"

"Not unless I make it," adds Konstantina.

"My Angelo here," Yiayia continues, "he also have nice figure, no?"

Angelo shakes his head in disbelief, but Mihaela only smiles and says, "Yes, he does."

"Well, then. I tell him not to eat too many sweets because I know that when he on his own, in maybe ten more years, all he will eat is sweet things. Unless he has good woman to cook for him."

Angelo still can't believe it, though he should have known it was inevitable that Yiayia would jump right in.

"Well," Mihaela responds pleasantly, "I'm not getting a Master's degree just so I can stay in the kitchen."

Yiayia cocks her head, raises her eyebrows, and puts a hand to her chest in astonishment. "You hear this, Konstantina?"

"*Nai, re, akousa!*" replies the bouffanted woman.

Angelo knows it's now or never and takes a deep breath. "How about we have lunch sometime. Then maybe hit a comic store? Y'know, work up to the whole home-cooked meal thing."

Mihaela's cheeks flush a little and her eyes lower, but only momentarily. "We can do that."

For a long moment no one says anything. Yiayia and Konstantina stare at one another, seemingly dumbfounded by the fact that, in the end, their grandchildren have initiated contact all by their innocent selves.

"You see, Konstantina!" Yiayia blurts. "I told you this would work. I win you. I win you bet."

Konstantina clasps her palms together. "Yes, Maria *mou*! You were right. I should never have doubted you."

Both Angelo's and Mihaela's faces flush. Despina laughs, and Yiayia leans in to take Angelo's hand and whisper in his ear, "Now, you treat this girl nice. And do you have, *em*, what is this word? I should know it. Is Greek after all. Ah, yes—prophylactics? You know how to use?"

"For heaven's sakes, Yiayia!" Angelo mutters back.

NINE

IN THE BIRD shop's storage room on Thursday afternoon, Angelo stands among the sacks of seed. Ms. Wheeler is in front of him, scowling and wagging her index finger, though he can't hear what she's saying, having long ago tuned her out. But then the woman does something she has never done, not in all her days of berating Angelo for one mistake or another: she touches him. It's not much, the slightest nudge of an open hand against his shoulder. But the gesture yanks him back to the present, at least momentarily, sound returning in a rush.

"Are you listening to me?"

Angelo blinks and steps back, bumping into a shelf. His cheeks go hot, and his body stiffens. Ms. Wheeler continues to bark and wag her finger. Angelo takes a deep breath, closes his eyes...

Suddenly, he's nine years old and on the playground, the other kids taunting him. *Ah, ha! You throw like a girl, Angelo! You dropped the ball and lost the game for us. Damn you're slow, Angelo...!*

He's still nine years old, but at home now, in his living room. As a boxing match plays on the TV screen, he stands before his father with balled fists. The man crouches to eye-level with Angelo, hands out in front of him. *Hit hard! Be tough, re!* And Angelo throws another punch, his fist landing in the center of his father's left palm with a whack. The man only laughs, shaking his head in disappointment...

The scene shifts a third time to reveal a more recent memory from this past Sunday. Father Stavropoulou is at the altar, his gaze aglow with the light reflecting off of his glasses. Meeting the man's eyes, Angelo feels strength and confidence transmitted...

He blinks again and finds himself back in the storage room. Ms. Wheeler is still yelling, flecks of her spittle spattering his face. But he's lost in thoughts of church. Had that subtle yet significant transaction between him and the priest actually occurred? Or has he only been dreaming up a scenario from which to gain strength in this moment? Perhaps it doesn't matter if the desired result is the same. He takes another breath then slowly exhales as he sidesteps Ms. Wheeler.

"Hey! What are you doing?" the woman shouts. "I'm not finished with you."

Angelo yanks off his apron. "I quit."

"What?"

"Find some other loser to take your chicken shit."

"W-wait. Angelo, I..."

But Angelo is out of the storage room, slamming the door in Ms. Wheeler's face. He strides to the front of the shop, the birds squawking as he goes, and waves to Carmen at the register.

"Hey, girl, hey," Angelo says, approaching Skipper's cage.

"*Haaa-looow*," the Macaw answers.

"Actually, it's goodbye." Through the bars, Angelo strokes the bird's beak. From atop her perch, she lowers her head to let him scratch between her neck feathers. Angelo locks eyes with Skipper and sees his reflection in hers, noticing how he is leaned forward as though poised for flight.

Twenty minutes later, he rests his elbows on the counter and watches the bartender, the same stout black woman from his previous visit, as she dries cocktail glasses. This is a first, deciding to have a drink at three-thirty in the afternoon, though it seems an appropriate way to celebrate the quitting of a shitty job. Yet another milestone for him. There isn't much of a crowd. At the far end of the counter, a gaunt, gray-faced man peels at the label of his Bud bottle. Meanwhile, a pair of men in faded jeans and tool belts plays a round of pool while a woman with a butterfly tattoo hovers at the jukebox.

"Hey, I remember you."

"This time," Angelo says, the bartender in front of him now.

"Last Friday, wasn't it?"

"Yeah."

"Whiskey and soda, right?"

"Right."

"Jack Daniels?"

"Jameson."

"Two out of three ain't bad."

When his drink arrives, Angelo savors that first sip. He takes another gulp as the weight of what he's done at the bird shop sinks in. His choice is at once surprising and not. It seems that over the last four days he has felt a certain weightlessness—maybe a new courage—not unlike what young birds must experience upon gaining initial trust in their wings. Angelo has soared through mid-week with the echo of Father Stavropoulou's sermon still resonating in his ears. He was excited about church and about the prospect of helping out with the Greek festival. Not to mention his date with Mihaela.

So, on the one hand, it makes sense that he should feel confident enough to finally stand up to Ms. Wheeler as if she'd been some kind of Turkish *Agha*. But on the other, his act of defiance feels so foreign that Angelo has to now drink fast to combat the anxiety. Not only is he newly jobless, but the date he has been looking forward to—at least in theory—is now only mere hours away. Mihaela agreed to meet for dinner at the Mediterranean restaurant next to the bird shop, and in hindsight, Angelo wishes he had picked another place. And what if Mihaela is tired of Greek food? No doubt she eats it all the time at home with Konstantina. Well, he can always suggest someplace else. But what will they talk about? And what if the conversation lags? Should he tell her he just quit his job? She hadn't seemed very impressed when he'd mentioned not exactly having plans post-graduate degree. And then there is the issue of not driving. Aren't all real American men expected to be drivers?

So much for the boost in confidence. Now it feels more like he's ridden an updraft too close to the sun. Angelo downs the rest of his drink then rings Bryce.

"What's goin' on, Greek?"

"Not much. I'm surprised you even picked up."

"Believe it or not, it's a slow night, my dude."

"No ladies on deck?"

"Watch it now. I ain't say all that. Just nothing top-notch, what it is."

"Come meet me for a drink. I'm at the bar we hit up last week."

Bryce pauses a long moment, exhaling loudly into the phone. "I don't know, man. I'm kinda beat here..."

"One drink, Bryce. C'mon, I need someone to talk to. I quit my job."

"*Ha*! 'Bout time you bounced that bitch."

"And I have a date."

"A what? Ho, shit, Greek! You ain't said all that now. I want details. This chick hot? I'll be down in a few."

Angelo is halfway through his second whiskey-soda by the time Bryce shows up.

"*Yiagas*, Greek."

Angelo crunches ice and nods as his friend slides onto the neighboring stool.

"It's *yia-mas*, by the way," Angelo says.

Bryce raises his hand to summon the bartender. "It's all Greek to me."

"How fucking original."

"Jeez, bro, who shit in your Fruit Loops? You must be really sprung over this broad, huh?"

"Sorry. It's not that. Just been a rough day, I guess. Anyway..." Angelo knocks back the last of his drink. He fidgets on the stool, his knee pumping like a piston.

"Whoa, man," Bryce remarks, pointing at Angelo's leg. "A little edgy there or what?"

"I am kind of nervous. It's this girl. And I'm not a Casanova like you."

Bryce clicks his tongue, taking a hit off his Rum and Coke as soon as it arrives. "Man, please. Who's this girl, anyway? Are you fucking her?"

"No."

"Then why is she even worth your time?"

Angelo makes a face. "We just met."

"So you're past introductions. All the more reason to be boning by now."

"Are you still fourteen, asshole?"

"No, but at fourteen I was gettin' ass. Know why? Because I didn't waste time thinking about the shit I wanted to achieve. I just did it. So my advice is to be less like Socrates and more like Superfly."

"You're serious, aren't you?"

Bryce tilts back his glass with one pinky finger extended. "Of course I'm serious. Women don't like guys who think too much."

"What?"

"Did I stutter? Look, when you meet this chick tonight, be aggressive but not too aggressive. Y'all are meeting for dinner, right? Okay, when the bread comes, don't think 'Oh, the bread's here. Should I offer her the first piece while it's still all nice and toasty?' Man, just grab you a hunk of bread and then toss her the basket like it ain't nothing."

Angelo glances around for the bartender. "I think I need another drink."

Bryce thoughtfully strokes the blond stubble on his chin. "And don't go givin' her too many compliments either. Women can sniff insincerity. Compliment her a little, for sure. But talk some shit, too. Like if she mentions her new earrings or something, you say, 'Sure, they're pretty, but they're a little too big for your ears.' Something like that."

Angelo scowls. "Why in hell would I say that?"

Bryce rolls his eyes. "You really this clueless, man? If so, I don't think even I can help you. 'Cause the girl is testing you, man. She wants to see if you're a chump who's gonna go along with everything she says, or if you're the type who'll be a challenge. An Alpha male."

"I guess so."

"Jeez, man. Where's your swagger? Know what you could try, though? That pick-up artist shit some of these dudes be usin'. Basic manipulation all it is. Personally, I feel like if you got to read a book or take advice from some guy wearing eye-liner and a *World of Warcraft* amulet in this day and age, when eighty percent of women don't even believe oral sex is really sex at all, you got major issues."

"I don't think I'll be going that route."

"Listen to me," Bryce says. "I hear Greek men are some suave cats, y'know?"

"*Kamakia*," says Angelo. "That's Greeks in Greece."

"We gonna play semantics? Ask yourself, 'Why ain't I carryin' the torch?'"

"Torch?"

Bryce rolls his eyes again. "The Olympic torch."

"Okay, okay. I'll try."

Bryce flashes his gold-toothed grin and slaps the counter. "My man! Think you're ready for this big date now?"

"I guess."

"My man! The game is to be sold not told, but I just gave you a freebie. Now, since I'm in a charitable mood, let me buy you a drink. Bartender!"

* * *

It's almost seven. Angelo finally decides—after walking five or so laps around the block to kill time—that it's all right to stand in front of the restaurant and wait. He posts up by the entrance, keeping enough distance to appear casual. He wonders if Mihaela will even show up, takes a deep breath, and considers Bryce's advice. It isn't the first time his friend has bestowed him with manly wisdom. Angelo has encountered similar philosophies built on the notion that women gravitate toward that which might be out of their reach.

Seven o'clock becomes seven-ten. Seven-ten inches into seven-fifteen. Angelo is all but convinced he's been stood up when he finally sees Mihaela approaching. He straightens his stance, squaring his shoulders and puffing his chest.

"Hey there," Mihaela says.

"H..." Angelo clears his throat, tries again. "Hi. You look great."

Mihaela smiles. "You, too. That's quite a coat you have there. Camel hair?"

"Yeah."

"I appreciate a well-dressed man."

"Me too... I mean..."

Mihaela chuckles. "Nervous?"

Angelo runs a hand through his hair. "Me?"

"I am."

"What should you be nervous about? If anything, people should feel nervous around you. Okay, that came out kind of strange."

Mihaela chuckles again. "Aren't you hungry? Let's go in."

"I wasn't sure if you were in the mood for Greek food."

"I certainly get my share of *pastitsio* and *spanakopita* at home," says Mihaela. "But, can you ever tire of the stuff? Besides, it looks like they have an eclectic menu."

"Okay, after you, then."

The host leads them to a corner table. Angelo remembers to pull out a chair for Mihaela, though Bryce would undoubtedly scoff. Angelo notices how tiny the table is. Not so good for food placement, but great for intimacy. Were the opportunity to strike, he could kiss Mihaela by barely leaning forward. *Baby steps, Greek. Baby steps.*

A candle flickers between them, casting Mihaela's face in a soft, golden glow. Angelo steals glances at her while pretending to study the menu. She resembles a younger Catherine Zeta-Jones with a bit of Maria Menounos mixed in. Angelo is reasonably certain that, if he can somehow find a personality between now and dessert, success will follow.

A handsome waiter brings ice water and bread, along with an *American Dad* jaw. Angelo checks for interest from Mihaela, but her eyes stay on the menu. Finally, she puts it down and reaches for the bread basket. But Angelo snatches it first, pawing around for the warmest piece then shoving the basket back. Immediately his heart dives into his stomach. Still, he's determined to give Bryce's methods a chance.

Mihaela raises an eyebrow. "Apparently, you are hungry."

Angelo bites the bread before an apology can escape his mouth. He chews a while and finally mutters, "Guess so."

Mihaela cocks her head. "Is something wrong?"

"Wrong? Why would you ask that?"

"You seem a little… agitated all of a sudden."

"Me? Maybe you're agitated."

"No. But if you'd like to see me get agitated, you're on the right track."

Angelo tears into the bread again, thinking absurdly of Popeye's spinach. "Those earrings are pretty nice."

Mihaela softens. "Thank you."

"But they make your ears look kinda big."

Mihaela frowns for a moment then laughs, Angelo relieved by her reaction.

"I get it," she says. "You're trying to be funny."

Angelo pops the last bite of roll into his mouth and talks around it. "I don't have to try."

Mihaela takes another glance at the menu. "You might be right."

"You enjoy my natural humor?"

"Your natural humor, maybe. Provided I ever see it. But whatever you're doing right now, I don't."

"Angelo nearly chokes on the bread but reaches for more. Mihaela pulls the basket away.

"Enough *psomi*, don't you agree? Do you think I'm stupid?"

"No. Of course not."

"Then why are you putting on this infantile act? I'm here to meet Angelo Koutouvalis, not Johnny Bravo."

Angelo feels heat in his cheeks. "Sorry."

Mihaela smiles. "I think Angelo just arrived. Are we ready to order?"

Angelo has a flash of seeing himself, for a change, as the guy who's just banished a creep from some pretty young woman's table. "Sure. If you are."

They sip red wine while waiting on the food. Angelo, boosted by his reviving buzz, leans back in his chair. He feels less like himself, yet not quite like his father. Whatever his father feels like.

"You have really beautiful eyes, by the way," Angelo says. "I guess that's kind of a generic compliment."

"I'm less concerned that it's generic and more concerned that it's genuine."

"It is." Angelo lowers his own eyes and says, "Sorry for acting like a pri... an ass earlier."

Mihaela smiles. "I forgive you. Something told me you might be worth waiting for."

Meals served, they begin eating. Angelo takes another sip of wine. Everything blends—the familiar, homey flavors, the plucked notes of the *bouzouki* in the background, the flicker of the candle's flame. All these elements stir in Angelo a sudden nostalgia...

He's three years old again, enduring a second baptism—metaphorically, at least—by way of his *yiayia*. She stands in shallow Mediterranean waters, holding him in her arms one moment, playfully dunking him the next. The warm water, the vivid blue tone—this vision caresses him now like an ocean wave, his heart a full moon...

Mihaela asks, "Food's good, huh?"

"Yes. So, tell me about yourself. I know you like comic books. I know you were born in Greece. I know you're studying civil engineering and living with your *yiayia*."

"That covers it, then." Mihaela watches his face and laughs. "I'm pretty laid back in general." A wry smile. "Fairly low-maintenance."

Angelo also smiles. "Low-maintenance in general or low-maintenance for a Greek girl?"

"Have you dated a lot of Greek girls?"

An anxious twinge tries to build in Angelo's belly, but he drowns it with wine. "I haven't dated a lot. Only had one real serious relationship, actually. Or semi-serious, anyway."

Mihaela seems genuinely puzzled. "Why is that?"

Angelo sips more wine to buy time. Should he mention the tube in his head, the scars marring his body? Should he admit to the desolation he feels? At least in this case, them both being Greek, he senses that to say he lives at home with his mother and *yiayia* wouldn't be a strike against him.

"I guess," he finally says, "I have trouble putting myself out there, y'know?"

Mihaela only shrugs. "It is a tough thing for a lot of people. But I have a feeling that's not all there is to it, with you."

Angelo clears his throat. "What about you? Had a lot of serious relationships? If you don't mind my asking, what kind of guys do you like?"

With her wine glass poised in one hand as she thoughtfully gazes at the ceiling, Mihaela for a moment resembles an ancient beauty offering a toast to Dionysus. "I guess I go for creative guys," she begins. "I've sort of always had a thing for somber, introspective artist types."

"You're in luck this evening," Angelo responds with a genuine chuckle. "And I suppose you only date Greek guys. Though somber, Greek, and artist kind of narrows the field, huh?"

Mihaela smiles again. "Remember, I'm from Queens. There aren't as many of us there as there used to be, but Astoria is still a center for Greeks, some of whom are artistically inclined. I've dated my share, I suppose, though many of them went around with their hair a bit too heavily gelled for my taste. I wouldn't say I'm only interested in Greek men, though. Actually, before I left New York, I was involved with an African-American guy. Really sweet. Charles was his name. A poet."

"Your parents weren't upset?"

"Well, my dad wasn't thrilled. But even he warmed up a little once he actually met Charles. My mom was okay with it. Except she did point out that nobody in America can make a living from poetry. Still, I think they'd prefer I settle down with someone who's Greek. And you're the first Greek guy I've been out with on an official date since I arrived in California."

Angelo smiles. "I'm glad this is official. Slim pickings?"

Mihaela smiles back. "Don't sell yourself short. And you seem to be a great guy… despite your initial attempt to show me someone else. I'd love to see some of your drawings."

Angelo laughs, truly relieved. "Glad to hear that. But I just meant that the community is so spread out here."

"True. But the church is beautiful, and I enjoyed the service on Sunday."

Angelo nods. "I wish I'd been more involved when I was younger."

"You don't have one foot in the grave, you know. How's your Greek? Did you take lessons as a kid?"

"I went to Greek school for a while. Made a few friends, but then I stopped going, and we lost touch. I can speak pretty well, I guess. It must have been nice living in such a big Greek community, *huh*?"

Mihaela considers. "It had its positives and negatives. It can feel a little stifling sometimes, like it's limiting your choices in life.

"As in dating black poets?"

"Or poets, period. As in 'you're in America now, so you must chase the almighty dollar.' That's part of the reason I decided to study in California. I wanted to be around different cultures and people. Greeks can be so judgmental about others. Though I guess that's not an exclusively Greek trait. A lot of the girls my age are bougie and snobbish, a lot of the guys are *malakas*."

Angelo realizes that, all other nice things considered, it's just good to have someone with whom to talk. "Maybe off-topic," he says, "but what's your take on the current situation in Greece?"

Mihaela considers. "I don't see it getting better anytime soon. They wanted to play with the big boys and get on the Euro, knowing full well they could never keep up. But the country's biggest problem may be its past."

"How so?"

"The world in general seems to look at Greece like there was the ancient golden age of democracy and philosophy and drama and then the Greece of today, with nothing in between. Modern Greeks either get idealized—like they're still walking around in togas—or unfairly slandered, as if they're all funny, lazy party people. Today's Greeks have to form their own identity somewhere between their glorious past and current slacker Zorba image."

"You folks all done here?" the *American Dad* waiter asks, appearing tableside.

Angelo looks at Mihaela. "Are we?"

The waiter adds, "Any dessert this evening? We have an excellent *tiramisu*."

"Your call, Mihaela," says Angelo.

"I'm full, but go ahead if you'd like."

"I'll think we'll pass, thanks."

The waiter leaves, and quiet ensues at the table, though the music comfortably fills the space. Then Mihaela asks, "How about a dance?"

"*Huh*?"

"Dancing," Mihaela says. "Would you like to?"

"Oh..." Angelo looks toward the open floor by the bar where people engage in a variety of traditional Greek dances. The feet of even those who perform the slower steps seem to dart around too quickly for him to follow, much less imitate. He remembers once being in similar surroundings, standing in awe of his father as he'd watched the man crouch to the ground, lean back and move his body to a slow *Zembekiko* tune, all the while balancing a plastic cup of Metaxa on his forehead. Tasso had held out his hand, beckoning for Angelo to try a few moves. But Angelo had refused.

"I don't know," Angelo says, eyes still on the dancers. "I'm not very good. Well... okay." He smiles and adds, "Just don't expect a Zorba."

They join the other men and women swept up in the swift steps of the *Kalamatiano*—the dance Angelo has watched many non-Greeks attempt at Greek Festivals. He and Mihaela link hands with the other dancers as they rotate the space in one big circle. Initially, Angelo feels as though he's being dragged along while trying to calculate each step. He stumbles twice, relieved when he doesn't throw everyone else off balance. Still, Mihaela is smiling at him.

Angelo feels as though he is out of his body, above the scene, looking down at himself. He's struck that somehow the night has turned out just fine. He closes his eyes, tightens his grip on Mihaela's hand, and lets his body fall into rhythm. He's back in his skin, back on the dance floor, turning, turning, turning, the music in his head and in his blood as he glides with arms spread like wings.

TEN

ANGELO SPENDS SATURDAY morning sketching at his desk. He smiles, nodding in satisfaction as he swipes away eraser residue and studies the picture. Helen of Troy as he imagines her. The face is unmistakably that of Mihaela, her likeness, he thinks, fitting for the role of Spartan queen.

The woman has occupied his thoughts since their date. Angelo springs to check the number whenever his phone warbles. Yet he is reluctant to become too enthusiastic: he's superstitious in that old Greek way of not tempting the gods. He kept his words to a minimum when prodded by Bryce for details, just as he's evaded Yiayia's persistent attempts at interrogation. And yet, beneath his strongest impulse to remain secretive lies an urge to open up to somebody. He cycles through his phone contacts. Maybe his father would be encouraged to know his son isn't entirely a lost cause.

He checks the clock to calculate the time difference: 10:30 already. His work has devoured the early morning hours, and he has to get to church for the festival prep. Still, he figures there is time for a call. It's past midnight in Greece, but his father is a night owl.

"*Yasou, Patehra,*" Angelo says when Tasso picks up.

"*Ela! Pos eisai, agori mou?*"

"Doing fine," Angelo answers. "Weren't sleeping, were you?"

"No, no. I'm down at the harbor with your *thio* Yianni. It's a beautiful night. We ate *barbounia,* and now we're finishing some *lefko krasee. Pes yasou sto thio sou!*"

Initial static and then Angelo can decipher voices joined in song. He shouts a "*Yasou!*" into the phone, but his greeting seems lost in the ether. Then a moment of silence as Angelo wonders if the call has been dropped. At last comes his uncle's "*Yasou!*" in return, and Angelo imagines the scene: his father, uncle, and the rest of their *parea* gathered at a seaside taverna, guzzling wine served from a ceramic jug while the moon beams above.

"Did you hear?" his father asks. "They all say hello and ask about you. All your *eikoyenya* here say to me, 'When will Angelo come to visit?' And I say to them, 'I don't know, he's anxious about flying.'" Tasso chuckles. "But your cousin Manolis always tells me, 'No, Angelo *einai manggas. Megalo palikari einai*!' You see how they love you?"

The word "anxious" lingers in Angelo's ears. He looks at the drawing, and now the proportions seem slightly off. He pushes the paper aside, tries to conjure an image of Manolis, but the memory is almost too dim. "Tell them I think about them all the time. And I hope to make a trip soon."

"Yes, that I'd like to see."

"So, how's things?"

"Everyone's doing fine, despite the financial turmoils. Your *yiayia* Eleni just had surgery on her eyes. She had cataracts removed, and she's much better now. And your *thia* Voula and *thio* Elia just got back from a trip to the island of Corfu. Elia has a house there, remember? No, of course not. You were too young."

"So, Dad, I actually have some cool news."

"Oh, yeah? *Pes mou.*"

"Well, the other night..."

"*Ohee, re, eimai sto telephono,*" Tasso cuts in, apparently addressing someone in the background. "*Nai, nai. Ola kala.* I'm sorry, Angelo, go ahead."

"So, anyway, the other night I went on a date."

"Really? Nice, Angelo."

"Yeah, the woman's name..."

"*Uh-huh,*" Tasso cuts in again.

"So, her name is Mihaela. She's a Greek girl."

"How nice. So, you are friends? From church?"

Angelo doodles on the back of an envelope, pressing hard with the tip of his pen. "Sort of. But it was a date. The romantic kind."

"Great, Angelo, great. Have fun, just don't fall in love. You're still too young. Panos, your cousin, has it right. He goes from one girl to the next. You remember Panos, don't you?"

"Sure."

"He's a good boy. Man, I should say. Strong. Doesn't fear nothing."

Angelo resists the urge to sigh. Then a long-buried memory surfaces: Angelo as a boy, standing in the yard losing a battle for Tasso's attention, as another boy, the son of a family friend, charms the man with some long-winded yet clever joke. Or was it some expert performance of boyish physical powers...?

"So, Dad," Angelo begins again. "This date was..."

"*Ela*," Tasso cuts in again. "I'm running out of juice on this damn battery."

"Okay, well..."

"We'll talk again soon, Angelo. Say hello to everyone there. Love you, *re*."

"Love you, too, Dad."

"*Andeh, kalinekta.*"

"Goodnight, Dad."

His father hangs up first, and for a long moment Angelo keeps the phone to his ear, listening to empty space.

* * *

He arrives at the church still thinking about Mihaela. He is anxious—that word again—over possibly having jinxed himself now that he's told someone about her. Although his father responded to the news with such apparently underwhelming interest that maybe it doesn't count. It wasn't the first time Tasso had seemed distracted during their conversations. Angelo supposes he should be used to the way his father seems ever-pulled in different directions, everyone vying for his attention.

Crossing the church grounds, passing the main chapel, Angelo checks his phone to make sure he hasn't missed any calls from Mihaela. Up ahead, a handful of young men in work clothes march about. Two of them haul two-by-fours; the other three wield electric drills. The sun seems to hover over them like a fiery-tempered foreman. As he approaches, he can hear their conversation:

"... *Ela, re, malaka*. You know my family's from Sparta. They still breed warriors there."

"Anyways! Like I was saying, this fool hits the gym and only works his arms. I keep telling him, 'You're gonna end up with Popeye biceps on an Olive Oyl body! What kind of Spartan will you be then?'"

"At least I don't go around with a spray tan, bro. I thought you were Greek. Not some guido, *Jersey Shore* reject!"

Laughter erupts, and Angelo feels uncomfortable, though knows they're not laughing at him. Yet, anyway.

"Hey," he manages. "Are you guys part of the festival crew?"

"We *are* the festival crew, boss," answers a tall, bony twenty-something with a bottom lip bulging with what Angelo figures to be chewing tobacco.

"So, I'm in the right place," Angelo says.

The crew speaks nothing in return, they just scan him while they put down their tools. Angelo feels like he often did on the playground, always the last to get picked for teams. Finally, a pot-bellied guy with a deep olive skin tone and hands the size of bear paws says, "So you came to help out? *Kalos orisete*. I'm George."

"*Hayro polee*. Angelo."

"*Harika*, Angelo. This is Jimmy," says George, pointing to the young man with the lip full of chew. Then he continues down the line, "Vassili, Niko, and Popeye-arms is John."

"Nice meeting you guys."

The group nods in return.

"So," George says. "Where you from, Angelo?"

"You mean roots-wise, like in Greece?"

Chuckling, George raises an eyebrow. "We can start from there. But I was thinking more along the lines of are you local or not?"

Angelo makes a smile. "Should've figured that. I grew up here."

"Really?" asks Niko, his stature stout and strong like a bulldog's. "Can't remember seeing you in church."

The sun glares. Angelo scratches the skin below his hairline, feels the moisture there. He hasn't exactly chosen the best work clothes: a Polo shirt and new jeans.

The rest of the group is clad in ragged old jeans and shabby T-shirts. He clears his throat.

"Yeah," he says. "My parents weren't much involved with church when I was growing up, but now I'm trying to get back into it on my own. Father suggested I help out here today, if I can." Angelo catches himself shifting his weight, one leg to the other and back again, like an unprepared kid whose turn to speak in front of the class has come. He notices John whispering something to George in Greek. George laughs then turns to Angelo.

"*Melas Ellenika*, Angelo?"

"Huh?"

"Guess not."

"I just didn't hear you."

"Just curious as to how good your Greek is."

Angelo feels put to a challenge and responds with, "*Etsi-kai-etsi. Katalaveno ola, kai boro na melao, alla siga-siga.*"

Vassili, sporting a colorful tattoo of an Athenian shield on his forearm, nods approvingly and then nudges George. "He speaks well. *Manggas einai.*"

George nods, seeming to approve, then picks up a drill. "John and Niko are bringing the boards while me and Vassili lay them down then drive the screws in place. We're making platforms for the booths. Wanna take my spot for a while?"

Though he accepts the tool, Angelo feels a long way from blue-collar. "Sure."

"All right," says George. "*Pame, paidia!* We've got a lot of work."

It isn't until he has the drill that Angelo realizes he has never used one before. He swallows as work resumes. The other guys recapture their previous momentum, lifting and carrying, crouching and pulling, marching past Angelo without so much as a glance. Finally he goes to where Vassili is on his knees drilling screws into wood.

"*Ela, re*, Angelo. This might be faster if I ready the screws and you drive them in."

"Sure." Angelo hunches to the ground.

"So," Vassili says, grabbing another fistful of screws. "You didn't tell us."

"Tell you what?"

"Whereabouts you have roots in the old country."

"Oh. The Peloponnese, mostly. My *papou* on my mom's side was from Crete."

"Nice. The Peloponnese, eh? My parents are from the island of Zakynthos. We go back to visit every summer. You been, I guess?"

The handle of the drill is chipped, and it pinches Angelo's palm. "To Zakynthos?"

"I just meant Greece, in general."

"Oh. We used to go quite a bit, but I haven't taken a trip in a long time. Not since I was, like, ten."

"Why not?"

"Money, mostly." Angelo looks at Vassili, something about him—his Greekness, perhaps?—causing him to feel a little more at ease. "Also, my dad moved back there after my folks split. About seven years ago. He and I didn't get along very well. At the time."

Vassili nods. "Greek dads can be tough. What did your old man do when he was here?"

"He was a contractor. Olympus Electric was his company."

"That sounds familiar. My dad's a plumber. Pegasus Plumbing." Vassili laughs. "We gotta fit Greek culture into the name somehow, right? It's like a requirement. My old man might know your pops. I'll ask him tonight."

Buoyed by the conversation, Angelo applies the drill with confidence. But instead of burrowing into the board, the screw spins out of the hole and flies away.

"Here," says Vassili. Taking Angelo's drill, he flicks a switch on the side. "Now try."

Angelo pulls the trigger and this time the screw whirls into the board.

Vassili nods. "Switch is weird on that drill. Should've warned you."

"No problem." Angelo, relieved, carefully spirals the next screw into place. Soon he gets the hang of the job.

Everyone works steadily through the next few hours, Mediterranean pop blasting from a boombox. Angelo is unfamiliar with most of the current hits from Greece, though he nods along to the music with the other guys. They pause once or twice to stretch and gulp bottled water. Jimmy spouts a steady stream of brackish tobacco spit, sharing his stash of chew with anyone who wants a lipful. Angelo isn't among the partakers. He gradually grows comfortable with the labor, and though his hands fumble a bit now and then, they gain proficiency.

Vassili is a steady source of encouragement, patting Angelo on the back every so often and playfully nicknaming him "The Machine" due to his increasing pace with the drill. The guys continue talking shit, Angelo joining the laughter as they include him in their jokes. At some point, between the driving of one screw or another, Angelo starts thinking of himself as one with the group. He watches his hand work the drill as though it's not his own, and then a shrill whistle startles him. He glances over to see George leaning out the driver's side of a battered pickup truck as it rolls into the parking lot.

"Break time!" George shouts.

Vassili drops his fistful of screws and motions to Angelo. "*Ela, re*! Lunch!"

Angelo follows Vassili to a corner of the grounds where George, Niko, John, and Jimmy occupy a picnic table. Burgers wrapped in wax paper and bags of French fries are spread like a bounty before them. Vassili plops down next to John and snags a burger. But Angelo, seeing that space is filled, remains standing. Everyone looks up from their food, and Vassili waves him over.

"*Ela*! Aren't you hungry, *malaka*?"

"I wasn't sure if there was room."

"Brother, we'll make room!" says Vassili. He and John scoot over on the bench, and Angelo slides in next to them.

George thrusts a cheeseburger toward Angelo, its wrapping stained translucent with meat juices. "Here, *re. Fai!*"

Angelo takes the burger and then grabs some fries. "Thanks."

George waves him off. *"Parakalo."*

"Hey, Yiorgo," Niko says, gesturing to George. "Didn't you get any drinks?"

"Yeah," George replies around a mouthful of food. *"Ena leptoh."*

Angelo watches him get up and waddle toward the truck, returning with two six-packs of Amstel Light.

"Whoa!" Jimmy exclaims, spitting his wad of chew on the ground. "Beer, *re pousti*? We still have work to do!"

"We got a lot done already," counters George, wiping sweat from his brow as he looks over at the platforms standing nearly complete. "We earned a drink. Besides, you gonna get *stupa* off just a couple light beers?"

"What we earned, brother," Jimmy begins, "are places in heaven through these deeds done on earth."

George rolls his eyes and opens a bottle. *"Endaxi,* Mr. Papas-in-training. You believe this guy, Angelo?"

"Just gimme a beer," Jimmy snaps. "I'm not worried for heavenly reasons. I, unlike some people, care about doing a good job on earth."

George slides Angelo a bottle, opens another for himself, then finally hands one to Jimmy.

"You guys are fuckin' unholy!" says John. "Gonna give Angelo a wrong impression so he won't want to come back next week."

"You been to the Greek Festivals before?" asks George.

Angelo nods, his mouth full of meat and cheese. "I usually go. It's just that I don't know many people."

"Now you know us," says Niko.

"For sure," Angelo replies.

"You heard that saying?" asks John. "'A Greek always has a home among fellow Greeks'?"

Jimmy takes a swig of beer. "I bet he knows this one—'Get two Greeks together and you'll have five opinions'!"

Angelo chuckles along with the others.

"Anyway," George says, "we work the festival every year. Set it all up then help out at some of the booths. I'm usually at the gyro booth."

"You can find me at the lamb sandwich spot," adds Niko.

"*Saganaki* is my gig," Vassili says.

"*Spanakopita*," says Jimmy.

Angelo looks to John, who doesn't answer. Following Angelo's eyes, Vassili says, "He does security. Likes walking around with a walkie-talkie. Plus, it gives him a chance to show off his Popeye arms."

"That's right," says John, taking a gulp of beer. "Chicks love 'em."

George tilts his chin toward Angelo. "We can put you at the calamari booth, if you want. You'll come out smelling like *psaria*, but it's fun work, I think."

"I'll give it a try," Angelo says.

The table falls quiet for a time, the group finishing their lunch as seagulls circle over the chapel and eye them in hope of leftovers. Following the gulls, Angelo's gaze drifts toward the distant Bay, golden with evening's approach. He thinks of Wings-n-Things and wonders how Skipper is faring in his absence. It feels like so much time has passed since he quit the job, yet it's only been two days. He still hasn't told his mother nor Yiayia that he's now unemployed. When Despina asked why he wasn't working this morning, Angelo lied, telling her that he had arranged a day off in order to help the festival crew. He still isn't sure why he hasn't told the truth.

Talk sparks up again as Niko questions the whereabouts of some guy named Kosta—apparently a mutual friend of the group—and they all theorize as to why he's absent. This Kosta person is apparently important or at least well known. His name triggers discussion of at least a dozen other names, all of which belong to local Greeks. This is fascinating to Angelo, if only due to the sheer amount of people cited. It seems a virtual six degrees of separation.

As if suddenly remembering Angelo, George turns to him and raises the last of his beer in cheers. "Sorry. We get to gossiping like hens in the *horyo* sometimes. You all right?"

Angelo nods. "It's interesting. You guys really know a ton of folks."

"I suppose," Vassili responds with a shrug. "We grew up with all these people. Went to Greek school together, Sunday school, church camp, danced in competitions, all that." He laughs. "Stuck with Greeks from the get-go."

Angelo considers a final fry. "You're all lucky."

Vassili says, "Angelo was telling me that his dad had an electrical contracting business before he moved back to Greece."

"Yeah?" says George. "You planning on continuing the family business?"

"Probably not," says Angelo. "I'm... in art school. I want to be an illustrator."

A moment of silence follows, and Angelo expects the worst. These guys will surely echo his mother's frequent sentiments about art not being a real job.

At last George asks. "You can get paid for that?"

Angelo tries to look wry. "Supposedly."

"Well okay, then!" bellows George.

Angelo thinks perhaps he should have substituted graphic designer for illustrator. *Maybe they'll lose respect for me now?*

Then Vassili asks, "Why don't you come out with us tonight, Angelo?"

"*Huh*?" says Angelo, stupidly.

"We're thinking of hitting the City. Probably go to a club or two. *Ela na pameh mazee.*"

"Sure," Angelo says.

George nods. "We'll scoop you up around nine, nine-thirty. *Endaxi*?"

Angelo smiles. "I'll allow for Greek time."

Everyone laughs.

"All right, *paidia*," George says, gathering the trash and throwing cold fries to the gulls. "Only a bit more, and we'll call it a day."

Together, they go back to work.

ELEVEN

AFTER CHURCH ON Sunday, Angelo walks to a florist's shop, still clad in his black slacks and jacket which absorb the sun's rays like a sponge. He chooses a colorful assortment, and the young woman at the counter smiles in seeming approval. Angelo smiles, too, as he hands her the money.

On a shelf behind the woman sits a small canary cage, the bird twittering between sips of water. "Never a quiet moment in this place," the woman says, following Angelo's gaze as it meets the bird's momentarily. "He belongs to the owner, and he must be so happy singing non-stop the way he does."

"How do you know it's a boy?" asks Angelo before he can worry about possibly being misunderstood.

"Well, I just assumed. He struts around that cage like I imagine a male would."

Angelo says, "Actually, the sexes of birds can't be determined without surgery. It's a simple operation and necessary if you want to avoid ending up with baby birds should the owner ever buy a second canary."

"*Hmm,*" says the woman as if deciding Angelo isn't trying to be funny. "I'll make sure Rebecca knows that."

"And it could be singing because it's annoyed about something."

"Really?"

Angelo nods. "Most of the time when we hear birds chirping in the trees, it's because they're competing for food or shelter or a mate. Not because they're having a great morning." Then he laughs. "Sorry, this's all probably way too much information."

But the woman is smiling. Then a flash of recognition comes over her face. "You work at that bird store, don't you? Rebecca sends me there to pick up seed and cuttlebones."

"Well..." Angelo straightens his posture. Quitting a job is nothing to be ashamed of. Especially a shitty one. "I don't work there anymore, but I think I remember seeing you."

"I'm Chloe, by the way."

"Angelo. Nice to meet you."

"These flowers for a special occasion?"

"Just want to make someone smile." Then Angelo gestures toward the bird. "Try putting a mirror in the cage. Birds love them. It's like they have constant company."

Chloe chuckles. "Who knew there was so much to learn about old Lemon here?"

"Lemon?"

"Rebecca's daughter named him... *er*, it. She's three. Her daughter, I mean."

Angelo smiles before turning to leave. "See you next time.

* * *

He finds his grandmother in bed reading the newspaper. He enters the room with the bouquet behind his back. "What are you doing under the covers on this beautiful afternoon, Yiayia?"

The woman glances up from her paper. "*Bah*. Is my hip. Half way through the service it start to pain me. Father Stavropoulou great speaker, but sometimes he talk for too long. I think, 'Get with the point, *re*.' We either headed to heaven or hell. Just tell me which one I going and how long it take to get there, so I have time to do my makeup."

Angelo laughs. "You're not going anywhere anytime soon, Yiayia." He reveals the flowers. "I hope these cheer you up."

"Wow! They are beautiful. You buy them special for me? You should wait until we dead to give old people flowers."

Angelo bends to kiss Yiayia on the forehead. "I'll put them in some water." He returns with a vase and leaves the bouquet on Yiayia's nightstand. He starts to leave but stops to peek back in the doorway. It's only when she thinks he is gone that Yiayia puts down her newspaper to smell the flowers one by one.

In his room, Angelo wonders if he should call Mihaela. They haven't talked since Friday, and he's unsure whether or not that means anything. He doesn't want to seem needy, but nor does he want to come off as disinterested. *Maybe a text will do?* But he already sent a couple last night. Besides, a text can seem careless, lazy. *And why can't she just ring me? If she's truly interested, she would make more of an effort, wouldn't she?* But then, a man should be assertive, and maybe she didn't want to come on too strong. Maybe right now, at this very moment, her thoughts are mirroring his. Perhaps she's also trying to calculate how much is too much, how little is not enough.

It seems a wonder people ever get together at all.

Angelo paces back and forth between his closet and desk. These must be the kind of problems Bryce had always warned him about, the troubles that occur when one hasn't amassed enough experience.

Finally he grabs paper and pencil and leaves the room. He stands shirtless before the bathroom mirror, relaxes his shoulders, puffs his chest a little. He ruffles his hair, just enough to wake up the curls. Then he puts the paper against the glass and sketches "The Greek," his alter-ego: square-jawed and muscular with an open shirt and a harpoon in hand. The Greek knows no fear. The Greek holds the powers of the twelve Olympians; Zeus's leadership and lightning, Apollo's gift for prophecy so that he can tell when the future will be painful or joyous and plan accordingly. The Greek always gets the girl.

Angelo goes into the kitchen and raids the cupboards and fridge, piling things on the counter. He puts water on to boil, heats oil in a sauce pan, goes to work chopping garlic and onion and tomatoes and basil.

"What are you doing?" asks his mother.

"Making lunch."

"Since when do you know how to cook?"

"It's only pasta and a salad. Pretty hard to mess that up."

Despina looks skeptical. "I wouldn't put it past you."

"Thanks for the faith."

"Does this have a reason?"

"I thought I'd invite Mihaela over."

"That's so romantic!"

"Mom, I..."

"I know, you're twenty-four."

Angelo prepares the table with the good china, the seldom-used set from the old country previously belonging to his great-grandmother. Only after the salad is dressed, the pasta warming on the stove does Angelo realize that in all the excitement he has yet to call Mihaela. But now he has a reason.

She agrees to come.

"What did she say?" asks Despina, reentering the kitchen.

"How'd you know she said anything?"

"I can see it in your face. Maybe I'll take Yiayia for a walk. If her leg's really bothering her, she should exercise it a little. We'll grab something out."

"Thanks, Ma."

A little later, Yiayia summons Angelo to her room. "How I look?" she asks, turning a circle. She wears a smart, dark wool skirt, black stockings, open-toe shoes, and a matching jacket. To top it all off, her signature brown headscarf with its purple poppy pin.

"You look *thavmasia*, Yiayia."

The woman smiles. "*Efharisto*, my dear boy. Now you be careful, all alone in this house."

Angelo rolls his eyes. "C'mon, Yiayia."

Finger to her lips, Yiayia shushes him. Then she leans out the doorway to make sure Despina is out of sight before opening the top drawer of her bedside table and withdrawing a His-and-Her Pleasure condom.

"I want to give you this," she whispers.

"Why do you even *have that*?"

"*Re*, I eighty-six, not dead." She places the condom in Angelo's palm then gives his hand a squeeze. "Okay, first you must be very gentle, little bit pressure like this."

"We are not having this conversation!"

"Mother, let's go," Despina calls.

Yiayia heads out but pauses to look over her shoulder. "Lightning up, you's. Starting to sound like one of those Anglo-Saxon people."

"It's lighten up," Angelo corrects.

"*Bah.* Whatever."

A little later, the doorbell rings three times before Angelo realizes it. He's fixated on the package in his palm, pondering its promise to bring "lasting intimacy that is mutually satisfying." That sounds like the claim of a good therapist. But latex doesn't charge by the hour, in the highly unlikely event a consultation would happen. At least today.

The doorbell rings a fourth time, and Angelo leaps to his feet, shoving the condom into his back pocket. Mihaela greets him with a smile when he opens the door. "Thought you might be in the shower or something."

"Just daydreaming, I guess. Sorry."

"I brought some bread and wine," she says. "I remember you like a full-bodied vintage."

Angelo considers making a joke but decides against it. "Thanks. You look awesome."

"You, too."

Angelo admires Mihaela as she strides into the room. Her hair is bundled atop her head, her face adorned with only a touch of lipstick, and she wears a strapless dress that exposes her beautifully toned shoulders and long, slender arms. Angelo feels a bit underdressed in only jeans, glad that he at least threw on a button-down shirt.

"This is quite a spread," Mihaela says, regarding the table.

"Hope it tastes half as good as it looks," Angelo replies. "I don't have much experience."

Mihaela looks playful. "With cooking?"

Angelo clears his throat. "Yeah. Here, let me get that." He pulls out a chair for Mihaela.

"I feel special."

"You are," Angelo says.

"Where's your mom and Yiayia?"

"They went out. Please, start."

"This is delicious, Angelo."

"It's hard to mess up salad and spaghetti. Even for me."

"You need to learn how to accept a compliment, sir."

"I'll try to remember that. Thanks."

Things go quiet as they eat. Angelo hasn't anticipated the sensation of being rearranged within his own mind, as if infatuation held the power to turn one inside-out, leaving vulnerable that which is usually safely concealed. It's different from the anxiety that customarily plagues him. He can't remember the last time he felt this way—not since Tracy, perhaps. Maybe Mihaela *is* special.

They realize they have neglected to open the wine. When they do, they go through the bottle fast. Loosening up, Angelo asks why he hasn't heard much from her much the last few days. He finds that between school and work she hasn't had a lot of time to herself. They move on to talk more about their respective lives, drawing many parallels between experiences. Angelo imagines that, if visually depicted, their days would take the form of tallies marking time until they ended up here, in his home, some oracle's prophecy fulfilled.

They go into the living room. While Mihaela settles on the couch, Angelo gets his Helen of Troy sketch. He hides it behind his back for a moment, recalling the incident with the girl at the coffee shop. But something tells him that this time will be different. Right away Mihaela recognizes it.

"This is me," she says, more in affirmation than surprise. "You drew it?"

Angelo nods. "Saturday morning. I had a certain image of you that I couldn't get out of my head. Sometimes I worry that if I don't draw the people I know, they might turn out to be figures in one long dream, and I'll wake up alone again. Hope that doesn't sound too weird."

"It's beautiful in a sad sort of way," Mihaela says, giving Angelo a kiss on the cheek.

"Thanks," he says.

"Don't you want to kiss me?"

"Can I?" he asks and feels ridiculous.

"I hope you would."

Their lips touch, Angelo only slightly surprised when there's no awkward attempt to find rhythm. The kiss deepens. Her fingers stroke his face, run through his hair. They pause for breath, and Angelo feels himself in full control. He lets his hands explore as they may, Mihaela sighing with pleasure at his touch. But then, something goes amiss. Like the phantom limb in that old horror movie, Angelo's hand moves of its own free will to his pocket. Next, he's holding the condom in front of Mihaela's face, dangling the shiny square like some Christmas ornament.

Mihaela says, deadpan, "I see you have a condom."

In horror, Angelo flings it away. "Sorry. I didn't know..."

"It's okay. I'm glad you're safe. I don't want to seem like a tease, but that's moving a little fast for me. Just making out is okay for now. Hey, don't be embarrassed. It's kind of flattering that you lost yourself in the moment like that. I hope it doesn't seem like I'm rejecting you, because I'm not."

Angelo smiles, though his cheeks stay warm. He rises from the couch. "Want some water?"

"Sure."

He returns with two glasses. They sit on the sofa, drinking slowly while gazing into each other's eyes.

"You're a great kisser," Mihaela says.

Angelo smiles. "Feels like I fumble through that like I fumble through everything else."

Mihaela clicks her tongue. "Now, now. None of that. Really, I mean it. I enjoy your lips."

"Yours are nice, too."

"I'm thinking of getting a dog."

"Kissing me reminds you of a dog?"

Mihaela laughs. "Not everything needs to be analyzed. Maybe I was thinking of puppies. And petting. Logical progression of thought. I've been researching and have my eye on a puppy at the shelter. Want to see him?"

"Now?"

"The afternoon's still young." She laughs. "Besides, I don't know if I can trust being alone with you."

Angelo lowers his head.

"I'm kidding, Angelo. C'mon. Hercules awaits."

"You already named him?"

"Of course."

* * *

Mihaela finds a parking space behind the shelter. They walk around to the front, Angelo holding Mihaela's hand. It's a small gesture but takes courage given that he still feels silly about the condom. Not a *kamaki*-worthy maneuver by any means.

Approaching the building's entrance, Angelo realizes he's never been to an animal shelter before. He pictures scrawny dogs pacing their barred cells like the stereotypical evil pounds. He wonders what type of dog Mihaela finds fitting of a name like Hercules, imagines a hulking Saint Bernard, a razor-toothed Doberman, or even a pit bull.

The shelter's front room, with its high ceiling and white walls decorated with colorful paintings of various animals, turns out to be a lot less depressing than Angelo envisioned. The corridor housing the dogs up for adoption is well-lit. The cages are spacious and clean. They're led down the passage by an egg-headed man, Mr. Shutterfield. Dogs gather at kennel doors, all wagging their tails and whining with, Angelo assumes, hope.

"This is the one," Mihaela says, pointing to the second to last cage.

"Tyson, we're callin' him," Mr. Shuttlefield says.

"I'm going to name him Hercules," says Mihaela.

"Nice name," Mr. Shuttlefield responds. He opens the door and a boxer pup scrambles out on huge, floppy paws, its coat a shiny red brindle offset with white. The puppy bounds about, wagging its stump of a tail. He runs in-between everyone's legs, while the other dogs scratch and bark.

Come here, you," Mihaela says. Angelo is momentarily uncertain whether she's addressing him or the puppy. She lifts the dog, beckons Angelo to come closer. Angelo strokes Hercules behind the ears. The pup looks up at him with its slightly bug-eyed gaze, eyes encircled by handsome, dark-brown patches. Its pink tongue lolls.

"What do you think?" asks Mihaela.

"I think he just peed," Angelo says, pointing to a spot on the floor.

"Just a little puppy mess," Mihaela replies, letting Hercules slather her cheek with his tongue. "Really, what do you think?"

"I don't know much about dogs, but he seems to like you a lot."

"I do believe I'll take him home."

"Do you already have the stuff you need? Food, bowls, toys, all that?"

"We'll stop at the pet store after."

"Have you told your *yiayia*?"

"*Ela re*, you're such a worrier."

* * *

Hercules lies sprawled across Mihaela's backseat like a prize fighter down for the count. They drive to a pet store where Mihaela loads a shopping cart with all the essentials. Angelo trails behind with Hercules on a shelter-provided rope leash. He's unable to get but a few feet before customers and employees crowd around to admire the dog. At first, Angelo's overwhelmed by the attention, left to answer a multitude of questions with few informed answers while Mihaela peruses the aisles. Then he warms up to the fact that many women are gathered around him. *Has the solution to fixing my love life been as simple as buying a dog?* He crouches and cradles Hercules in his lap so the ladies can stroke the pup's belly, their eager hands grazing Angelo's legs. It's low-down to be sure—even Hercules looks up at him with what seems an occasional smirk—though it's not as low as using a baby, exploiting motherly instincts.

Baby.

Angelo repeats the word in his head, overcome by an absurd paranoia. Mihaela, meanwhile, piles her cart—or is it *their* cart?—with items sure to domesticate both Hercules and Angelo. He knows this is ridiculous. Yet it continues to play in his mind like a slapstick segment of a sitcom.

This is what I wanted, he thinks, *to finally find a woman I connect with*. But maybe he isn't ready to help take care of a puppy. Much less a baby. A damp warmth breaks Angelo's reverie. Hercules has piddled in his lap.

"Did poochy pee-pee?" A woman inquires in the sing-songy voice reserved for puppies. And babies.

"Yeah," Angelo says. At least a baby would have a diaper. He alerts an employee of Hercules's puddle. Then he lets the dog lead him to Mihaela—in line at the checkout counter—its nose apparently already having uploaded her scent into memory.

"There you are, little one," Mihaela says, bending down to stroke the dog's head.

"Little one had a little accident," Angelo says.

"Puppies do that." Then Mihaela cocks her head. "Everything cool? You look kinda pale."

Angelo quips, "Naw. Just tired, I guess. Up early for church, y'know."

He helps Mihaela carry the supplies out to the car then they take Hercules to be examined at a clinic next door to the pet shop. During the ride home Angelo wonders if he's been coerced into accompanying Mihaela to her *yiayia*'s place to help the dog acclimate. They park in the driveway of a two-story Victorian fully restored to resemble a gigantic doll house with ornate gables and gingerbread trim.

Hercules barely stirs as Angelo unloads the things. He balances bowls atop chew toys and a big bag of puppy food then lugs it all up to the high front porch. Mihaela follows with Hercules' sniffer in hyper mode. Mihaela opens the front door, and Angelo is amazed at the sight of so much crystal and glass. The entire front room appears as a prism reflecting light. The chandelier's translucence combines with that of the table top, flower vases, and picture frames so that each surface is linked by a fragment of rainbow. And there are many other items: a dozen dolphin-shaped crystal figurines lined across a window sill, a graceful glass swan, and, in another corner, an oversized string of *komboloi*. The blue and white beads drape around a spiraling blown-glass candle holder.

Angelo remains on the threshold, uncertain whether to enter for fear of shattering something. Then he feels Mihaela's hand around his wrist, pulling him forward. Meanwhile, Hercules stretches the length of his leash, scampering in to inhale all the new scents.

"I guess your *yiayia* likes crystal?"

Mihaela laughs. "What gave you that idea? My room is a lot less fragile."

Angelo follows Mihaela down a short hallway into her domain. By the time he's set her purchases on a chair, Hercules has peed in a corner.

"Can I make a suggestion?" Angelo asks.

"Of course," Mihaela says, bending to spray the soiled area with cleaner.

"You might want to lay some newspaper down until he starts getting the hang of things."

"Yeah."

"Can I ask you something?"

Mihaela laughs again. "That's something already." Then she regards him seriously. "Angelo, you don't have to ask me if you can ask something, just ask it."

"Well, what made you want to get a dog? I mean, why now?"

"I think it's the right time. I feel I need more responsibility in my life. Like, I should be accountable for something, you know? And I've always wanted a puppy."

"What about grad school? That's a lot of responsibility, too."

"It's different, though."

"You needed to be accountable, so you got a puppy? Why not volunteer for a good cause or something?"

"What are you trying to say, Angelo?"

"Nothing, never mind. Sorry."

"You don't have to be sorry for that."

They work in silence for the next half hour, puppy-proofing the room. Hercules, his belly now full of kibble, sleeps atop Mihaela's bed as if it had always been his.

"Mihaela! What have you two done?"

Awoken abruptly, Hercules yaps a warning. Angelo and Mihaela startle at the sight of Konstantina in the doorway.

"Yiayia, this is Angelo," says Mihaela. "You remember him."

Konstantina's red-tinged bouffant resembles a bush on fire. "I no mean *aftos*! What is this *skelee* doing here?"

"His name is Hercules, and he's quite friendly."

"Yes, but why it here?"

"We picked up him just now from the shelter."

What's this "we"? "I thought you already told Konstantina," Angelo blurts.

"I never said that," Mihaela responds. "You asked me, and I said that you worry too much."

"Apparently justified in this case."

Hercules leaps off the bed and races around the room, attempting to scramble up everyone's legs and into their arms. He first tries Angelo then Mihaela and lastly Konstantina, who shrieks and nearly tumbles on her bottom. Finally, Angelo corrals the dog, slinging him over his shoulder like a sack of rice. Hercules writhes playfully in his grasp.

"Don't be scared, Yiayia," Mihaela says. "It'll be fine. He's my responsibility, and he'll be out of your way. No need to babysit, I promise."

Konstantina ponders for a moment then finally gives a half-hearted nod. "Okay. But make sure he train well. I had a dog in Greece who knew to use the toilet."

"I'll take care of him, Yiayia. Don't worry."

Angelo says, "I should get home." His Yiayia is no doubt worrying, but he says this more as if to make sure that leaving is still an acceptable option.

A short while later, Mihaela's car idles at the curb in front of Angelo's house. He tries to unlock his door, lowering and raising the window twice before finding the right button. He starts to get out, but feels Mihaela's hand on his arm and turns to her.

"Everything okay?" she asks. "Really?"

Angelo nods. "I had a nice time. And I'm glad you're happy with Hercules."

Mihaela smiles. "I also had a nice time, and thanks for helping me."

"Maybe we can see each other this week? Like, for lunch or something?"

"That sounds nice."

Angelo slides out and begins to shut the door, but Mihaela leans across the passenger seat and stops it with her palm.

"Aren't you going to kiss me goodbye?"

"Oh, yeah."

TWELVE

THE DAYS PASS. Angelo accompanies Mihaela and the puppy to the park and invites Mihaela to San Francisco's Greek Independence Parade. Those festivities prove more meaningful than he could have imagined. There are floats shaped like ancient battle ships and temples. Participants dress in patriotic blue-and-white attire. Even more exhilarating are the Greek flags displayed in the windows of shops and stores, offices of real estate and other businesses—places Angelo would pass on any other afternoon oblivious to the fact that they were owned by Greeks. It feels as if an excavation has taken place, leaving Angelo to witness the unearthing of a community he didn't know was there.

On the Monday following the parade weekend, Angelo, no doubt emboldened by this new awareness, visits a travel agency. The woman seated at a desk across from him taps computer keys then says, "All set. You're scheduled to leave Wednesday, July 7th, returning Thursday, August 15th. Departing San Francisco International on July 7th, arriving at London's Heathrow on July 8th. You've got a six-hour layover there, then departing at seven AM, arriving in Athens at 9:30 AM local time. How does that sound?"

Angelo tightens his grip on the arms of the chair. Hearing the trip laid out like that lends it finality. Maybe too much. He wishes he could somehow bypass flying and still cross the ocean; a nice thought, but a thought with no power. "Sounds good. Are people still traveling to Greece? Even with all the turmoil?"

"Travel is down across the board," the agent says. "We have our own economic problems. Greece has seen a drop in tourism since their economic crisis, but people still crave those Mediterranean beaches and ancient ruins. How would you like to pay for this? Personal check? Credit or debit card?"

A ripple in his stomach, Angelo feels for a moment like he's buying a ticket on Charon's ferryboat. Still, he hands the agent his card.

"Enter your pin. Great, here's your receipt. And call us if you don't receive your ticket in the mail within the next week. Anything else I can help you with today?"

This is more than enough. "I think that's it, thank you," Angelo says, rising to leave.

"Sir, your card."

Angelo retrieves his plastic, thanks the woman again, and exits into the sunlit afternoon. Leaving without an actual ticket seems somewhat anticlimactic—or maybe noncommittal. This allows him to pretend that the trip is still merely a consideration. He supposes that, though there would probably be obscene penalty fees, he could still cancel.

Unlike many people with phobias about flying, he isn't so much afraid of the plane falling out of the sky; his fear has more to do with the claustrophobia that ensues in confined spaces. Even in a BART train under the Bay. There's also the foreboding of having so many hours to fill alone, hours that pass so slowly.

What will he do with himself for half a day in the London airport? Six hours will feel like six days in such a situation. Airports—with their stark walls and shiny floors, their sterile corridors and half-heard summonings over raspy P.A. systems—remind Angelo of hospitals and surgery. Circumstances during which he was held against his will, waiting desperately to go home. Even the previous trips to Greece as a child with his parents were anxiety-provoking. He'd been overcome by homesickness as soon as he'd boarded the plane, even with his hand in his mother's. He shudders now at those memories as he approaches his house.

"Welcome home."

Angelo looks up from the bottom of the stairs to see Mihaela on the porch cradling Hercules, manipulating the pup's front paw so it appears the dog is waving to him. Climbing the steps, Angelo strokes Hercules behind the ears.

"Can't I get some love, too?" Mihaela asks, spreading her free arm to invite an embrace, which Angelo obliges.

But then, his mind still unsettled by what he's just done—the challenge, perhaps, he's made to himself—Angelo asks in a voice that sounds rude to his own ears, "What are you doing here? Did we have plans that I forgot about?"

Mihaela puts the dog down, Hercules proceeding to diligently sniff the space between Mihaela's and Angelo's feet.

"No plans," Mihaela says, apparently not thinking it rude. "We didn't get a chance to talk yesterday, and I didn't want to go another twenty-four hours without seeing you. Hope that's all right."

Angelo watches Hercules nip at his shoelaces. He'd just begun to think of telling Yiayia and Despina about his trip, steeling himself for his grandmother's likely hysterics and his mother's probable concern. Now he's been thrown off balance by Mihaela's unforeseen visit. "Sure, it's fine," he says. "Why didn't you just knock and go in? Long as you must have been standing here."

"I only drove up ten, maybe fifteen minutes ago," Mihaela replies. "Your mom said you weren't home, and I told her I wouldn't mind waiting out here. Besides, I like hearing the birds sing in the trees."

"Birds don't usually sing out of happiness."

"Fascinating," Mihaela says with a smile.

Angelo manages a smile, too. Unlocking the door and gesturing for Mihaela to lead, they find Despina and Yiayia in the kitchen and stand in the doorway a moment unseen, watching Despina open the oven and withdraw a pan of roast chicken and potatoes. Meanwhile, Yiayia stands at the counter squinting at a newspaper.

"Oh!" Despina jumps, turning to see Angelo and Mihaela.

"Sorry, Ma," Angelo says.

Despina smiles, coming over to Mihaela and scratching the puppy under its chin.

"His name's Hercules," Mihaela says.

"Great name," says Despina. "Mother? You remember Mihaela, of course."

Yiayia lifts her head from the newspaper to greet Mihaela with a grin. "Ah, *pos eisai, koukla mou*?"

"Fine, thanks," Mihaela says. "How are you, Ms. Lambros?"

Yiayia chuckles. "So beautiful and polite, too."

"Just in time for dinner," says Despina. "Angelo, go grab some plates. You'll join us, won't you, Mihaela?"

Mihaela glances at Angelo, who of course makes a smile despite whatever complications Mihaela's presence might cause.

"Love to," Mihaela replies. "Should I tie Hercules somewhere?"

"Oh no, just let him roam free. I love dogs."

"He might have an accident."

Despina shrugs. "Puppies will do that."

Angelo sits at one end of the dinner table, Mihaela at the other, Despina and Yiayia rounding out the sides. No one says much with the meal commanding attention, though Angelo notices Mihaela trying to catch his eye. He's reluctant to meet hers, still slightly irked that she's come unannounced. *Why? Isn't this what I'd wanted so much, a real relationship?* But, will she soon be checking his whereabouts? Trying to read his phone messages like jealous girlfriends on court TV shows? Or maybe just because he's been raised to think it's polite that someone should call before visiting? Maybe that's the least of all possible evils?

Still, he's reminded of how the girlfriends of his high school buddies were always around. Since he'd never had many friends, that had become an annoyance. Forking another bite of food, he considers that he should be happy—even grateful—that there's finally a woman in his life. And maybe he's just not yet accustomed to that responsibility. A friendship, or relationship, is about sharing. Was this why Bryce had warned about getting too involved? Or maybe just involved too fast?

Then Yiayia is doing something with her hands under the table. She's hiding scraps in her napkin the way a child might: forking food into her mouth, chewing, and then spitting into the cloth as she swipes it across her lips. It's a new low in Yiayia's rebellion against sustenance. Angelo is about to call her out, but his mother speaks instead:

"Must have been a nice surprise, finding Mihaela waiting, Angelo."

"It was," Angelo says, smiling at Mihaela.

"He seemed a little irritated, actually," Mihaela says with a chuckle. "I had to explain my presence."

Angelo gives Hercules a scrap of chicken. "I wasn't."

Despina laughs. "It's not often Angelo is welcomed home by a beautiful lady."

"Other than yourself, of course," says Mihaela.

Despina laughs again. "This one's a keeper, Angelo."

Like I've thrown so many back? Angelo smiles. "Don't I know it, Ma."

"I had a story ready," Mihaela continues. "I was going to tell him I was in the neighborhood searching for something for a friend's birthday. It's next week, and seeing as how this area is full of so many great boutiques. But I just confessed that he'd been on my mind."

Angelo blushes, and everyone laughs. Yiayia forgets to keep her napkin concealed, placing it back on the table in full view, scraps and all.

"Mother!" Despina snaps. "That's disgusting! And you haven't eaten anything!"

"I have, Despina! I have!"

Angelo decides that now is the time. He announces loud and clear, "I bought a ticket to Greece."

Everything comes to a halt. Even Hercules freezes. Angelo's shocked when Yiayia waves her soiled napkin like a flag and cries, "Bravo!"

Angelo turns to her in wonder. "Did you hear what I said?"

"I not deaf!" Yiayia laughs. "You surprise I want you go to Greece?"

Despina says, "Not quite sure I heard you. You bought a plane ticket?"

Angelo isn't certain if he feels silly or annoyed. "I don't think you can get there by train. Not from here, anyway." *Though I wish I could.*

Despina cocks her head, glancing between Yiayia and Mihaela as if still seeking confirmation that her ears haven't deceived her. "You bought a plane ticket," she finally repeats.

Angelo spreads his arms like wings.

"When?"

"This afternoon."

"Did you shop around for the best deal? Look on the Web? You do realize how much a trip like that costs? Well, obviously you do now, but..."

Angelo glances at Mihaela, wishing—at least at the moment—she wasn't there to hear him say, "I'm twenty-four, dammit."

"Well, why didn't you ask me to go in on it with you? I would have paid half as a present for completing your first year of grad school."

"It's okay, Ma." Angelo glances again at Mihaela. "I wanted to take care of something by myself."

"Oh. But what about flying?"

"I guess the desire to go is finally greater than the fear telling me I shouldn't."

"You could travel by ship," Mihaela suggests. "Just fly or take a train to New York. There must be cruise ships. Also freighters that take passengers, even if there aren't any more Queen Marys."

"Or Titanics." Angelo makes a grin. "Maybe I could have one of those quickie shipboard romances."

"Angelo!" Mihaela exclaims.

"Just kidding." *At least I think so.* Angelo shrugs again. "I've considered that, but it's not the actual flying that bothers me. It's just thinking about the length of the journey, the trip itself. A ship would probably take a week or more."

"When do you leave?" asks Despina.

"July 7. And I return on the 15th of August."

"That's a good stay. Any stopovers?"

"I've got six hours to fill at Heathrow on the way to Athens. But only a two-hour layover on the way back."

"Heathrow can be a madhouse."

"That helps, Ma."

"Just warning you, so you'll be prepared."

"Is okay," Yiayia announces. "You have Mihaela with you! You see? This is why I now think is good idea to travel to Greece. Angelo have company for the big trip."

Despina raises her eyebrows. "I didn't know Miheala was going."

Mihaela looks as surprised as she should. "Neither did I."

"Yiayia just volunteered you," says Angelo.

"Oh."

Would she want to go? Angelo still isn't sure what to think.

But, Mihaela only smiles. "Sounds great anyhow, but I have to work this summer. Though I'll miss you."

Another thing he hadn't considered. Should he have told her as soon as he decided to go?

Yiayia cries, "C'mon now! Work, work. Is all I hear in America. You young and beautiful. Have lots of time to work when you older. Now is time to enjoy vacations, be free, swim, jump on rocks like a goat!"

Angelo raises an eyebrow. "'Jump on rocks like a goat?'"

Mihaela chuckles. "That sounds fun, but, really..."

"*Bah!* I don' want to hear excuses!"

Despina sighs. "Mother. Leave the poor girl alone."

"What, Despina? I just..."

"This is a trip to Greece, Mother, not a weekend at Disneyland."

Or, Angelo thinks, *a quickie shipboard romance.*

THIRTEEN

AFTER DESSERT, ANGELO and Mihaela retire to Angelo's room where they lie together, fully clothed, on the bed. Hercules settles down for a puppy nap on the floor. They remain quiet for a long while, Angelo unable to fully relax. His muscles suffer an occasional twitch. It seems that his body is playing out the conflict that so often occupies his mind: wanting closeness, desiring it intensely, yet somehow resisting. He's always been aware that gaining access to a relationship is a problem for him, though he's never expected this new anxiety. Here in the shadows he tries to analyze it, but, like his fear of traveling, it remains somewhat obscure. Obviously in this case he's afraid of being hurt. Or hurting someone else. Maybe it's selfish, but he wonders what if, in his relationship with Mihaela, he loses a sense of himself? What if he has to give up too much? Or, what if he just can't meet her needs? And not in the way Bryce would define them.

At least the trip to Greece will give him time to think.

"What are you thinking about?" asks Mihaela.

Synchronicity? *Already*? *"Huh?"* Angelo says, buying time.

Mihaela strokes his chest with her fingertips. "Your face looks so distant."

"Sorry. Just spacing out, I guess."

Mihaela kisses Angelo's temple. "Mean you weren't planning the perfect moment to dangle another condom under my nose?"

Angelo smiles. "We've established that I'm not a smooth operator. Don't you wish you'd settled on one of those Greek boys back in New York?"

"Are we fishing for compliments?"

"Like a *kamaki*?"

"What?"

"Nothing. No fishing for compliments, just landing the fact of my lameness."

"Shush, sir. Maybe if you behave, I'll take you with me to Queens after your Greece trip."

"You really can't go, huh? Assuming you'd want to."

"Afraid not. But I would love to be trekking with you through the Peloponnese. How long's it been?"

"About fourteen years."

"Your relatives must really miss you. And you stayed away all that time because you don't like traveling?"

"Part of the reason, at least."

"Tell me about your dad."

"What do you want to know?"

"Just tell me about him. What's he like?"

"Thought I did the other day."

"You said he was a contractor when he lived here, but now he's back in Greece. That's about it."

Angelo gazes at the ceiling, finding himself without words to describe the man to whom he so often made comparison. To say he's godlike would be overly-dramatic, while to simply list his human attributes would do him little justice. Finally, he says, "I think I have an idea." He goes to the desk and returns to the bed with his drawing pad and pencil. He lightly sketches a circle atop the page. "So, my dad has this big personality," Angelo begins again, keeping his eyes on the paper as he speaks. "He carries himself in a way that commands everyone's attention."

Mihaela sits up now, too, watching Angelo draw. "Does he have a lot of that stereotypical Mediterranean machismo? Like a *kamaki*?"

Angelo glances up from the page, wondering if Mihaela had glimpsed that prized photo of his father from the glory days—if perhaps Angelo had left it out on the bedside table. But, no, it's safely in the drawer. "Dad says they're kind of a thing of the past."

Mihaela smiles. "They may call themselves something different these days, but Greek men have always maintained their flirtatious charm."

Angelo huffs air through his nose. "I never had…"

But Mihaela cuts him short. "Let's get back to your father."

"Well, he's not a stereotype," Angelo says, adding heft to his pencil line, the circle darkening into the promise of a face. "He was fun when I was growing up. He'd play games and sort of think like a kid, y'know? He'd tell Greek myths as bedtime stories. It's pretty impressive how he'd actually recite passages from *The Iliad* and become all the characters, make it seem like the story had been created just for me. But I was also afraid of him. That big, powerful voice that brought life to Achilles and Agamemnon and whisked me there among the clashing swords and spears, it could also snap me back to reality when he was angry. He'd lose his temper a lot. I don't really remember what he would get so mad about. Maybe he wasn't even sure. I swear, sometimes when he'd grab me by my shirt collar and my body would just go slack while I looked in his eyes, I'd see in his face this kind of… loneliness, I guess. Like, I wasn't even there, and he was trapped someplace screaming for the sake of hearing his own echo. The only sound he could trust, the last thing able to assure him he wasn't entirely alone without even himself to confide in."

Angelo feels Mihaela touch his face, and he looks up from the page.

"That must have been so scary for a kid." Mihaela says, softly.

Angelo reexamines the paper, leaning back a bit to gain perspective, impressed by how quickly he has rendered his father's likeness. All the details are there: the man's slight widow's peak, his full lips and deep-set eyes. Looking at Mihaela now, Angelo says, "Scary for sure, but I don't mean that's all there was."

"Of course not," Mihaela reassures him.

"Because we had plenty of good times, too. All the stories he'd tell. Not just the myths, but the ones that were his own. He'd have people hanging on his every word. They would speak about him like he was more than a person. I know it sounds strange, but they'd talk like he was some phenomenon. I remember, one time, he did the lighting for this upscale neighborhood bar. He took me along one day, and I played out front while he worked. I went in to tell him something but didn't see him anywhere. Finally, I asked the owner of the place, and the guy goes, 'Your daddy? He just blew through here, left the door swinging and the women trailing after him!' Isn't that something?"

Mihaela nods.

"Even then, small as I was," Angelo continues, "I wanted to walk like my father, fill out my clothes like he wore his."

Mihaela smiles. "The Most Interesting Man in the Universe?"

"Hey, I'm serious here."

"If that looks anything like him," Mihaela says, regarding the drawing, "he's certainly handsome."

"Tell me about it."

"But so are you." Mihaela touches his face again. "You know, it's okay to feel affection and anger toward someone at the same time. It doesn't mean you love them any less."

"I'm definitely trying to learn that."

"So, how did your parents meet?"

Angelo suddenly realizes that, for all his anxiety over intimacy, he's revealing information that he hasn't shared with many of his closest friends, not even Bryce. But now he can't stop himself. Mihaela's soft touch and sympathetic gaze seem to bring it out. "They met while my mom was vacationing in Greece. I guess they had a mutual friend who introduced them one summer."

Mihaela smiles again. "And look what that union brought to the world."

Angelo smiles, too. "I'm working hard not to make another self-deprecating joke."

"Then I'm training you well. Why did your dad end up going back to Greece?"

"I guess... Where do I start? Mom and him split up when I was still in high school. Seems like it had been a long time coming, given all the arguing over the years. Things ended badly." Angelo pauses to lean back again while checking the sketch's progress. He's momentarily startled by its realism, as though face-to-face with the man for the first time in nearly a decade.

He begins anew. "Dad and I got into it that day, too, as he was leaving. Since my teen years, our relationship had been rough. A lot of it had to do with plain old adolescent moodiness on my part, probably. And Dad was overbearing. He'd want to hang out a lot, like we did when I was little, and of course I wasn't having that."

He looks momentarily self-conscious then continues. "He left for Greece about a year after moving out and finalizing the divorce. Guess it was always where his heart had been. He was the only one in his family to ever leave there. But, for all his talk of the old country, I don't know why he didn't push me harder to get involved with the local Greeks as a kid. That's one of the reasons I want to go back to Greece now. To ask him why." Angelo almost admits that another reason for reuniting with his father is to hopefully learn the ways of the *kamaki*, but even he knows to keep that to himself.

"What do you think he'll say?"

Angelo forces a chuckle. "If I knew, I wouldn't have to ask."

Mihaela strokes Angelo's hand. "Whether or not you were on good terms when he left, I'm sure he'll be so proud of the man you've become."

"Hope so."

"I'd bet on it. But if for some weird reason he isn't, that isn't your problem. You do know that, right? Despite what they say in church about honoring thy mother and father, we weren't put on earth to please our parents or live up to their expectations."

"I guess I know that, too."

"And I think you should give him this portrait. It's awesome."

Angelo regards his drawing. "It is pretty good, isn't it?"

Mihaela playfully punches Angelo's shoulder. "That's what I want to hear, sir! I do believe your confidence is rising slowly but steadily."

"Wait until you see some of my other work."

"Can't wait."

Angelo goes to the desk again, retrieves a stack of manila folders, and spreads them atop the bed, picking through to gather an assortment of his best grad work. There are still lifes of flower vases and fruits, portraits of classmates, comic strips featuring centaurs and depictions of the underworld Hades, and, in finale, a few sketches of his newest creation, that Super-*Kamaki*, The Greek.

"These are impressive," Mihaela says.

"Aren't they?"

Mihaela chuckles. "Hope I'm not creating a monster."

"I have a long way to go before there's a risk of that."

"If I hadn't seen my dad in seven years, I'd be anxious about the trip. It is a big deal, really." Angelo nods. "Bigger than I probably even realize. We talk a lot on the phone. Still, it's not the same. But I've always been kind of an anxious person."

"You don't seem chronically anxious."

Angelo shrugs. "Maybe I hide it well. Probably lots of practice."

"I hope I don't make you anxious."

"You do," Angelo admits. "Mostly in a good way, though."

"Well, you make me anxious, too. But, I'm not scared of falling for someone."

"Maybe lots of practice?"

"Not so much. But it does help."

FOURTEEN

ONE EVENING, ANGELO arrives home with an envelope in hand from the mailbox and announces, "I hold the golden ticket!" as he strides into the dining room. Apparently no one gets the *Charlie and the Chocolate Factory* reference. Yiayia barely glances up from her newspaper, and Despina, carefully applying eye-liner with the aid of a little mirror, offers only a nod.

Angelo, feeling a bit unsupported though he probably should have made himself clearer, flops into a chair across the table from Yiayia. He opens the envelope to scan his itinerary. Everything seems correct, though he's somewhat surprised to not feel as nervous as he'd anticipated; perhaps it has paid off to have continually reminded himself over the last few days that the trip entails few risks and that time will surely pass in the air, however slowly. Or, maybe his calm demeanor in the face of this oh-so-significant event is the result of a particularly good day of classes. It culminated in the semester's final round of critiques, Angelo reaping an ample harvest of positive feedback on his latest drawing.

"A really strong sense of line," Trevor had said while examining Angelo's work. "There's an energy that I haven't seen in your previous pieces."

"I agree," the professor had chimed in. "There's a story here, a sense of things happening, even as the figure itself is the only clear image on the page. You're ending the term on a real high note. I'd like to see you continue developing this idea over the summer."

"I have to ask," another classmate had added. "Is it you? We know you're Greek, but are you The Greek?"

"Aren't we all in our own work?" Angelo had replied while sitting there overwhelmed, his mind swirling as it always did when his turn came, trying to absorb so many opinions at once. But he'd left campus with new energy, feeling certain today would bring the ticket. Now it's here, and he will be getting on a plane in a little less than eight weeks.

"Sorry for not saying hello when you walked in, hon," says Despina, finally completing her makeup. "Ticket finally came?" She's wearing a strapless, navy-blue evening dress. It's been a long time since Angelo has seen his mother in such fancy threads.

"You don't look bad, Ma. What's the occasion?"

"'Not bad' isn't exactly what I was shooting for. And does there have to be an occasion?"

"I mean you look really nice. As always."

Despina chuckles. "Thank you. I have a date tonight."

"A *date* date?"

"*Nai, re*! A date. I didn't want to tell you earlier because I knew you'd react like this. *Asamai tohra*."

"A date with who... or is that 'whom?'"

Despina fiddles with an earring. "A gentleman whom I met online."

"I think I'm gonna lose my shit."

"Watch your mouth, young man!"

"*Nai*," Yiayia speaks up, "I gon' lose my shits, too."

"Mother! What is it with you two? Almost everyone is getting together via the Internet these days. Hard as I work, don't I deserve a life?"

Angelo spreads his palms. "Of course, Ma. Guess I just figured you'd meet somebody the old-fashioned way."

"What's that supposed to mean?" Despina snaps, standing up with arms akimbo. "You want me to get an arranged introduction like we're living in the *horyo* in 1920?"

Angelo sighs. "You know that's not what I'm saying. But you can't blame me for being surprised. I can't remember you going on a date since... Dad left."

"You're right, and I've waited too damn long."

Angelo watches his mother fix her lipstick in the mirror. "Is he Greek?"

"Actually," she says, "he isn't."

"Wow!"

"What does it matter as long as he's nice? May I remind you that, before you met Mihaela..."

"Which was an arranged introduction."

"You don't seem to be regretting it. But I didn't see you running around exclusively with Greek girls."

Angelo sighs again. "You didn't see me running around with hardly any girls."

"What about Tracy? She was sweet, though I knew she wasn't the one."

"You implying Mihaela is?"

"Well, not necessarily, but..."

"Tracy was back in college. And Halie was just a rebound right after that. Nobody before them and hardly anyone since."

"Until Mihaela now."

"Yes."

Despina continues primping. "And why do you think that is? You're certainly more than handsome enough."

"I don't have any game, Ma."

"Game?"

"What is this, hunting?" asks Yiayia.

"Game, like in smooth talk," Angelo says, feeling even more gameless now. Why did cool expressions always sound so uncool when explained in standard English?

"Oh, Angelo, you're plenty charming," says Despina.

"A hottie!" adds Yiayia.

Angelo sighs once more. "You're my mother and grandmother. What else are you going to say?"

Despina shrugs. "I don't have to say anything. How is Mihaela, by the way? She hasn't come around much since that dinner."

Angelo decides to change the subject. "So, where are you meeting this *xeno* tonight?"

"Here, as a matter of fact."

Yiayia's eyebrows shoot up. "He coming to this house?"

Despina frowns. "Is there another 'here'?"

"But, Despina, what if he a serial killer? Axe murder!" Yiayia holds up the paper. "It say in this article that these days so many psycho killers!"

"Enough, both of you! He's just a regular guy. A nice man. We've met for coffee a few times, but this is our first real date."

"Coffee?" says Angelo. "When?"

"Enough!" Despina marches out of the room, glowering at Angelo over her shoulder. "You want to be treated like an adult? Then treat me like one, too. Craig should be here soon, so be on your best behavior, please. Both of you."

"'Craig?'" Angelo says into the emptiness his mother has left behind. "He certainly isn't Greek, is he?"

"*Ela, re,*" Yiayia whispers, her face holding its trademark mischievous grin. "Let's give this *xeno* a hard time, eh?"

"No." Angelo goes to his room to tinker with another sketch of The Greek, though he's unable to focus. He supposes that when it comes to men, his mother has far better standards than he gives her credit for. But should her suitor assume he will be running the show, Angelo is prepared to inform him otherwise. He's on his feet at the sound of the doorbell, almost beating Despina to the door.

"Back off, you," Despina says, shooing him away as she turns the knob.

"Just making sure he wipes his feet," Angelo mutters, remaining within proximity of the entryway.

"Come in, please, Craig," Despina says.

Angelo feels Yiayia creep up behind him.

"Meet my son and mother," Despina says, ushering her guest into the room.

"My pleasure," the man replies.

I bet, Angelo thinks, briefly shaking Craig's hand, all the while taking note of the man's stiff posture and clammy palm. He follows him into the dining room to watch as he surveys the decor: first the Medusa sculpture, then the framed photos of the Parthenon and Peloponnesian village, his gaze finally coming to rest on the marble figurines by the window. Angelo scoffs at the newcomer's apparent inability to appreciate all the cultural significance, the man's own Wonder Bread roots probably running about as deep as a kiddie pool. No doubt part of Despina's appeal to this guy is her exotic Mediterranean background. So different from the WASPy types to which he's likely accustomed. Angelo is waiting for him to drop a *My Big, Fat Greek Wedding* reference or an anecdote about his favorite diner. Or mention of Greece's dismal economy.

And yet Angelo—ever the diplomat—considers that his mother had been right: ultimately, it just matters that the guy treats her well.

Angelo is a little surprised his mother has gone for someone so plain. Craig resembles Bill Gates with a beard, and unless the guy also possesses a brain capacity and bank account comparable to that of his lookalike, that's not saying much.

Things continue like that for a while: Craig examining the figurines, Angelo observing him from the room's opposite corner. Yiayia stands behind Angelo, breathing down his neck as if seeking protection should their visitor suddenly produce an axe. Despina has left the room, perhaps making a last-minute wardrobe switch. The silence begins to scream. Still, Angelo makes no attempt at conversation, suddenly—if ridiculously—feeling obligated to make sure Craig doesn't steal one of the figurines. Even someone totally ignorant of ancient history might recognize their value.

Then the man finally speaks. "Beautiful, aren't they?"

Angelo's startled but quickly composes himself. "They're from Greece. Underground, I mean. Artifacts. Not some gift shop. A relative found them while working with archaeologists. We're not sure how old..."

"Oh, they're real," says Craig. "Look, I'll show you."

Angelo, again surprised, steps forward but feels Yiayia grip his arm.

"Careful, *re*," she whispers. "Remember what I read in the paper."

Ignoring her, Angelo joins Craig at the small table by the window. "How do you know?" he asks, trying not to emphasize 'you.'

"See this line here?" Craig says, pointing to a faint configuration in the stone. "It's made by a very specific tool. You wouldn't see such a line if this was a fake or even just something made in the recent past."

Angelo cocks his head. "How do you know?" he repeats, this time the "you" sounding natural.

"I majored in archaeology in college. And went on a bunch of digs in the Mediterranean."

Craig puts the figurine back, and Angelo says a natural, "Wow."

Finally, Despina returns, a purse slung over her shoulder. "We're going to dinner and then to a play. Should be a few hours, don't worry if it gets late. And Angelo, make sure Yiayia drinks one of those nutritional shakes, okay?"

"Yeah, Ma. Have a good time. Both of you."

Craig says goodbye, follows Despina to the door, and in that moment, Angelo is hit with an odd familiarity. Something indecipherable in Craig's demeanor reminds him strikingly of his own.

* * *

To pass the time and keep Yiayia from conjuring up schemes to bring a premature end to Despina's date, Angelo engages his grandmother in a couple rounds of blackjack, the two of them sitting at the dining room table playing for candy. Were Yiayia to succeed in making trouble for her daughter, Angelo, having been left in charge, would be responsible. And it wouldn't be the first time Yiayia—ever resourceful—had foiled Despina's plans from afar.

So far so good, in regard to grandma-sitting tonight, though Yiayia proves to be a horrible bluff at cards. She chuckles and nods whenever she has a favorable hand, flipping it around to share her good fortune once or twice before Angelo gets annoyed. When Yiayia starts to eat her chips prior to betting them, Angelo figures it's time to switch activities. He sits her on the couch to watch *Rembetiko*, one of her favorite DVD movies. Angelo, having seen the film numerous times, lets his mind wander.

He still can't tell what's more surprising: the fact that his mother is on a date, or that she met someone via computer, Angelo unaware that she was even Internet-savvy beyond navigating her email and an occasional Google search. Angelo did a bit of Internet surfing himself tonight in order to double-check Craig's claim about lines in marble. It seems to be true.

And what of Craig, the unassuming archaeology whiz? What if one date leads to a couple and a couple leads to more? What if they really hit it off and Craig persuades Despina to see three as a crowd? Sure, Angelo plans on getting his own place. Eventually. But this is his home as much as it his mother's—he's next in line to inherit the house—and should he leave, he wants to do so on his own terms.

That, he decides, is pure paranoia.

"Pause the movie," Yiayia commands. "I going to the toilet."

Angelo does so then assists his grandmother up from the couch. "Do you need help?"

Yiayia clicks her tongue. "C'mon, *re*, I eighty-six."

"Now you know how I feel when you want to follow me around everywhere."

"That's different. You just a boy."

Angelo watches his grandmother shuffle toward the bathroom then plops back down on the couch. He stares at the static on-screen image of a rag-tag group of musicians. They look more like a mafia gang than a band, clustered on stage in their tilted fedoras and shoulder-draped suit jackets.

A sudden thud from down the hall and Angelo bolts into the bathroom to find Yiayia on the floor, crumpled in a puddle of urine. He drops to his knees, asks if she's okay then carefully pulls her into a sit. He clutches her limp shoulders and calls in her ear, but she doesn't stir. He nudges her gently and gets no response, nudges a bit harder, still nothing.

Now panic sets in. He doesn't know CPR, can't even remember how to check a pulse, and the bathroom walls seem to inch ever closer. She had seemed fine when getting up from the couch. And yet he should have known to accompany her. He tries to shake her conscious to no avail, and now tears are blurring his vision. Despite his fear, he gently lays Yiayia back down then runs to the couch for his cell. Just as he flips it open, Yiayia groans and lets out a terrible cough. Pocketing the phone, he runs back to the bathroom. She's still on the floor, though with eyes open now. He feels a great wave of relief, crouching again to help her sit up.

"What... the... hell... am... I... doing... here?" Yiayia says, staring around.

"You came in to use the bathroom and must have fainted or something," Angelo explains.

"Or something. Help me up, *re*! Is all wet here!"

"Wait, maybe you shouldn't move yet."

"Get me up!"

"Okay, here we go. Ready?" Angelo drapes his grandmother's arm over his shoulder then slowly gets to his feet, lifting her as he rises. With the ebbing of adrenaline, he realizes how heavy she is, despite being so thin. He sits her on the edge of the tub then helps her out of her wet clothes as the bath water runs. When it's full, he gently lowers her in. He lathers a sponge and begins washing her back. "You don't remember what happened before you fell?"

Yiayia shrugs. "I go in to use toilet, and all the sudden I feeling dizzy. Next I waking up on the floor covered in the piss. Damn! I do remember washing you when you were a *moro*."

"Long time ago, *huh*?" Angelo says. "Maybe I should still call an ambulance, just to be safe."

Yiayia thrusts her arm up in protest. "*Ohee* ambulance, *re*! I okay!"

"But..."

"No but! I just pass out for a little bit. Is not like I miss anything exciting."

"I do have to call Mom, y'know."

Yiayia shrugs. "Call her. Maybe she ditch that *xeno*."

"I see you remember that."

Angelo dials his mother but doesn't get an answer. He tries again, equally unsuccessful. *Has she turned off her phone on purpose, expecting Yiayia to pull something?* Yiayia has, though apparently not on purpose.

After assisting her out of the tub and into bed, he spends the rest of the evening at the dining room window, save for periodic checks on his grandmother, who now seems fine. As the hours pass, Angelo goes from fearing for Yiayia to growing increasingly frustrated at his mother for leaving them alone. And then his frustration shifts to Craig, the man somehow responsible. Had Despina stayed home, Yiayia wouldn't have worried and probably wouldn't have fainted.

Eventually, Angelo gets so worked up, ala his grandmother, that he contemplates waiting out front of the house, silly as that would be. But he goes in to check on Yiayia instead, impressed that she's propped herself up in bed to sip her nutritional shake, something she ordinarily won't do without diligent prompting. This calms him, and he sits on the edge of her bed. He knows she might not have much longer on earth, and this time should be cherished, despite how much she may try his nerves. He's never known her to pass out like that. Her last doctor visit revealed a strong heart and good lungs, near perfect health overall, at least for her age. Yet Angelo regrets not calling an ambulance.

At last comes a rattling of keys. Angelo greets his mother at the door, a bit surprised when she enters with Craig. Before they can share the highlights of their evening, Angelo relays an account of Yiayia's accident. Alone with Craig after Despina goes to check on Yiayia, Angelo gives him a helpless shrug. He tries to muster ill feelings toward Craig, but, as before, identifies too closely with something in Craig's manner. Then, just after Despina comes in to inform them that Yiayia seems to be fine, they turn at the sound of footsteps coming up the hall. Yiayia seems steady on her feet, but Despina moves to help her.

"Mother, you should be resting."

"*Asamai, re,*" Yiayia says, frowning at Craig. "Usually," she growls, "when people leave someone's house, they know not to return so quickly without new invite."

"Mother! That's rude! Craig was just walking me in."

"Don't worry..." Craig starts to say.

"Don't tell my daughter what to be doing, you's!"

"Mother! I'm really sorry, Craig."

"Despina," Yiayia begins, hands defiantly on hips, "you want me respect this man, and I don't know who is he? A stranger who comes to my home to take out my daughter without saying but few words to me first?"

Angelo now feels sorry for Craig but knows better than to interject. The guy seems to be taking it pretty well, standing with hands clasped behind his back and looking pretty neutral.

"First of all, Mother," Despina starts again, "this is my house, and I'm a grown woman, just like your grandson is a grown man."

"Don't bring me into this, please," says Angelo.

"And I can invite in whomever I want. And Craig has been polite to you."

Yiayia narrows her eyes, seeming to gear up for a grand finale. "Maybe, Despina..."

Yep, here it comes.

"Maybe I fall in the bathroom because of this..." Her fiery gaze locks in on Craig. "*Xeno.* He cause me to worry, and I hitting the ground."

"My God!" cries Despina. "You just can't stand to see me happy, can you, Mother?"

Yiayia spreads her palms and innocently says, "Despina, how can I see you happiness if you leaving me here alone all the time?"

Despina just shakes her head.

Everything is still for a long moment. Finally, Angelo goes over to Craig and murmurs, "This might be a good time to make your exit." Then he smiles. "Don't worry though, Mom is worth it."

FIFTEEN

OVER THE NEXT several nights, Angelo has a recurring dream in which he goes through all the motions of air travel. He checks in at the counter and receives his pass, traverses security, boards the plane, and prepares for take-off. Each step is rendered in vivid detail, from the metal detector's screech when he forgets to empty a pocket to the glint of the stewardesses' lapel pins to the cramped legroom of his coach seat. And he always awakens right at the moment of ascension.

Angelo suspects that the dream is his mind's attempt to pre-navigate what it perceives as an ordeal. He knows the size and congestion of the airports will be intimidating, so each evening before bed he has been researching them, just to reduce the number of nasty surprises he may encounter. In addition, he obsessively checks his ticket to make sure it's still where he's left it. He does this not out of any real fear that it's lost, but rather to reassure himself that the ticket is not just another figment of his ongoing dream.

One morning, opening his eyes just as the plane lifts off the runway, Angelo is met by a splitting headache. He slowly rises from bed, staggers into the bathroom, downs a few Tylenol. Then he returns to his mattress and shuts his eyes, fireworks exploding in the black. Over time the pain lessens but remains a dull, throbbing nuisance throughout the day, accompanied by an unflinching nausea.

He goes to class but leaves early, his anxiety mounting as he's reminded of Yiayia's fainting spell and wonders if it was something contagious. But exiting at his train station with stars in his vision, he suspects a malfunctioning of the tube in his head.

Back home, he explains the situation to his mother. Leaving Yiayia under the supervision of a neighbor, they rush to the nearest emergency room. Angelo experiences flashbacks from childhood: white glare all around; the pierce of a needle entering his scalp; the winding corridors leading him further away from loved ones, further into the unknown.

He and his mother sit in the waiting area. The sky outside grows black. Angelo endures with his head in his hands, temples pounding. Seated beside him is a man swearing to himself while clutching a wad of tissue to his eye, the paper stained red and darkening. Further down the line, a teenage boy sits with a skateboard in his lap. His face is contorted in a grimace, his left arm dangling at an unnatural angle. Angelo gets the feeling that both of these injury victims are regarding him with some resentment, given that he is ahead of them in line while displaying no visible damage.

Despite his discomfort, Angelo thinks about his mother's broken plans for this evening. Apparently, Craig was supposed to take her out on what would have been their third date. Angelo hasn't seen Craig since the first, but according to Angelo's mother, the man has taken Yiayia's attitude in stride. Angelo understands, of course, that this sudden affliction isn't anything he can help. He's had the tube long enough to know trouble can strike at any moment, and he hopes to be healed and in flying condition when the time comes.

Finally, someone calls his name. A nurse leads him down yet another corridor and into a small room, his mother staying behind. He waits alone, seated atop one of those typical doctor office tables covered with the waxy paper that makes annoying crinkling sounds every time he moves. His head still throbbing, he looks at the art on the wall. One piece is a classic Georgia O'Keefe floral painting, the petals rendered in vivid detail, flowers at their most vagina-esque. The other piece is a painting of Superman. Angelo stares until the images begin to merge, the Man of Steel entering a rosette cavern.

A slim, East-Indian neurosurgeon enters and introduces himself as Doctor Buhari. He checks Angelo's reflexes then has him perform a series of simple drills: following the movement of a finger in front of his eyes; walking across the room on the balls of his feet; touching his finger to his nose. Angelo, seeking distraction from his rising anxiety, jokes that he probably wouldn't be able to pass one of those drunk-driving tests even while sober. This gets a chuckle out of Doctor Buhari, but the fun ends when the man recommends Angelo get a CAT scan. Angelo feels the same helplessness he felt as a child when not even being a good boy could spare him from suffering because of his condition. But he takes a deep breath and sets his jaw. *I'm a man now, and men aren't supposed to be afraid.* Something his father would probably say.

Angelo lies at the mouth of a giant, buzzing cylinder that sounds like a tunnel full of bees. A tech at the opposite side of the room flips a switch, and Angelo's breath catches in his throat as the mat beneath him moves forward. Inside the cylinder now, Angelo is told by the tech to stay perfectly still.

It has been years since the last surgery to replace his tube. Still, it seems in all that time he has only been leasing his body, his flesh remaining the property of the doctors and the surgeons. Angelo has simply been maintaining things until the next operation, knowing the rent will have to be paid. He dreads the prospect of another surgery. What if something goes wrong? What if he doesn't wake up? What if he wakes up mid-procedure but can't move, can't cry out, left to endure? He recalls a magazine article that Yiayia once cheerfully shared that went into detail about the rare phenomena of anesthesia wearing off too early; it left Angelo nearly convinced he should be so unlucky.

Released from the tube at last, he is told by the tech not to move, though he doesn't suspect he's able to anyhow. His skin feels artificial, like plastic. The rapid beat of his heart echoes in his ears with a seemingly metallic clang. Angelo, near delirious with apprehension now, considers that perhaps his entire being has been rendered of foreign matter, created in some laboratory when he was an infant.

He's assisted off the mattress and led back into the room with the paintings to find his mother seated in a chair across from the newly re-gasketed table. She smiles and says something, but Angelo is surprised when he can't hear. The room feels suddenly like a vacuum. Eventually, Doctor Buhari comes in. He greets Angelo's mother then sifts through a manila folder to withdraw a stack of X-rays, the first of which he holds up to the light.

In wonder, Angelo examines the image of his own skull, the white of bone and brain stark against the black background. The faint outline of his head encapsulates it all. Then, he notices the tube itself, the brightest component of the X-ray: a glowing bulb just above and behind his ear with a cord running the length of his neck. The bulb—the reservoir where the excess brain fluid is collected before being drained—resembles a small, round eye. *Mind's eye*, Angelo thinks; *holder of X-ray vision*.

Studying the cord now, he tries unsuccessfully to spot any rupture. Again, there is the reservoir's eye, Angelo interpreting its unrelenting stare as one holding threat, a promise of more pain to come. And yet he can't look away, forced to face what is being reflected back at him: a glimpse of himself as a newborn on death's brink, convulsing with a seizure, tiny fists clenching in an attempt to grasp what can't be held. No matter that he knows the scene will end happily, he's struck by its tragic tone. He wishes he could reassure that baby of better things to come.

But then he's brimming with rage, fighting an impulse to snatch the X-ray out the surgeon's hand, destroy it in hopes of blinding that all-seeing eye. His body acting of its own accord, Angelo feels himself rise from the bed and step toward Doctor Buhari, slow and deliberate, trying to anticipate what his arms will do once they are within reach of the doctor. Hopefully, they'll go for the folder and not the man's throat.

Then, Doctor Buhari lifts another X-ray. This one appears to be a bird's-eye view of Angelo's brain. He's struck by the abstract quality of the image, like some alien landscape seen from above. Buhari replaces it with a third photo, this one showing Angelo's brain close-up: a spongy shape vividly white against the black background. A Rorschach inkblot in reverse. Compared with a fourth image in which large black gaps abound in the white space, this spongy brain seems healthier.

Angelo just stands in the middle of the room blinking, his mother and the doctor regarding him curiously. "Just wanted," he begins, "to get a closer look."

"It is a pretty sight," Doctor Buhari says. "In this particular photo, the ventricles are quite tiny, and that's exactly what we want to see. But when we look at this one..." the man pauses, referring now to the photo with all the gaps in the white space, "we are looking at a brain overwhelmed with fluid. These enlarged ventricles are the cause of your discomfort during shunt failure. But as you can see in the other picture, there is no enlargement of the ventricles at all."

Angelo stares blankly at the Doctor. "And?"

"And the good news is this photo of an optimally-functioning brain is what came back from today's CAT scan. In fact, the tube is barely visible here. I'm not sure it's even being utilized any longer."

"God, that's wonderful news!" Despina says.

Angelo almost echoes his mother but holds back, overwhelmed.

"How old were you at the time of your last revision surgery?"

"About fifteen," Angelo says.

"I don't want to give false hopes. As you know, hydrocephalus is not a 'curable' condition. But there is a chance you won't need another operation. However, it is best we don't go in and fiddle with the tube—or attempt to remove it, I should say. We can't be certain you wouldn't have an adverse reaction." Buhari withdraws the first X-ray again—the side view of Angelo's brain in which the tube is visible—and holds it to the light. "I'm not sure what is the cause of your current headache, but we can rule out the tube."

Angelo stares at the eye again. Just a harmless bulb. "What do you think's causing it?"

"Have you been under much stress lately?"

"He's finishing his first year of grad school," Despina answers. "Also planning a trip to Greece this summer."

Buhari smiles. "Go out and enjoy the rest of your evening. Try to relax and drink plenty of water. Should the headaches get more frequent or severe, let us know. But you may find they're simply an after-effect of all the ouzo you'll be drinking while traversing the Greek Isles."

* * *

In celebration of his happy diagnosis, Angelo and his mother decide to have dinner out. They share a table at a Mexican restaurant near the hospital and clink water glasses to the good news, though Angelo remains hesitant to fully relax. Optimal functioning of his tube aside, it doesn't seem like stress is sufficient to cause a headache like his current one, though the pain does lessen as he continues mulling over all that has happened in the past few hours. He stares at the colorful tablecloth, which rather unpleasantly—at least in his present frame of mind—depicts a Day of the Dead celebration. He fails to hear his mother the first time she speaks.

"Sorry, Ma. Lot on my mind, I guess."

"I asked how you're feeling."

"A little better."

"I'd toast you with a margarita, but that wouldn't do your head any good."

Angelo lowers his eyes to the skulls and bones on the table again. "What if it's something worse? Like a tumor?"

Despina clicks her tongue. "You sound like Yiayia. I won't tell you not to worry because I know it isn't that easy. But trust the experts. The CAT scan would have seen anything like that."

Angelo nods then sips more water.

"I used to drive the neurologists crazy when you were small," Despina says, touching Angelo's hand. "Call them whenever you'd so much as mention a headache. Finally they said that unless you were in complete agony and experiencing all the key symptoms, they didn't want to hear from me. I guess it was then that I realized you weren't really so fragile. You'll never be a football player or an astronaut, but all the better for that, I say."

Angelo nods again. "Just as long as I don't become a professional artist like Papou, right?"

Despina clicks her tongue. "Angelo, I never..."

"Dad always says I shouldn't worry," Angelo cuts in. "Maybe he's right. But, just because the tube is on the inside, under what everybody can see, doesn't mean it's been easy to deal with."

"No one's saying it is."

But Angelo presses on, "Because I was the one going through the surgeries and hospital stays. You guys were there, but the toughest parts I had to endure alone."

"You're absolutely right."

"Don't being patronizing, Ma," Angelo blurts.

Despina touches his hand again. "I'm not. I'm sorry if it seems that way. I just want you to know that I'm willing to try and understand, even if I'll never truly be able to."

"That's more than most people will admit," Angelo says. He thinks of the surgeries endured during his elementary school years, recalls returning to class after his hospital stays and attempting to explain why his head was bandaged.

"Remember those acrobats who once performed at the hospital?" Despina asks. "And the salty chicken broth you were given while recovering? You wanted me to make that even after you'd gotten back home."

Angelo smiles. "Yeah."

The food comes, and Angelo is grateful for the distraction. Only then does he realize the extent of his hunger, his appetite returning after having been nonexistent most of the day. He eats fast, the headache almost gone by the time he's halfway through.

"You think it's possible I'll never need another surgery?"

Despina shrugs. "I don't think anyone can say for sure, but you heard Doctor Buhari. You're very healthy today, knock on wood."

Automatically Angelo taps the table. "They have good hospitals in Greece, right? I mean, for the worst case scenario?"

"Of course. We are talking about the land that brought the most medical advancements to the world."

"But that was a long time ago."

Despina laughs. "The way you usually talk, one would think it happened yesterday."

"Time is relative."

Despina laughs again. "I can tell you're feeling better."

"Maybe. Let's not talk about the tube anymore."

They finish their food in silence. Angelo dabs his mouth with a napkin then scans the dessert menu.

"Still hungry?" asks Despina.

Angelo shakes his head. "Just browsing."

"That was good. Seems like this is the first evening in a while that we've been out, just the two of us. I'm sorry it had to come after such a traumatic day."

"I'm older now, Ma."

"But even in the last year I feel like we used to spend more time together."

"We've both been busy," Angelo replies, still eyeing the dessert selection. "And now, with Yiayia around..."

Despina snatches the menu. "Look at me. How do you feel about Craig? Really? Are you okay with our situation?"

"I didn't know it was a situation already."

"Be serious, Angelo. I know Yiayia doesn't seem to approve, but she rarely approves of anything."

"Well, it is a little weird seeing you with somebody after all these years, but if you're happy, that's what matters."

"That's certainly a cliché. What about your happiness?"

Angelo shrugs. "You're not responsible for my happiness anymore. I'm happy that I don't need to have surgery, but I'm sorry you missed out with Craig."

"Never mind that. There's tomorrow or the next day. Is it weird because you feel like he's getting between you and me? Or because he isn't your father?"

Angelo considers. "Neither. You and Dad had your time. I guess you just weren't right for each other in the long term."

Despina seems genuinely surprised. "I didn't realize that's how you felt."

"About you and Dad? C'mon, Ma."

Things go quiet again. Despina looks for the waiter. Angelo checks his phone.

"I just hope," Angelo says finally, "the guy doesn't try to kick me out."

"I don't think he's the type," says Despina. "As if I'd let him! Besides, he's a long way from earning the privilege to move in. And why would you even think that?"

Angelo shrugs. "Healthy paranoia."

"What's healthy about paranoia?"

"Paranoids have enemies, too. Speaking of earning, what does he do?"

"He's a museum curator."

"Maybe he can help me get an art show."

Despina smiles. "History museum, not art. Though his job is somewhat artistic, seeing as how he's around all those ancient artifacts."

"He's not like Dad at all, huh?"

"I never thought about that, but no."

Another moment of silence passes, then Angelo asks, "Do you think Dad is proud of me?"

"Of course, Angelo. Why would you think he wouldn't be?"

This time it's Angelo who touches his mother's hand, fixes his gaze so that she's forced to meet his eyes. "Really, Ma. Just like you wanted my true feelings about Craig."

"I know he's proud. The man brags about you all the time. I'm sure all of Greece knows of your achievements in school."

"It's not just school, Ma. I'm talking about who I've grown up to be. Is he proud of that?"

"Angelo, you should already—"

"Because," Angelo cuts in, "I remember that day you guys had your last big fight."

Despina finally looks away. "Why bring that up?"

"Because he and I got into it. He asked me why I was always avoiding him, and I said I was trying to find my own way, tired of wanting to be him, because I *wasn't* him. Remember? And I wanted to explain more, because I was frustrated. But he cut me off and got so angry. And then I tried to apologize, but he pushed me away. And said he was disappointed in me."

Despina doesn't respond for a while, only stares down at the Day of the Dead. Then Angelo blinks as if just waking up, wishing there was a way to retract the words he has spoken. "I know it was a really difficult time. And it's not like I never said bad things to him or that I had no part in all the troubles between him and I as a teenager. Sure, it was a long time ago and our relationship is much better now. I even forgave him for all that. I'm just saying..."

Despina smiles. "It's okay, hon. He was the adult in the situation, you were the child. You can feel the way you feel and still love him."

"That's sort of what Mihaela said the other day."

Despina raises an eyebrow. "You have such deep conversations already? That's pretty special."

Angelo shrugs. "It just came up in passing. I didn't tell her the details."

"Angelo, I don't blame you for feeling hurt. And you're entitled to some animosity."

"But I really don't have any, Ma, that's the thing. I haven't seen him in seven years. Yeah, we talk on the phone, and he knows what's going on in my life, but what if he sees me when I get off the plane and none of that matters? What if we're face to face and he just shakes his head?"

Despina shrugs. "What if you get off the plane and none of the past matters? I'd say that's more likely, wouldn't you? You're both adults now."

Half to himself Angelo murmurs, "Maybe he'll be disappointed in me for not being a ladies' man, like he is."

"Oh, please, Angelo. Anyway, you're dating now."

"Yeah, *now*. But he used to ask me how I was doing with girls, and I'd lie. I'd say I had a girlfriend when I didn't."

"Big deal. Your father wasn't all that suave." Despina laughs. "Remember, he used to ride a donkey."

"When he was a boy."

Despina cocks her head. "It's like you think he had some magic power. But if that was true, wouldn't we still be together? I think you were right in that last argument. Learn to be yourself not your father."

* * *

They reach the porch to find a flat, rectangular object wrapped in blue paper and tied with a white bow leaning against the front door. Angelo eyes it curiously, then looks to his mother, but Despina appears equally perplexed.

"It's probably for you," Angelo says.

"I imagine you've got more secret admirers than I," Despina replies. She examines the package then nods at her son. "Yep, it's yours."

Angelo frowns. "Doesn't say who it's from. What if it's anthrax?"

"That's not healthy paranoia."

"What if it's the real X-rays from the hospital? The ones bearing bad news."

"With a *bow*? Just open it, *re!*"

Angelo carefully removes the wrapping paper. Both his and his mother's eyes widen at the sight of his most recent drawing of The Greek now behind glass in a black and gold frame. The colors perfectly accent the pencil line, the image appearing bold and strong. Angelo searches for a card and finds none, but then turns the picture around to reveal a note taped to the back. "It's from Craig."

"Read it!"

"*Angelo: Sorry to hear that you aren't feeling well, though I hope this brightens things. I think this piece deserves to be hanging in a gallery someday. Maybe even a museum. I thought I'd get it framed, so you'll at least have the first step taken care of. Best, Craig.*"

"Isn't that thoughtful?" Despina says.

"Yeah. But, how did he get this?"

"I showed him some of your recent work when he came over the other night. You were still in class. He said he really liked that one, but I never saw him leave with it."

"Better make sure he didn't swipe anything else."

"Angelo!"

"I'm kidding. This is great. Except, I thought you said he isn't with an art museum."

"That doesn't mean he can't appreciate fine art. Let's go find a nice place to put it up. Just until it's gallery-bound."

"I don't think he was serious about that part."

"Doesn't matter if he was. It's your piece. Have to admit, though, I didn't realize how spectacular this drawing is until just now. Something about seeing it framed like this. It's really great, Angelo. Is this character a *kamaki*?"

Angelo feels his cheeks darken. "Maybe. Anyway, that means a lot coming from you, even though you're just my mom."

Despina raises an eyebrow. "*Just* your mom?"

Angelo chuckles. "What I mean is I know you haven't always been happy about my decision to try art as a career, so for you to recognize my potential means a lot."

Despina sighs. "Angelo, it's not that your choices make me unhappy. I just worry, like most mothers would, that you're choosing a very difficult road for yourself. I know how tough a life in the arts can be, clichéd as that might sound, being that I'm the daughter of a painter. But ultimately you have to live for yourself. Like you said before, I'm not responsible for your happiness, nor are you responsible for mine. Stop worrying so much about what I or your father think. Okay?"

Angelo manages a smile. "I'll try."

SIXTEEN

SOMETIME AFTER HIS hospital visit, Angelo gets a call from Mihaela informing him that they need to talk. When he says he's all ears, Mihaela clarifies that she means an in-person discussion, and he can't just sit back and listen while she does all the work. Angelo suggests they meet at his house, but Mihaela says no, she would rather meet at a restaurant. The Mediterranean place. Angelo agrees, though upon hanging up, he's immediately anxious. *Why did she sound so formal?* And why choose the place where they'd had their first date? Isn't that what someone does—usually a man—when planning to propose? *No, too early for that. Way too early.*

Pacing the living room now, trying to draw a satisfactory conclusion, Angelo glances up at the framed sketch of The Greek as though seeking guidance. Do *kamakia*, while wooing woman after woman, ever find themselves in awkward situations? Or do their powers render them invincible to romantic adversity? Maybe the journey to Greece will provide answers, though until then it seems he's on his own.

He and Mihaela haven't talked much over the last several days, which he attributes more to her busy schedule than any reluctance on his part. Paranoid, perhaps, but with his romantic history, he can't help being pessimistic.

Then it hits him. How can he be so self-centered? Maybe this meeting has nothing to do with him, or them, at all. What if Hercules has come down with an illness or been hit by a car? What if Mihaela's *yiayia* is sick? The circumstances need not even be so dire. Maybe Mihaela has decided to move back to New York.

Tired of speculating, Angelo leaves the house and heads for the restaurant. When he arrives, Mihaela is already inside. Once he sits down, it seems that, despite his anxiety, everything is fine. Mihaela smiles at him, compliments his outfit, even has ordered him a beer—an enticingly cold glass of Peroni beside his bread plate. Angelo peers at Mihaela over the rim of his glass, not quite ready to fully relax. He has mixed feelings upon discovering that all is well with her *yiayia*, and that Hercules is rapidly growing and responding fine to his training classes.

"You seem apprehensive," Mihaela says after a time.

Angelo clears his throat. "You were the one who sounded tense on the phone. Why do we need to talk here?"

"I was hungry."

Mihaela doesn't raise any topics of serious discussion as they order, the food arrives, and their meal progresses. Finally, Angelo leans back in his chair to enjoy the music. Right then, something flashes in Mihaela's eyes. Before Angelo can react, she launches like a Spiderwoman who has waited for the perfect moment to pounce on her prey.

"I didn't want to mention this up front, because it's obviously a sensitive issue for you, given that you seem reluctant to talk about it."

Angelo readies himself for the worst. Not that he hasn't heard it before; some variation of, "You're a very nice guy, but..."

"Why you didn't tell me you'd gone into the hospital?"

"Is that all?"

"*All*? Don't you think it's a big enough deal?"

"I guess I didn't before just now. And it was just a false alarm."

Mihaela frowns. "It was real to me. I had to find out from your mother. Because you didn't call me. Because you haven't called me in days. I didn't even know you were sick."

"I'm not sick. It's just a condition I have that needs to be taken care of once in a while. I haven't even had surgery since I was a teenager."

"*Surgery*?"

"It's not something I usually tell people until I really trust them."

Mihaela sighs. "How can we have trust if you won't share anything with me? What if we were out somewhere and you got one of these attacks, and I had no idea what was going on or what I should do? Does that seem fair?"

"I guess not."

"Angelo, I'm not saying you have to dump all your secrets right away or keep me informed about everything that goes on. But I'd like to believe that I could someday be important enough so you'd want to reveal personal things and know that I'd be there to listen. Just like I hope you'd do the same for me."

Angelo fidgets in his chair, overcome by that all-too-familiar sense that he's somehow being suffocated. Again he reminds himself that this is part of a real relationship and that Mihaela is right, yet he can't shake off the urge to flee. But of course he doesn't. Instead, he listens as Mihaela goes on to say that she feels he is avoiding her. That—in female-speak—his "energy" has been different lately, and perhaps the day when they can be important people in one another's lives is still quite a ways down the road. Maybe, just for now, they are better off being friends, which, in female-speak, is usually the kiss of death.

Angelo nods in all the right places. He really hadn't thought the hospital visit was a big deal, and his hesitancy to phone over the last few days—the hesitancy she apparently sees as avoidance—was only due to the fact that he didn't want to bother her while she was busy.

But, Mihaela claims, it is more than the hospital visit or the lack of phone calls. Something just doesn't feel right.

"I've been taking time to process, y'know?" Angelo says. "I've been single so long, I'm used to doing my own thing. Guess I need to work on communicating."

Mihaela takes a breath. "I've got no desire to be with someone who makes me second-guess myself, to constantly wonder if it's okay to call or text or come over."

Angelo says nothing. *What's the use*? It appears that he's blown a relationship again. Then he gives it a last, desperate shot. "Shouldn't we take more time? We don't even know each other that well. I'm sure when it's all more comfortable..."

"I've had enough time now to decide this isn't right." Mihaela takes his hand across the table top. "It's not that I don't think you're a great guy and we..."

Angelo sighs. "Please don't say 'can still be friends.'"

* * *

The travel dreams continue. Angelo suffers all the pre-flight angst over and over again but never actually leaves Earth. The semester ends, and there is nothing to distract him from memories of Mihaela. He's surprised to be thinking about her constantly now. The worst part is not having anything concrete on which to pin his failure. Except maybe being himself. Being him, not his father, who had promised that the powers of the *kamaki* would be revealed to Angelo. Yet it appears the man had been woefully wrong.

He finds that many of the qualities that had initially evoked feelings of claustrophobia—her impromptu visits, her constant desire to touch and be physically close—are the very things he misses. And he recognizes the irony that, while she was busy much of the time, he had still felt crowded, but now that she's gone, he's left to cope with too much space. Again. Every time the phone rings, he hopes that she is calling to say she's changed her mind and misses him. But no such luck. Finally, on the fifteenth day, he calls her but gets no answer and leaves no message.

He wonders, sometimes guiltily, if he should look for another job. But what of his forthcoming trip? Who would want to hire him for only a few more weeks? No real need to find work given his savings. The one thing that keeps him from sinking into total despair is the Greek Festival to come. All the preparations are complete, and event fliers are appearing in restaurant and store windows all over town. As he'd mentioned to the work crew, he's attended the festivities before, but this will be his first experience as a booth volunteer.

Come that long-awaited Friday morning—the first day of the Festival that takes place over a three-day weekend—Angelo is up early, having eaten and showered before Despina or Yiayia are even out of bed. He isn't scheduled to work until one o'clock, but he's too anxious to sit around anymore. The morning marks the first in a while when he doesn't check his phone in hopes that there might be a missed call from Mihaela. On the drive up to church, when his mother asks him if he will see her this afternoon, Angelo mutters obtusely that he isn't sure what her plans are.

Curiously, it doesn't appear that Yiayia has gotten wise. It would seem that, with their grandmothers being such good friends, Konstantina would have told Yiayia something was amiss.

While meandering the church grounds, Angelo recognizes many of the booths he helped assemble. Seeing them now, manned by volunteers as festival-goers line up for food or buy craft items, he is joyous at being part of something larger than himself. He waves at a few familiar faces, Jimmy and Niko among them.

Despite it being a hot day, the event has drawn a large crowd, diverse in both culture and age. Angelo watches a group of school children be led along a path studded with poster boards displaying historical tidbits about ancient Greece. Nearby, a group of elderly men occupy a table, sipping coffee and chatting in the shade of a tree. And there are women in abundance, many around Angelo's age and enticingly clad due to the heat.

Arriving at the calamari booth, he's greeted by his co-volunteers and issued gloves and an apron. The work proves fast-paced but enjoyable. Angelo is initially given the task of slicing lemons for the garnish. Proving competent at that, he moves up to the fryer, and then helps serve the baskets of squid, scooping the hot, golden rings as customers line up. Finally, during a brief lull, someone makes a beer run, and Angelo leans against the mobile freezer at the back of the tent, downing the cold brew in thirsty gulps. One of his co-volunteers, an elderly man with sad eyes and drooping jowls, comes up beside him and raises his beer. They clink bottles and exchange utterances of *yamas* before taking sips.

"*Toh onoma sou pali?*" the man asks.

"Angelo," Angelo replies. When the man continues to gaze at him expectantly, he adds, "Angelo Koutouvalis."

The man fingers the whiskers on his chin, his eyes narrowing in calculation a moment before popping wide. "*O patehras sou ton lene* Tasso?"

Angelo nods. "That's my dad. Tasso Koutouvalis." He coughs as the man abruptly whacks him on the back with a palm and introduces himself as Sophocles Maragos then goes on to explain that he'd worked with Angelo's father in the days when Tasso first arrived in the country. The man says he remembers Angelo as a baby, and now, having seen him as a young man, he knew he had recognized a strong resemblance to Tasso.

Angelo tells the story of his father's return to the old country, and Sophocles fingers his whiskers a second time.

"When you going to visit Greece?"

"I'm traveling in July for the first time in many years," Angelo says.

Sophocles whacks Angelo on the back again. "Tell your father I said hello! He was a very good man, always. I could tell you many stories about him. You know he used to coach some of the guys on how to meet women?"

"Really?"

Sophocles nods. "Not me, of course. I was too old for all that, even then. But many of the others hung on his words. *Ela, fileh mou.* We have more customers."

Angelo returns to work. They establish an easy rhythm, with Sophocles taking orders and collecting money, Angelo dishing up the calamari, and a third volunteer manning the fryer. The lines get longer as the hours pass, and Angelo, perhaps inspired by the earlier conversation, interacts more comfortably with the customers. When a trio of young women approaches, he boldly steps up and tells Sophocles that he'll handle it.

Sophocles moves aside with a wink and murmurs, "Just like your father, *eh*?"

Smiling at the new arrivals, Angelo asks, "What can I get you ladies?"

"Three combos, please," replies a bright-eyed brunette.

"Sure thing. I'm waiting on a fresh batch." He looks over his shoulder toward the fryer and calls out, "*Re, Yianni, posa lepta yia ta kalamarakia?*"

"*Mia stigme!*" The fry cook hollers in return.

"It'll just be a moment, ladies."

"That's okay," the brunette says. "That was Greek you were speaking, right?"

"Yes."

"That's really cool. Were you born there?"

"In Greece?" Angelo asks, and then thinks, *Duh*. "No, I wasn't." He tries to think of something cool to say, but then the orders are up and he loads the baskets onto a tray. "Here you go, ladies."

"How do you say thank you in Greek?'" another woman in the group asks.

"*Efharisto*," Angelo says.

"*Efharisto*," the women repeat in unison.

Angelo smiles. "Your pronunciation was pretty good." Then, as the trio start to leave, something clicks in his brain. "Wait up, ladies, I forgot something on your orders. Can I have your trays for a second?"

Angelo carries the baskets over to the cooler and takes out a container of crumbled feta cheese. Liberally sprinkling the cheese over the fries, he adds a little lemon juice and oregano then returns to the women. "Greek Fries. Enjoy."

"Thank you." The women depart, smiling after giving Angelo appreciative looks that might have gone beyond upgraded food.

"Greek Fries, *re*?" Sophocles says, standing at Angelo's side now. "That's not on the menu."

Angelo still watches the women. "Maybe we should try it out as a special."

"Your mother cooking those at home?"

"No. Just came to mind."

Sophocles winks. "That was original."

"Thanks," says Angelo, and realizes it was.

Toward sunset, and despite the trial of Angelo's new item proving a success, the booth experiences another brief lull in business. This time Angelo offers to make the beer run. En route to the bar booth, he is shocked upon spotting Mihaela. Has she come to see him?

But then he sees she is with a young man. She'd known he would be here, so maybe this sighting with another man hadn't been accidental... Angelo keeps his head down and veers away.

* * *

Days later, when he looks back on the festival, Angelo feels vexed despite his pleasant experience. It seems as if all the volunteers—himself included—somehow resembled caricatures of themselves in the end: plate-breaking, party-loving Greeks, all expected—at least in the eyes of attendees—to dance like Zorba and speak like Aristotle. Gifting those three women with his "Greek Fries" now feels less like a charming gesture and more a cartooning of the cuisine. Maybe it had been the patrons constantly erupting with shouts of "Opa!" and "Open wide for ouzo!" Or the couple who asked if people in Greece still wore togas, only to receive affirmation from a volunteer.

Or, perhaps more likely, spotting Mihaela was to blame for these negative reflections. Yes, it had all gone south after the Mihaela sighting—Mihaela with that other man. Angelo had moved sluggishly through the remainder of his shift after that then wandered alone among the crowd until well after dark, stopping to chat only briefly with Vassili and George.

If the mystery man was a new love interest, Mihaela had certainly moved on quickly. But of course that wouldn't be as hard for her as it was for him. He retreats into solitude for days at a time—maybe a fortress of solitude—holing up in his bedroom with his drawing pad, feverishly sketching to combat the loneliness.

SEVENTEEN

AT LAST, ONE QUIET EVENING in early June, as Angelo sits at his computer half-heartedly browsing a dating website, he gets a call from Bryce inviting him to a going-away party the next afternoon. Of course he'll be there, Angelo says, though he's astonished that it's already that time.

"Tell me about it, partner," Bryce replies. "Shit, we coulda kicked it a bunch in the past few weeks, but you been AWOL. Doin' your own thing, I guess."

Angelo thinks of all the time he's been brooding alone in the house, but says, "Busy there for a while, but lately I've been around."

Bryce laughs. "Funny how nobody noticed."

"What?"

"I'm just fuckin' with you, breh. We fixin' to get started about four, five o' clock tomorrow. I'm gonna barbecue. Lotta ladies RSVP'd, so we need your Greek charm."

Angelo snorts. "You got jokes. Should I bring anything? Drinks?"

"How 'bout your best pick-up lines?"

"All I seem to have are the worst."

Bryce sighs. "Always so serious. Bring drinks, lots. And dress nice, feel me? I've already told someone about you. Someone special. A female someone."

"Who?"

"Later, man. Gotta roll."

"Wait. Bryce? You were kidding about no one noticing I'd been out of touch?"

"Don't know why you trippin', considering you only got, what, two, three friends including me?"

"Yeah, never mind."

"Now, don't go sounding all down and out. I was just playin'."

"For sure."

* * *

Upon waking to sunlight through the curtains, Angelo tosses back his covers but hesitates to get out of bed, his chest weighed down by a vague sense of foreboding. He feels that he will be tested in the coming hours. And then he leaps up and frantically searches for his suitcase. It's the morning of his flight to Greece! But where are his bags? He hasn't even packed yet! And what about his passport?

He bolts into the kitchen to find Yiayia customarily perched over her newspaper, Despina sipping coffee, still in her robe. Panicked, Angelo demands if anyone has seen his luggage, but Despina only gives him a puzzled look.

Then it hits him. It's still June, and the only place he needs to be today is Bryce's party. He tries to downplay his mix-up, but Despina and Yiayia give him funny looks all through breakfast. As morning transitions to afternoon, Angelo continues to cope with a feeling of disquiet. Helping his mother with the house cleaning chores and later fleshing out the beginnings of a new sketch, he's distracted by thoughts of Bryce's imminent departure for boot camp. It's almost as if his friend's send-off is propelling him closer to his own; the momentum of Bryce's journey forcing Angelo to more closely confront the truth that his time is soon to come. But his future remains hazy beyond the Greece trip, while Bryce seems to have his priorities mapped out.

Finally, the hour of celebration arrives. Angelo takes his buddy's advice to dress up for the occasion. He grabs the case of beer from the fridge and heads out to hunt for Bryce's departure gift. He hits a hole-in-the-wall record store, reasonably certain Bryce would appreciate some vintage hip-hop, but then he remembers his friend's music collection is already vast.

Next, he goes into a bookstore. He knows Bryce is not the most avid reader but does crack a novel every once in a while. Angelo spots one called *Way Past Cool* and considers it based on the title alone. But maybe Bryce has already read it? He moves on to the non-fiction section and pages through a big, glossy coffee-table book about genealogy. Angelo recalls that night at the bar when he'd asked Bryce if he knew from where his people had arrived on American soil, and the shrug he'd received in return. His buddy might get a kick out of this.

When Angelo finally arrives at the park, the fog has burned off, and the sun flares hot as he saunters up a dirt trail thick on either side with foliage. He comes to a point where tree branches crisscross overhead and birds call to one another in boisterous warbles. Dappled sunlight filters through the leaves. He passes the lake and ascends a grassy slope toward scents of grilling meat. In the distance, a pair of barbecue pits fronts a cluster of picnic tables that have balloons tied at the ends of their benches. Erasing any doubt that he's found the right party is a banner of jungle camouflage hoisted along the branch of a nearby tree. The military colors inspire visions of Bryce lying bloody off some dirt road. Angelo tries to will them away, telling himself that in all probability Bryce will safely return, just as he will enjoy an easy trip back from his own tour of familial duty.

Thirty or forty guests mill about the picnic ground; a majority of them are African-American and strangers to Angelo. He wades through the crowd, shyly exchanging pleasantries but mostly keeping his head down. Finally he spots Bryce at the rear-most table, a plastic cup in one hand, iPod in the other. The MP3 player is hooked up to a set of jumbo speakers throbbing out an old Outkast tune. Angelo thinks he sees stress in Bryce's expression, but it may just be that his face is scrunched against the sun. Then Bryce looks up at him, and whatever tension may have been there is gone now.

"The Greek!" Bryce exclaims, offering his hand. "Glad you could make it, brotha!"

"Of course, man," Angelo says, taking his friend's hand. "Look at you, all decked out."

Bryce glances down at his baby-blue linen top and bottoms and the blue alligator shoes that complete the ensemble. "Ain't no thing."

"This stuff is for you."

Bryce checks the bag. "Corona. Good choice. And what's this?" he asks, taking the present.

"Just a little going-away gift. Everything okay? You nervous about shipping out?"

Bryce sips from his cup, and his eyes go distant. As if reading Angelo's recent thoughts, he asks, "Why? Are you?"

Angelo feels his cheeks go hot.

Bryce chuckles. "I don't want to talk about leaving quite yet. Food's almost ready. You hungry, bro? We got chicken, beef ribs, hot links. Go grab a plate."

"Will do," Angelo replies. He heads for one of the grills and waves at Bryce's sandy-haired parents. They return the greeting but appear to be in conversation with someone, so Angelo moves on. As long as he has known Robert and Molly Davis, he's never once seen them criticize any of their son's choices. Not his insistence on wearing the gold grill, not his music, his collection of black friends, nor his taste in women. But given their tense postures—lips pursed, arms identically crossed over chests—Angelo imagines that Bryce's decision to enlist has caused some grief.

Plate loaded with barbecue, Angelo selects a beer from a cooler and looks around for a place to sit, hoping to come across as less shy than he feels.

"Over here, if you like."

Angelo turns to see a shapely young black woman smiling and beckoning him toward her table. Could this be the woman Bryce had mentioned wanting Angelo to meet? He walks over and sits down. His hand shakes just a little as he raises the beer to his lips, now wishing he had something stronger.

"I'm Tatiana."

"Angelo."

"Nice to meet you, Angelo."

"Me, too. I mean, you, too. I mean, nice meeting you, as well."

"So, Angelo, how do you know Bryce?"

"We went to high school together." Angelo tightens his grip on the bottle, his palm going moist. *This isn't going to cut it,* he thinks. He has to come harder or the woman is going to get bored. Why can't it all be so simple as, Hello, mademoiselle, you are beautiful... "So, how do you know Bryce?" he finally asks, then suppresses the urge to slap his forehead. *Way to go, Greek, deflect attention onto another guy!*

"We met through a friend."

"Awesome." *Seriously?* Still, he says it again. "Very awesome." Panicked now, he starts in on his food to shut himself up. He catches Bryce's eye across the way as he waits at the nearest grill. His friend flashes a thumbs up, but Angelo thinks, *If you only knew.*

Once everyone has enjoyed their first round of barbecue, Bryce's mother steps into the center of the picnic area and raises her hand. "I just want to say how much I appreciate you all joining us this evening. It was important to get everybody gathered together to show Bryce how much we love him."

Cheers and applause from the tables. Bryce smiles and takes a bow, his grin glinting.

"Over on that far table," Molly continues, "there's a stack of envelopes with a card inside them. Before leaving tonight, please take a moment to fill one out. I'm going to slip them into Bryce's bag so he'll have something on the plane to remind him of home." At the word, "home," the woman's voice breaks, and she gestures for her son to stand. "Come up and say a few words, hon."

Bryce ducks his head. "No speeches, Mom."

Robert wags a finger at Bryce in what appears to be mock anger. "Don't back-talk your mother, young man. She's still your sergeant for one more day."

Bryce struts over to where his mother had been standing, suddenly claiming the spotlight and surveying his audience. "I didn't prepare no statement or nothin'," he says, "but thanks to all my people for supporting me. Thanks to my parents, and thanks to my future fans who don't even know they're fans yet. Because when I get back, I'm fixin' to do big things, believe that."

Another round of cheers. Angelo exchanges a smile with Tatiana as they clap for their friend. Angelo can't help wonder if he, too, will do "big things" upon returning from Greece.

"I know coming out of the Army," Bryce continues after the applause dies down, "I'll be a better man. Now, before I sit back down, I want to remind everybody to please enjoy more food. I can't take all this to boot camp!"

Clapping again, Angelo looks at Tatiana. "He certainly has a way with words, right?"

"Certainly does," Tatiana agrees.

Angelo notices the woman smiling expectantly, but he can't think of anything else to say, though he senses something stirring below the surface. It's as if the perfect one-liner, twenty-four years in the making, is catching in his throat.

"I'm going to the cooler," Tatiana finally says, rising from her seat. "Want anything?"

Angelo shakes his head and watches her go. He sees Bryce coming, scoots over to make a spot for him.

"How you feelin', Greek?"

Angelo shrugs. "Weather's nice. Food's good. Can't complain."

"How you feelin' about Tatiana. Saw y'all chatting it up."

"She was doing most of the talking, but what's new there, right?"

"So, she told you, then?"

"Told me what?"

"Come on, man. She must've said something."

Angelo doesn't have the heart to say that they hadn't gotten that far yet. Mihaela hadn't been the one, and neither is Tatiana, apparently. "Look, man. At least you gave it a shot, right? I just don't know if she and I can click like that."

Bryce momentarily frowns, but then bursts out laughing. "Ho, shit, Greek! That's funny! I'm sorry, dude, but big mix-up. The chick I was hoping you'd vibe with couldn't make it. Shoulda said somethin' earlier, but it slipped my mind."

Angelo laughs now, too. "Wow! I really misjudged there."

"It's nothing, Greek. But I might as well tell you. Tatiana is my baby mama."

Angelo cocks his head. "But you don't have any kids."

"Not yet," Bryce clarifies. "Girl is pregnant, though. About a month along."

"Oh. I don't know what to say, man. That's huge news. Congratulations."

"Now you know why it seemed like I was kinda overwhelmed earlier. I just recently found out."

"You still gonna go? To the Army, I mean?"

"Shit, I gotta go at this point. But I don't know how things are gonna go down when I'm away."

"You told your folks?" Angelo asks.

"Not yet."

"Bryce, you have to tell them...! She's planning to keep the baby?"

"Of course," says Bryce. "And I'm cool with it. It'll force me to really get out and grind when I'm back."

"I'll say."

"Think I'll be a good father?" Bryce asks "Not just providing what the kid needs far as money's concerned, but like raising it up. Think I'll do all right?"

Angelo puts a hand on his friend's shoulder. "I think you'll do great."

Bryce nods, though tentatively. "'Cause, if it's a boy, the relationship between father and son seems especially tough. I don't want my child growin' up resenting me and shit."

"You resent your dad?"

"No, but I'm just saying."

Angelo is surprised by a sudden embrace from his friend. After, they both go quiet. Then Angelo asks, "Are you scared?"

"Of being a dad or going into the Army?"

"Both seem scary prospects to me."

Bryce picks a dandelion stem off the bench and twists it around his index finger. "Yeah, kinda scared. But either situation is gonna be what it's gonna be. Just have to take them as they come. I've tried to prepare myself, but you forget all that when you're going through it, y'know? Be so busy adapting once I get off that plane, probably won't have time to be scared."

Angelo hopes he can adopt a similar philosophy when it comes time for him to leave. He may not be headed to the military, but travel anxiety will surely wage war on him.

He looks over at Tatiana selecting food, tries to see if there is a fullness to her belly that he hadn't noticed then realizes it's far too early. He tries to picture her and Bryce's child, a beautiful baby no doubt, with vibrant, bronze skin.

"Mind if I open your gift?" Bryce asks. "Or want me to wait until after?"

"Go ahead. It's nothing major."

Bryce goes to the back table and returns with Angelo's present. He appears slightly confused after opening it and examining the book. "What's this?"

Angelo shrugs. "I thought maybe someday you'd want to trace your roots. Beyond Anaheim."

Bryce seems to weigh the suggestion while paging through the text. "Lotta pictures. That's always good. Actually, this might prove useful. I want my baby to know where he or she has descendants. Can't just be black or white people. Like you always sayin'."

"You really have no idea about where your ancestors came from? Parents never said anything?"

"Nope." Bryce laughs. "Maybe I got a little bit of Greek in me."

"You don't look Greek."

"Ain't they some blond ones?"

"Yeah. But mostly in the north. But your nose is too small."

Bryce laughs again. Then he excuses himself to mingle with his other guests but pauses and turns back. He asks if Angelo wouldn't mind keeping an eye on Tatiana while he is away. Angelo's momentarily uncertain as to whether or not Bryce is serious. But what seems to be genuine gratitude warms Bryce's eyes when Angelo agrees.

He watches Bryce walk up behind Tatiana, kiss her neck, and clasp his arms around her waist. Then, he recalls an old joke about a knight in medieval times leaving his castle to join a crusade. With his lady in a chastity belt, he gives the key to his most trusted friend for safekeeping. Then, after riding away on his steed, he sees his friend galloping after him calling, "It's the wrong key!"

People continue having conversations around him, but Angelo feels content to only be an observer. He picks up the wrapping paper from Bryce's gift then retrieves a pen from his pocket. He sketches the scene, capturing the partygoers in careful, lucid strokes. At some point it gets hard to see his lines, and he looks up in surprise to find that twilight is falling. He watches the guests gather their belongings and line up to wish Bryce a final farewell. Bryce remains Bryce, shaking everyone's hand. Once the crowd has lessened, Angelo goes to his friend.

"This is it, I guess."

"Guess it is, Greek."

"Good luck, man. And be safe. Don't they say, 'never volunteer'?"

"That's what my dad said, too. And to keep my head down. I'll do my best."

"I'll miss you," Angelo says.

"Not for a while. You'll be too busy partying it up in the land of your ancestors. Still nervous about the flight, *huh*?"

Angelo forces a smile. "Guess I can't hide it."

"Don't worry, bro. Just enjoy yourself. Time passes for better or worse. You'll be back before you know it."

Angelo's mouth forms a genuine smile this time. "So will you."

Bryce nods. "Anyways, I'll miss you, too. But I'll have phone privileges at some point."

"Sounds a little like jail."

Bryce smiles. "You can't get to be all you can be without giving up something."

"Yeah," says Angelo. "I've heard that before."

EIGHTEEN

FOR ANGELO, DAYS pass far too quickly, despite the fact that, with school out for summer and his having no job, there should be infinite time to fill. He establishes a regular drawing schedule during which he tinkers with existing sketches or creates entirely new ones. The Greek continues to feature as his main subject, the character evolving into a curly-haired, olive-skinned, bare-chested lothario who says the right things, makes the right moves, and has all the right powers, his only flaw being an unappeasable appetite for the full range of life's carnal pleasures.

As the steady stack of artwork mounts on his desk, he figures that he's on pace to craft an entire graphic novel, a wordless one at that. And while he is currently unclear as to what might be the plot, there is little doubt that a narrative structure is taking shape. No harm in getting a head start on what might evolve into his Master's thesis project.

Angelo notices that during post-work—yes, work—walks, he always looks up whenever a plane passes, tracking its flight as he would a bird's. Then, upon returning home, he lies on his bed and stares at the ticket while tension builds in his chest.

One evening, after putting aside his latest sketch, he digs out of his closet a long-neglected photo album. A collection of pictures from those earliest Greek summers, many of them featuring Angelo as a young boy playing on the beach, his skin tanned a rich bronze, as if he himself was a shore-washed artifact. He braves the surf buoyed by a pair of orange water wings. In most of the shots, his mother looks on from a few feet away, her head bobbing among the waves like a watchful mermaid. Now, he basks in these carefree expressions captured at a time when his anxieties must have dissipated as quickly as they'd come, perhaps washed away at sea.

In another picture—this one marked with the caption, *Angelo, three years old*—he's looking over the edge of a low wall bordering a restaurant's patio while a stray cat props on its hind legs gazing up at him. And in the next photo, he stands, a couple years older, among a cluster of taverna tables. He smiles at the camera while arms and hands jut into view at either side of him, some pointing into the lens as if to direct his attention, others reaching at him, Angelo positioned like some child messiah.

Further along there are photos of his mother and father as a young couple. There are also images of his extended family: Angelo's cousins, Tasso's brothers and sisters, Despina's first cousins; so many faces that it's hard to keep track of who's who. Will Angelo recognize them now? And perhaps it's foolish to think he can just show up after all this time and expect the family to embrace him.

Scattered throughout the album's pages are snapshots of Tasso's hometown: the small, white houses with the terracotta tile roofs, bougainvillea scaling the outer walls in shocks of pink. And in just about every shot, glimpses of the sea, its expanse shimmering like a mine of blue diamonds.

After emerging from his room in the wake of a particularly engrossing session of drawing, Angelo goes to the kitchen to find his mother washing dishes. He pours himself a glass of juice and proceeds to tell of his break-up with Mihaela.

"What do you mean?" Despina almost demands. "You two seemed to have so much fun together."

Angelo shrugs. "I guess relationships need to be sustained by more than fun."

"Did you have a big fight? How did it end?"

"Just a goodbye. On her part. Pretty smooth, actually."

"What was her reasoning?"

"I didn't call to tell her about the hospital visit."

"I thought that odd, myself," Despina says. "She phoned here that day and I..."

"It's all right, Ma. She told me. She also said it seemed like, in general, I was avoiding her."

"Were you?"

Angelo frowns. "I don't think so. But I guess I can see why she might assume that." He considers. "I tried telling her I'm so used to being alone that it doesn't occur to me that other people aren't... that they need more time with their friends and significant others."

Despina nods. "That may be true, though not necessarily a bad thing." She smiles a little. "At least for you creative types. But it's unfortunate. Especially so close to your trip."

Angelo drinks the last of the juice. "Well, it is what it is, whatever it is. I guess I've accepted it."

Despina studies him. "Is that really so? I suppose that's why you've been looking so glum lately and holing up in your room."

"I've been drawing a lot. That's all. I'm getting into this new work."

Despina doesn't seem convinced. "You could have gone to Greece. Before now, I mean. I don't want you to think I was holding you back, or that I would have resented you wanting to visit your father. It was never my intention to make him out as the bad guy, Angelo. I hope you don't think that."

"I don't. It's fine, Ma."

"Let's go to the airport," Despina says unexpectedly, as though suggesting a walk in the park.

"*Huh*? Now? Why?" For a second Angelo feels new fear. "What did you do, bump up my ticket?"

His mother only shoulders her purse and snags her car keys. "Don't be silly. I'm picking up Craig. He's been on business in New York. I was going to ask if you'd stay home with Yiayia, but now I think it's better we all go."

"Don' this Craig know to taking a taxi?"

Angelo and his mother turn to see Yiayia in the doorway. Balanced surprisingly well on her tiptoes, she grabs a roll of toilet paper off a high shelf.

"I was just passing through on my way to move a bowel and I hear you's talking."

"Move it fast," says Despina, glancing again at the clock.

"I just stay here alone. You go."

"No, Mother. You have to come with us. Now hurry."

"Like I'm saying, Craig can be taking a taxi."

"He's not taking a taxi, Mother, and you are coming."

"Hokay," says Yiayia. "I can stay home and wait quiet for the mercy of my death any night. I get my coat."

"I thought you had to move a... use the bathroom?"

"It can wait. At my age is a lot of waiting and little reward."

* * *

In the back seat, with the window down, Angelo feels better getting out of the house. Falling into a reverie as they cross the Bay Bridge, it isn't until multiple roars sound off from above that he realizes they are near the airport. Despite himself, a new tension seizes his gut.

"Oops! I crap my pants!" Yiayia announces, her first words since getting in the car.

"Mother!" cries Despina, momentarily swerving the vehicle and getting a squawk from the horn of another. "I knew this would happen! I told you to go before we left!"

"Ha. I'm just kidding! You should see you face."

"Very funny, Mother."

"And why you put on so much makeup?"

"Mother..." Despina warns, taking the next exit. The road forks, marked by yellow signs: one reads *Departures*, the other *Arrivals*. Despina chooses the latter and heads for Short Term Parking.

"I think you can park there behind those taxis for a few minutes," says Angelo. "If he's coming right out."

"No, I want to meet him after he gets his bags." Despina raises an eyebrow in the mirror. "Now we're an expert on airport etiquette?"

"I've been doing some research."

"Good for you."

"I'll wait in the car with Yiayia."

"No. All three of us are going in."

"Why?"

"Just stop. You sound like a little boy."

Angelo helps Yiayia along while his mother leads the way, pointing things out like a tour guide.

"Back there is where you'd pass through security if you were boarding... and here, on the other side, is the terminal for international flights. That's where you'll be going. Up ahead is reserved, obviously, for incoming flights..."

Though she's been going on like this since they entered the terminal building—"terminal," comforting term for people flying—only now does it dawn on him that this tour, of course, is for his benefit, that she's trying to ease his anxieties. He recalls her walking him through his first school a week before classes began.

"I think he's traveling light, so we probably won't have to wait very long," Despina says as they reach the baggage claim.

"If he travel light, he could take the BART if he too cheap for a taxi," chirps Yiayia, but Despina just ignores her.

Angelo gazes around at all the people waiting for their loved ones. There must be a few who are here unwillingly, meeting people they loathe, maybe to fight over wills. Still, the sight is calming; something about this collective welcoming reminds and reassures Angelo that journeys end mostly without incident, and no matter who or what you leave behind, they are almost always there for you upon return.

"There he is," Despina announces, straining to look over the shoulders of those in front of her.

"You sure is him?" Yiayia asks. "I don' know how you can tell that *xeno* apart from all these other pale Anglo-Saxons." A couple people glance at Yiayia as she utters this, but the old woman scowls, and they quickly avert their eyes.

Craig emerges from the crowd with a free arm spread wide as if to invite a hug, his other hand towing a small suitcase, while a carry-on bag is slung on a strap over his shoulder like a mega man-purse. He looks tired—hair ruffled, suit jacket and trousers rumpled—but the fatigue lends his features a certain cragginess, making him look less like Bill Gates and more like the aspiring archaeologist he had apparently once been. *Why had he left that dream behind?*

"Missed you," Despina says, leaning into Craig as the man wraps her in his unoccupied arm.

"The feeling is quite mutual," Craig replies.

Then they kiss briefly; the sight still causes Angelo's stomach to dip ever so slightly. For an instant, all the other people around them disappear, and it's just Craig and his mother. He feels Yiayia stiffen next to him but ignores her, smiling as Craig turns to greet him.

"How was your flight?" Angelo asks.

"Very nice, actually. I usually fly coach, but this time I splurged on Business Class. A lot more legroom, seats that tilt almost entirely flat like a bed. Food wasn't bad either, but I never seem to have an appetite while flying. Something about the cabin pressure, maybe. But they had chicken tarzini, and if I'd been hungry, I would've gobbled it up."

Angelo is surprised to hear Craig go on like this. Perhaps the man reads Angelo's expression, because he smiles a bit self-consciously.

"This is how I get when I skip a meal. I go all talky."

"Looking like you skip more than one," Yiayia says. *"Polee kondos eisai!* You looking awful."

"Mother!" Despina snaps.

"It's all right," Craig says. "What did that mean?"

"She said you're really skinny."

Craig smiles at Yiayia. "I look forward to fattening up on some of your daughter's Greek cooking in the future. Hey, let's grab something. My treat."

"McDonalds?" asks Yiayia.

"Mother!"

* * *

They dine family-style at a Vietnamese restaurant in San Francisco while Craig does most of the talking, Angelo surprised that the man can be so chatty.

"...It's a funny thing," Craig says between slurps of noodles, "but I find that whenever I mention to anyone, even strangers, that I'm with..." He pauses, maybe to correct himself for Angelo and Yiayia's benefit. "...friends with a Greek woman, I almost always get an interesting response."

"How so?" Despina asks, dipping a spring roll into a small pool of hot sauce at the corner of her plate.

Craig shrugs. "It could be I'm just imagining things or projecting my own enthusiasm onto others, except it really seems that upon hearing the word 'Greek,' most everybody's eyes light up."

Despina smiles. "You don't spend a lot of time chatting up freaks, do you?"

"Only after dark." Met by blank looks, Craig clarifies with, "As in 'The Freaks Come Out at Night?' Remember that song?"

Angelo offers the olive branch. "I do."

Craig appears properly grateful. "You might be surprised at how many folks have a story to tell."

Despina playfully rolls her eyes. "Memories of their favorite diners, as in, 'the Greek's down the street'?"

"Well, a few of those, for sure," Craig admits, and Angelo admires his courage. "But one woman told me about her lifelong dream to sail the Greek isles. And a man mentioned that Greek history and mythology were his favorite subjects in school. Another guy went into this whole deal about how he'd seen a TV special on Grecian sculpture that discounted a recent theory that the ancients had used plaster molds of real bodies and then set them into bronze in order to achieve that fabulous level of realism."

"But nobody actually asked about me?" Despina cuts in. "A real, flesh-and-blood Greek person?"

"No, most didn't."

Despina sighs resignedly. "Isn't that how it always is? No one is prouder of our history than us Greeks, only there's so much emphasis on the past. But what about today's generation of Greeks? The ones blazing new territory in their fields, only most of them are enjoying such achievements abroad because conditions at home are far too bleak. And the Greeks of the six-hundred euro club? No one wants to shine light on them either, the people struggling to make a living on such a small salary. It's only Plato and Socrates and Achilles and Agamemnon and Pericles. May we never forget them, but let's remember there's hopefully a future."

"Of course," says Craig.

Angelo's suddenly conscious of the fact that he rarely gives thought to the current generation. When he does, it's often in comparison to the ancients. He remembers Mihaela's statement about the country being haunted by its past.

"Good point, Despina," says Yiayia, who has actually been eating for once. "At same time, we can't forget that in the Athens of a five-hundred B.C., people..."

"Mother, skip it, all right?"

Yiayia clicks her tongue. "You never letting me have no fun."

"It's certainly a fair point you make," Craig agrees, gesturing with his chopsticks. "More positive attention should be paid to the common people of today's Greece, not just its beaches or its ruins."

"Cheers to that," Despina says, lifting her wine glass. "I wish I wasn't so cynical."

Craig raises his own. "Cheers to that. And cheers to you and me, to our friendship and budding romance."

Despina and Craig clink glasses. "You're so sweet, Craig."

Craig turns to Angelo and asks, "Do you have a girlfriend?"

"Not at the moment," says Angelo.

"I'd think girls would be after a smart, good-looking guy like you."

Angelo only shrugs, like a little boy asked about school.

Despina glances between her son and Craig, saying first to Angelo, "I hope I'm not overstepping my boundaries..." then to Craig, "Angelo recently ended things with a young woman he was seeing."

"*Ah!*" exclaims Yiayia.

Angelo feels his cheeks go hot. "She wasn't really my girlfriend. We weren't going out that long."

"Still, it's always sad when things don't work out," Craig offers.

"Yeah," Angelo agrees.

"I never dated much in my younger years," Craig goes on, maybe carefully. "But the few breakups I endured were pretty nasty. At least for me. I walked around really bitter and angry."

"Maybe Angelo will meet a woman in Greece," Despina says.

Maybe. If I can learn to cast a line like a kamaki.

"Oh, yeah," says Craig. "When are you going?"

"In a week and a half."

"He going to see his father," Yiayia chimes in. "Let's hope he remember to pick up Angelo from the airport."

Craig smiles at Angelo. "It should be a great trip."

Angelo wonders for a moment if Craig will be glad to have him out of the way then decides that's paranoia.

"Angelo's nervous about the flight," Despina says.

Angelo feels heat beneath his cheeks again. "Ma! I'm right here!"

"I'm sorry. Just being a mother, I guess."

"Well, he is... what the word... freaky about it," adds Yiayia helpfully.

Angelo sighs. *My big, fat Greek family.* "I guess I'm not a good traveler. I get claustrophobic and sort of homesick."

Craig nods in what seems genuine empathy. "Transatlantic flights are no fun for anybody now. Crammed in a stuffy aluminum tube with a bunch of other fidgety people. Not like the old 747 days when you could walk around or go up to the lounge for a drink. Have you tried taking an herbal supplement or even a sleeping pill?"

"I wouldn't want to make a habit of anything."

"We're not talking opium here. These herbs are non-addictive, and there are a lot of really gentle sleep aids on the market. It's tough to get rest on a plane no matter what, but taking something might help you relax, at least."

"Or you can use my medical marijuana card," Yiayia offers.

"Mother!" exclaims Despina. "Where did you get one of those?"

Angelo gives Yiayia a wry glance. "You're not allowed to smoke on a plane."

"Since when?"

"Apparently since the last time you flew." Angelo turns to Craig. "I'll look into it. The supplement, I mean, not the weed."

"I think you'll be glad if you do," Craig says. "Probably won't even need it on the way back." He smiles. "Especially should you, as your mother said, meet a nice young woman over there. She'll occupy your thoughts the entire trip home."

"You're way more optimistic than I am."

"It isn't optimism, it's only experience. Experience anyone can acquire. The real difficulty lies in convincing yourself that you deserve whatever you desire."

"No offense, but that's easy for you to say, seeing as how you seem to already have many of the things you want. At least, that's what I assume."

"And you wouldn't be incorrect," agrees Craig. "But of course, it wasn't always this way. My brother and I grew up with the type of father who let us know when we had done wrong but never praised us when we had gotten something right. By the time I was older and out on my own, I was a mess. I went around flinching when someone gave me criticism *or* praise. Never mind the fact that I no longer held anything against my father. I'd figured he was only going by the way he'd been brought up. He'd even apologized, and when I got old enough to where we could basically see each other as equals, things were a lot easier."

Angelo has a brief vision of being met by his father, the air entirely different between them, seeing as they are both adults now.

"But," Craig continues, "a new understanding between my dad and I hardly mattered by then. Things got so bad that I signed up for one of those self-help workshops. The ones advertised on late-night TV. I got hooked on the whole spiel and attended all the sessions. Practiced all the mantras and code words, participated in every role-play, and committed to transforming into my new self. Come to find out, about a thousand dollars poorer, that once I used my "Friend Requests" and "Closers" on new people with whom I wanted to develop relationships, I was still left with my old self. I suppose it took wasting that thousand bucks to teach me that I had been pretty okay to start with."

"Yeah," agrees Angelo. "I guess it's pretty foolish to think some course can change in a few weeks what it took a lifetime to establish."

Despina says, "I didn't realize you had such a difficult relationship with your father, Craig."

"There's still quite a bit you don't know about me," Craig replies. "Maybe Yiayia and I have something in common."

Yiayia perks up. "You having cannabis card, too, *re*?"

Despina shakes her head. "Mother..."

Angelo laughs, noticing after a moment that Craig is laughing with him.

NINETEEN

"I'LL SEE YOU in a couple days, *re mangga*. The sun won't burn your wings, my son. You're ready now."

That had been his father's goodbye prior to hanging up the phone last night. An exchange of formal farewells had already taken place, but those final words seemed the most meaningful, though strange since his father rarely spoke poetically or used parables. Angelo had expected, or at least hoped, that an answer might come in his dreams; maybe an image of himself as Icarus flying dangerously close to the sky's blazing heart, yet no damage done to his wings of wax. But last night there had been no dreams. At least, none he can remember. He hadn't even experienced that all-too-familiar airport routine.

Now, his bedroom aglow with morning at last, he lies amid the rumpled blankets and gazes at the ceiling, trying to determine if it hadn't *all* been a dream. But no, his father's last words were real. All the more curious, given that Yiayia had said something similar yesterday during an outing together. Angelo had accompanied her on a department store errand downtown, and they had just mounted an ascending escalator, Angelo holding her hand. She had said, "I know you ready now."

Finally, he sits up in bed and considers that nearly everyone has been vaguely commenting on his sense of preparedness lately. He tosses his covers aside, gets up, and goes to the window, gazing out at the morning sunshine. Today is the day.

Accompanied by the chirping of birds, he goes about giving his suitcase and carry-on a last inspection. Morning transitions into afternoon, and then it's time to leave. Angelo is packed and ready, though not in the all-encompassing sense that everyone else assumes he is. A brief feeling of déjà vu as his mother takes the airport exit off the freeway. Despite thinking himself prepared, his heart pounds as they find a parking space. His stomach becomes an aviary of fluttering things while Yiayia and his mother accompany him to the check-in.

"How do you feel?" his mother asks when they step into the line.

Angelo shrugs, feeling so many things simultaneously that it's useless to try and articulate them. Reaching the counter, Angelo hands over his suitcase, and the clerk checks his ticket and passport. Then, with another dark sense of finality, the time comes to move on. He embraces Yiayia and then his mother. He reminds himself that he can change his mind, that he's not going to prison or into the Army or surrendering to surgery. He could simply walk out of here. But that's ridiculous.

"Relax," says his mother. "Everything will be fine."

"I know," says Angelo, wishing he believed it. "I'll call when I get to Athens."

"We'll be expecting it."

"And," Yiayia says, "bring me back some goodies, all right? I can't find good *lathee* here. Not even at Vondas's store."

"I'll try and fill up a jug or two," Angelo says, smiling. He starts to turn away, but Yiayia grabs his arm.

"Remember, if you meet a girl in the village, use prophylactics or the pull-out method."

"Mother!"

"I just want he be careful, Despina!"

"On that light note, I'd really better go," Angelo says. One last wave and he steps across the line separating passengers from bystanders. He passes through security quicker than expected, and then he's walking down the corridor leading to the plane, reminding himself that despite its white walls and narrow confines, it isn't a hospital hallway.

* * *

Angelo has a window seat, though he prefers not to look out, even though the plane is still on the ground. If his mother and Yiayia are watching from some observation window, he doesn't want to see them, fearing, perhaps, he might yet change his mind, demand to get off, and make a huge scene. He distracts himself by listening intently to the flight attendant's standard routine about emergency exits. Veteran travelers pointedly ignore the spiel as if that gives them sophistication. At the moment of take-off, he shuts his eyes, trying not to imagine the jet nosediving back into the tarmac. By the time he opens them again, the earth's surface lies distant below.

Ten or so minutes into the flight and he supposes it isn't actually that bad, though he does have approximately ten hours and fifty minutes left to endure. His legs already feel cramped for room, and the air seems to have turned stale. The guy in the adjacent seat, a broad-shouldered, doughy-faced man, seems to have gone right to sleep. Not that Angelo is in the mood to chat, but he is envious of those who are able to nod off no matter the situation.

As soon as he'd stowed away his carry-on, Angelo asked for some water and downed one of the herbal pills Craig had recommended. Hopefully it will take effect soon, but all Angelo can manage now is to look at the seat back in front of him, too jittery to draw or concentrate on a book. A shift to his left and he bumps against the fleshy shoulder of the sleeping man; turn to his right and his own shoulder grazes the window. He tries to reach his carry-on beneath the seat, but his head hits the tray table. He just stays like that, doubled over, listening to the low drone of the engines. For a moment he thinks he might get sick and wonders what he would do if something were to happen with his tube right now. *Even if a doctor is on board, would they be able to help? Would the plane have to land somewhere? Where? Could I make it to a hospital in time?* He tries to find reassurance in his most recent visit with the neurologist, but even experts can be wrong.

Angelo takes a deep breath. This trip might have been a bad idea. His muscles twitch, and he has to concentrate on not springing out of his seat. He closes his eyes, counts to ten, then twenty, then fifty. *Let it pass*, he tells himself. *Let it pass*. When the panic finally does subside, he sits back and checks on his neighbor. Still sleeping. He requests another cup of water from an attendant whose smile seems too bright and too reassuring and sips it slowly as he watches the small video screen which, in all his anxiety, has gone unnoticed. An image of a tiny plane blips across a map of the world. It seems they don't have far to go. But before Angelo can get excited, the picture zooms out to an alternate view; the actual distance left to travel looks vast and daunting.

At some point—minutes or hours later—while Angelo practices the circulation exercises illustrated in the in-flight magazine, rotating his ankles and arching his back, a stewardess brings out the meal cart. It's only then that Angelo realizes to what degree he has been immersed in his anxiety. If nothing else, this flight is full of beautiful women willing to give him attention—their curvaceous figures barely contained in their tight uniforms. He watches as they undulate up and down the aisle; he suffers a strange combination of horny and sleepy, head dropping downward, dick jutting upward. He wonders how one goes about joining the Mile-High Club? Is there some subtle look one must give or a secret password like "Animal Style"?

In the end it isn't the herbal supplement, the belly full of indifferent food, or the blip of the video screen that lulls him to sleep. The only thing that works is watching the sway of the stewardesses' hips.

* * *

By the time he disembarks the plane at Heathrow, Angelo is near zombie-like with fatigue. He has managed to sleep a bit, but it doesn't seem to have done him much good. For a few moments he can only stand numbly amid all the bustle around him, the passing travelers blurry in his vision like extras in a comic book panel. Dimly he comes to the realization that he's facing one of his greatest fears: lost in limbo far from home, alone and vulnerable among strangers in a place where anything can go wrong.

He gazes out at a view of tarmac below a heavy, dark sky. At last, he ventures further. He's somehow a little reassured by the British accents from speakers' voices. He really has made it this far. Two escalator trips and a short tram ride, and he's at his next departure gate. Eleven hours spent in the air; now another six to fill here in this realm of the in-between. He wonders what time it is in California but is too exhausted to do the math. If it's night here, it must be afternoon there. He's tempted to call his mother but decides that would be childish: of course he's made it this far, like all the other people around him, like thousands of people every day, like millions of people every year.

He periodically gazes up at the nearest information board, its screen ever in flux with new departures and arrivals, as well as a number of cancellations and delays.

He closes his eyes, lids feeling like dragging sandpaper, and considers that having a meal could occupy sixty minutes or so, but he isn't hungry. At this hour there is no possibility of leaving the airport for a tour of London via a sightseeing bus. He could explore some of the Duty Free shops, though he's reluctant to wander around and get lost. The signs seem more confusing than helpful, and having to lug around his bag would quickly grow tiresome. Or would they say "bothersome" here? He decides to stay put.

Across the corridor, at a table out front of a small tea shop, a lanky young man wearing a long leather coat with a lambskin lining and a sort of top hat of black velvet or velour has just approached a young woman sitting alone. The woman, a cute, petite blonde who looks very British while sipping from a cup of tea and skimming a paperback, doesn't notice the man at first. He's positioned himself with his back to her in a manner of seemingly casual disinterest, though he addresses her over his shoulder and then gives her his full attention. He points to something in the distance, his lips moving and the woman nodding. Then they exchange a quick handshake, and the man joins the woman at the table. Angelo watches him lean away while speaking, as though preoccupied with something else. But each time the woman diverts her attention, the man gives her the slightest touch on the hand. When this raises no objections, he risks a touch on her shoulder and then her knee. The woman seems to lean in closer to him now, batting her eyes and giggling.

From Angelo's vantage point, it is clear that this guy is running a game. He's surprised that the woman appears to be falling for it, though he's also intrigued that something so obvious can seemingly work so well—like the success many Greek men enjoy while being so forthright with their intentions when approaching women. This man shakes the woman's hand again and then gets up to leave. Angelo watches to see if any numbers are exchanged. There apparently aren't. The woman goes back to her tea and book, and Angelo sits there gazing at her. He counts to fifty then to a hundred before finally going over and standing dumbly in front of her table, almost losing his nerve.

"This might sound weird," he begins, "but I have a really long wait until my next flight. Mind if I join you?"

The woman greets him with a smile and says naturally in an English accent, "Not at all."

"I'm Angelo."

"Josie."

"So, where are you headed, Josie?"

"New York. My first trip to America."

"I'm from there. America, I mean. Not New York. But I hear it's a nice place."

"Where are you from exactly?"

"California. The Bay Area. Oakland... San Francisco?"

"Yes. I know of it. And where are you off to today, if I may ask? Not here to visit London?"

"I'm going to Greece. I have family to see."

"How nice. It's a beautiful country. In a bit of a rough spot now, *eh*?"

"To say the least."

"I've spent a good number of holidays there. I don't suppose it's your first time?"

"No, but I haven't visited in a long while."

Josie smiles. "Won't you sit down?"

"Oh. Thank you." Angelo pulls up a chair and then there's awkward silence. As usual, he can't think of anything clever to say.

"It's a shame you're unable to accompany me to New York."

"Why's that?"

"You seem like an ideal travel companion. Polite. Unassuming. I wish you'd come by a few minutes earlier to rescue me from that rather creepy fellow. Did you see his hat?"

Angelo smiles. "Sort of like Willy Wonka."

"My thoughts exactly.

"What was he saying to you?"

"He wanted to know if I had witnessed some commotion down that way," Josie says, gesturing in the direction in which Angelo had seen the man pointing. "Two men fighting, he claimed. When I said no, he took it as an invitation to sit down. He wasn't polite enough to ask. I must admit, though, he was quite the conversationalist. Very witty."

Angelo feels a familiar pang of envy.

"But," Josie continues, "one could tell he was quite insincere, and I tired of him rather quickly."

"I hope I don't give you a similar impression."

"Not in the least. You seem perfectly nice."

The story of my life. Perfectly nice. Like vanilla ice cream or the color beige. "Can I ask you a question?"

"Do you always ask permission? Not typical of most Americans I've met."

Angelo considers that he's thousands of miles from home and will never see this woman again, so why be concerned of appearing uncool? "In your opinion, how can I...?" He pauses to rephrase. "Do you think a guy like me, 'perfectly nice' and all, can get girls without adopting some other persona, becoming more outgoing and, well, sort of a bad-boy type? I mean, I guess, what do women want in a man? Really? And what if I can't give it to them, the way I am now?"

He's posed these questions quickly, before he could change his mind, and now cowers a bit in his chair, ready for the rebuff.

But Josie cocks her head like a sparrow. "Are you asking me seriously?"

"Yeah. I kind of do serious pretty well."

Josie regards him seriously. "Of course I can't speak for all women. But, given the evidence and the very short time I've had to regard it, you seem perfectly all right to me."

Angelo sighs. "I don't want to just be perfectly all right."

Josie touches his hand across the table. "I didn't mean perfectly all right as in barely above average. We British do have a reputation for understatement. I meant that you seem like a man more than a few women would find appealing. Myself included."

Angelo full-on blushes.

Josie laughs. "If I had needed any further proof. Why would you want to be anything other than what you already are, which is perfectly nice? Most women desire someone who is genuinely themselves. That might sound clichéd, but I think it's true. Why would you entertain the idea of being with a woman who attracts 'bad boys'? What does that say about her? And would that be the sort of woman you'd want?"

"I see your point."

"That's perfectly nice, too—you actually want a woman's opinion and value what she has to say." Josie smiles again. "If you really want my advice, Angelo, stand up a little straighter. And smile more. Definitely smile, you have a nice one."

"Thank you, Josie."

"And do be yourself, Angelo. And if you find that doesn't seem good enough for the people around you, then perhaps you should find a better sort of people." Josie smiles again. "Birds of a feather, you know."

TWENTY

AT THE END OF HIS FLIGHT, when the pilot announces they're descending toward Athens, Angelo turns to the window; the view proves to be less than spectacular. The modern city sprawls out from below the ancient Acropolis in thousands upon thousands of boxy white apartment buildings like some child's haphazard Legoland. Angelo tries to romanticize the scene, imagining scraps of marble scattered in a great ripple effect around the Parthenon, recycled in the construction of the current urban center. But he knows this isn't true. After landing and leaving the plane, he expects a feeling of further disillusionment, but instead is surprised by a new charge of energy.

I made it! At last I'm in Greece!

Compared to Heathrow, navigating Athens International is a cinch. For a while, the sound of Greek all around seems odd: Angelo is used to his second language spoken in occasional spurts, not the rapid-fire phrases he hears now, half of which he can't decipher. Most of the passengers on his flight had been Greek: *yiayias* in black scarves, men of swarthy complexions fingering *komboloi*, women engaging their small children in games of *paklamathi* to pass the time. But Angelo had barely been able to hear them speak over the engine's drone. Or perhaps they had all sat nearly quiet, as fearful of the skies as he was. Hearing their chatter now, Angelo is struck by a new awareness of his dual identity as both outsider and insider; more than a tourist in this land, yet far from being a native. Still, it isn't a loneliness he feels, but a new sort of freedom to move between the two worlds in a way he hasn't since he was last here as a ten-year-old boy.

Sighting his bag on the luggage carousel, he worms his way to the front of the crowd and snatches it. Emerging from the mass of people, he comes face to face with an image from his future as though he's seeing himself as he will appear twenty-five or so years from now. The shock is such that he drops his suitcase.

"*Ela, re.* What are you waiting for?"

Angelo blinks, rubs his eyes.

His father stands before him casually dressed, hair combed back and flecked with silver. Still, Tasso has maintained his striking good looks. Hesitantly, Angelo approaches. His father opens his arms, and Angelo falls against his chest, breathing the familiar scent of the man's aftershave. It's one of those last lingering aromas from childhood, provoking recollections of his dad in front of the mirror on the mornings he had skimmed a razor across his face, Angelo watching from the doorway with a mixture of admiration and fear.

"Let me look at you, *palikari*," Tasso says, grasping Angelo's shoulders. "You're a man now!" Tasso's hands are trembling, his eyes wet, face beaming. "Let me just look at you for a while."

Angelo shyly glances away. It seems funny now that, in all his time spent pondering how this very moment might actually happen, he hasn't once imagined his father being elated to see him. Or maybe he hadn't expected his own apprehension falling away so quickly.

"You must be hungry after so much flying," Tasso says, speaking Greek now. "Would you like something to eat?"

"No, thanks, Dad. Can we just get out of here? I'm sick of airports. It's morning, but all I feel like doing is sleeping."

Tasso slings Angelo's carry-on bag over his shoulder then takes the suitcase. "Yes. You must be very tired with jetlag. I should have realized that. Let's get to the car."

Once they're out on the road and leaving Athens's bustling sprawl, Angelo lets his eyelids droop. He has been anxious that his father might want to talk the whole ride, Angelo unsure what to say. But Tasso lets him rest, tuning the radio to a station playing old

Kazantzidis hits, then rolling up the windows and blasting the AC.

Angelo was surprised to find that the car is a scarred old Peugeot, a vehicle rarely seen in the States, and if so, often driven by aging ex-hippies and trailing tails of oily blue smoke. He has usually pictured the man rolling a vintage Alfa Romeo or MG, maybe even a classic Mercedes. This battered French relic doesn't seem worthy of Tasso's prowess. Still, Angelo has to admit that the ride is relatively smooth. He's napping before he realizes it. Then, upon waking an hour or so later, he looks out at golden-brown hillsides, sun-blanched and only sparsely dotted with green. He has a vague memory of this same scenery as viewed through his much younger eyes, his head and shoulders out a car window, the hot country breeze bathing his face, his arms out-stretched as if guiding flight. At the height of spring, these same hills must appear stunning in full bloom, but he knows them only as summer terrain, dry and dull as they are now.

When they reach the Corinth Canal, that great chasm separating the Peloponnesian peninsula from the rest of the Greek mainland, Tasso stops on the bridge so they can step out and admire the view. Angelo savors lungfuls of the Mediterranean air while gazing down at a pair of ships that traverse the waters far below. It's difficult to fathom how man-made tools could create such a deep cleft in solid rock. Peering at the jagged cliffsides, Angelo imagines a massive cyclops, like the one featured in that old *Clash of the Titans* movie, forcing the earth apart with its strength.

As his father goes into a bit of the history about this great divide, two children—twelve at the oldest, their genders indeterminate—timidly approach in rags, hair matted about their shoulders, grubby palms extended in gestures of want. Angelo gives them each a single Euro coin.

"They're just kids," he says, watching them wander on.

"The face of the economic crisis," Tasso replies. "Sad, but we can't save every child we see."

"I've seen news, but I didn't think there were homeless kids in Greece."

"*Ande, re*! It certainly has been a while since you've been back. Are you thirsty? There's a gas station ahead, we'll grab some lemonades."

After stocking up on refreshments, they continue on their way, Angelo still thinking about the young beggars while pressing the icy bottle of sparkling lemonade against his cheek. Did they have parents around somewhere? Anyone to look after them? Of course, the streets of Oakland and Berkeley teem with homeless people, but children begging are seldom visible, as if America—at least thus far—won't allow that shame to be seen.

Taking a sip from the bottle, he is almost in the mood to talk. He watches his father from the corner of his eye, wanting to tell him something, though he can't remember what. He knows they have much to discuss, but there doesn't seem to be any urgency on either of their parts. He turns to the window and feels his eyelids droop again but resists the urge to sleep. Here and there, signs appear to announce the nearing of a town, though some of these places hardly seem more than a few houses set back from the road.

As the car grumbles up a steep incline, the road grows winding and narrow, and before long he's shaken by the sheer height. At the highest point, there's a small roadside shrine at the cliff's edge. A hundred yards further, they pass another and then one more. Each of these is almost identical: miniature, peak-roofed structures containing candles and colorful icons of the Virgin Mary. These have been put up by people wanting to remember their loved ones who have died or been saved along this path.

As they head down the slope and round a curve, the sea comes into view, its blue expanse shimmering under the sun.

"We must go for a swim as soon as we get to the *horyo*, eh?" Tasso says. "The water should be wonderful on a day hot as this."

"I haven't swum in so long, I've probably forgotten how," Angelo replies.

"You're Greek, *re*. The sea flows in your blood."

"I might need a nap first."

"Yes, of course."

They round another curve, and a great gust of black smoke comes billowing off an adjacent hillside. Tasso gestures to its peak. "You see this? They set fires in order to claim the land under their insurance and then build on it." He shakes his head. "Desperate for money."

Angelo watches the smoke. "Economic troubles again?"

Tasso nods. "We don't feel it as much as those who live in the cities, but it's difficult times all around."

* * *

Further along the coast, Angelo can sense they're approaching the village—his village. Something in the air reminds him of the place, just a subtle impression carried on the wind like a whisper from afar. And then there it is, the *horyo*, marked by a sign more colorful than most they have passed on the way. It's hand-painted with images of a woman sunbathing on a beach, the words *REST. EAT. PLAY* stenciled beneath in Greek and English.

Tasso steers along the harbor road. People wave, and he returns their greetings. Angelo recognizes no one, but maybe that shouldn't surprise him. At last they pull up at Yiayia Eleni's two-story house, which faces the sea.

Tasso says with a chuckle, "You can get out now."

Angelo does and reaches for his luggage in back, but his father takes it and waves him on. Angelo climbs a short flight of deeply worn stone steps that lead to a fragrant garden of rose bushes and citrus trees. Jetlag in combination with the heat causes him to weave slightly, once almost falling as he tries to avoid trampling the tomato plants and dandelion greens, though the cement pathway is wide.

"*Opa, re*," Tasso calls from behind. "Been drinking?"

Angelo laughs and stumbles on, his foot sliding over a stone that appears to be moving like a tortoise, though maybe only to him. But, upon closer inspection, he finds the animate rock *is* a small tortoise retreating into its shell; Angelo lifts it to make sure no harm has been done. Setting it gently down, he moves on alongside the house and under a canvas canopy. The air is a little cooler here, and laundry is strung out to dry on a clothesline. Reaching a narrow, wrought iron door, Angelo lifts his fist to knock.

Tasso laughs. "What are you doing, *re*? It's open."

The door leads into a living room, light there mellowed by curtained windows; it's meticulously clean and minimally furnished. Angelo stops to stare at a framed image on a wall: his class picture from sixth grade hanging next to photos of his cousins at similar ages. It's not the photograph itself that surprises him, but the fact that it's arranged as if all the pictures were taken at the same time and in the same place; as if Angelo has grown up right alongside Manolis and Yiorgos and Katerina; as though he never left at all.

The floor of the next room is plain, smooth cement. It's larger than the first room and contains a bigger table laid with place settings and more family photos. In the far corner, a TV screen glows, and at first Angelo doesn't notice the bed in the farther shadows. He feels Tasso's hand on his shoulder.

"Go to her, Angelo."

Angelo moves to the bedside where Yiayia Eleni lies, delicate among the sheets like a nested bird. She turns to him, skin stretched over bone, her face deeply lined with years. Her hair is whiter than Angelo has ever seen. Only her eyes and the brows above them remain fiercely dark. She barely moves, though her gaze seems to miss nothing and fixes on Angelo long enough for him to grow uncomfortable. But there is no sign of recognition; in fact, she tugs at the top of her blanket as though to shield herself before looking to Tasso.

"*Pios einai aftos*?" she asks in a raspy voice barely above a whisper.

"*O Angelos einai*," Tasso replies.

"*Alithia*?"

Angelo swallows, looking back to see his father nod at Eleni. Turning to her again, Angelo finds the woman still regarding him with that unflinching gaze. But her thin arms are spread wide now. For a moment, Angelo doesn't move, her gesture failing to register. Then he understands, bending low to let his grandmother embrace him, gently slipping his own arms around her. They stay like that for a while—an entire minute, perhaps more. Eleni seems to not want to let go for fear that Angelo may vanish again.

"He must rest now, Mother," Tasso says gently.

Angelo stays by Eleni's bedside for a few moments more to hold her hand in reassurance. He enters the next room, and his eyes widen.

"You remember, *eh*?" Tasso says.

Angelo nods, gazing at the two mattresses on either side of the room fitted atop wooden frames. In over nineteen hours he hasn't glimpsed a sight so inviting. He claims the bed closest to the door, flopping down to feel his muscles spasm with new exhaustion. Then, in those last lucid moments before sleep comes, he gazes at the wooden beams overhead. These aren't yet dreams that play across that familiar ceiling, but recollections from a time when, as a young boy, he shared this space with his father and mother, one family, one room. Then he's overtaken by slumber, and strangely he dreams of the bird shop, and none of the birds are in cages.

He awakens with a start, for a moment expecting to find himself in his own bed at home, and maybe hearing his mother call that it's time to get up for school. His T-shirt is sweat-sodden despite the open window through which he can hear a dove cooing somewhere nearby, the sound soothing and familiar. He feels refreshed, though still a little disoriented, and wonders where his father is.

In the next room, Yiayia Eleni lies as he left her, eyes tracking images on the TV screen: a fat man in a cream-colored suit and giant, novelty sunglasses with neon-green frames cackling into a microphone as bikini-clad Greek babes dance around tossing a beach ball back and forth. Angelo can't tell if Yiayia is truly paying attention, but the sight makes him picture Tasso in a similar scene, playing the jester while girls prance about. In fact, Angelo begins to wonder where his father keeps his current harem. *Surely the man has women waiting in the wings someplace...*

Entering the front room, Angelo nearly jumps at a new sound emanating from out in the yard. A man's voice belts forth in deep baritone, vocal chords thrusting out a slightly off-key tune.

"*Dadadi-Dada-Daaaaaa! Dada-Deeee!*"

Angelo exits a side door and creeps around the house, intrigued by the violent, bleeding notes. What he sees next lights a grin, and he cups a hand over his mouth to smother the kind of childlike laughter that hasn't burst out since he was a boy.

Seated on a bench under an orange tree, like some sort of Mediterranean Buddha, is his Uncle Elias. The man is clad in only boxer briefs, possessing a relatively thin—even fit—physique in contrast to a tremendous round paunch, as if he might have been Atlas, tired of holding up the world and deciding to swallow it instead.

"*Thio!*" Angelo calls.

Uncle Elias looks up in surprise, though he must have known of Angelo's arrival; he has his cell phone in one palm, *komboloi* in the other. "*Ela re*, Angelo! *Pou esouna tosa hronia*?"

They embrace. The last time he saw Elias, Angelo had been small enough to sit on the man's lap, his uncle letting him practice steering his big truck down the dirt road on the mornings when they drove out to the fields to harvest the fig trees; Angelo had gorged on the ripe fruit in effort to gain a belly as godlike as his uncle's.

"*Kaloston agori mou!*"

Angelo turns to the house, his Aunt Voula appearing at the top-floor balcony; she is big-boned in a yellow sun dress and possesses one of those laughs that seems to require an entire body's participation.

"*Yiasou, Thia!*"

Angelo dashes up the steps, leaping the stairs two at a time to reach his aunt and wrap his arms around her. Then his father appears, cradling a small cup of strong, dark coffee.

"Feeling better now, Angelo?"

"A lot."

"Ready for a swim?"

"Sure."

"Not too long," Voula says. "Lunch will soon be ready, and the child must eat well."

"*Ela re*, Voula," Tasso responds. "The child is twenty-four now."

"Ah, yes."

Angelo follows his father across the narrow road in front of Yiayia Eleni's house and down a short slope to the beach. Children splash in the surf just as Angelo once played there, their bodies so bronze beneath the sun that at times it's difficult to determine where their flesh ends and the sand begins. Way out in the depths, a trio of heads bobs above the blue waves like crowns of otters—three elderly women whose voices carry on the wind, their chatter concerning the critical issue of what each has chosen to serve as the midday meal. At least as far as Angelo can translate.

He studies his father as the man stands at water's edge contemplating the sea. A memory long buried surfaces now...

Angelo at four or five years old, thrashing in a swimming pool, chlorine burning his eyes as he sputters and chokes, desperate for air. His father appears poolside, leaping in fully clothed to come to the rescue. And then, after Angelo is safe and dry, his father's hands—those same hands that pulled him to safety—swat his behind in anger as Angelo cries. He had been warned not to drift into the pool's deep end, but had, of course, disobeyed. He remembers being confused, unsure if his father was a man to be idolized or feared, the fact not occurring to him then that both options were possible, even simultaneously...

Gazing at him now, Angelo wonders if anything has really changed.

Tasso dives underwater, resurfacing about twenty yards off shore, shaking droplets from his hair and waving to Angelo. "Water's beautiful."

Angelo pokes his foot in but quickly withdraws. "Cold!"

Tasso chuckles, rolling his eyes. "Cold," he utters. "Come on! Be a man, *re*."

I was kind of hoping you wouldn't say that. Sighing, Angelo bends to splash water onto his legs and torso in effort to acclimate. This only provokes more laughter from Tasso.

"Come on! You looking like a total *Amerikano!*"

Finally, Angelo takes the leap, ungracefully flopping into the surf, failing to execute his dive as planned, and then doggy paddling toward his father.

Laughing again, Tasso asks. "Are you serious? Sure you're my son?"

Angelo goes red in the face, water splashing into his eyes. Panting now, he pauses to tread. "I'm rusty, that's all. Like I told you, I haven't been swimming in a long time."

"Let me remind you how it's done." Tasso dips back under, emerging a few seconds later to demonstrate a perfect crawl stroke, surging atop the waves, arms and legs thrusting to increase speed. "If you're not going to try," Tasso shouts from a distance, floating on his back now, "maybe you should just sit on the beach like one of those Scandinavian tourists struggling to get tan."

Angelo takes a breath, feeling a sudden rage surge within his chest like a flare of heartburn. He hasn't traveled this long, come this far, to be belittled by his father as he was so many times as a boy. He moves toward the man in a half-hearted breaststroke. Tasso takes off again, and soon they're both swimming furiously, pitted against one another. Angelo's determined to prove that he's truly a *man* now—a *Greek* man—that whom his father has expected and goaded him to be.

They head farther out, the ocean appearing to stretch on infinitely to the horizon. In the briefest moment when Angelo allows himself a look back, the shoreline is just a distant strip of sand, like some wavering desert mirage. His father leaves behind a ripple of foamy waves that seem to slow Angelo's advance. Despite this, or perhaps because of it, Angelo's stroke gradually gains confidence, as if Tasso's challenge has awakened within him some forgotten aquatic instinct. *Are we racing or attempting an escape?* Angelo isn't sure. Whatever the motive, it seems this challenge has been a long time coming. Angelo doesn't want to fail. But no matter how hard he kicks and slices the water with his arms, his father retains the lead. The man comes to a stop a few times, rolling onto his back to check Angelo's progress.

"C'mon, *re!*" Tasso calls, not breathing hard in the least. "Haven't you any strength?"

But Angelo can't seem to catch up, his breath burning in his throat like something toxic—like the swallowed chlorine from his close call at the swimming pool. And yet he refuses to stop. Then Tasso switches direction, heading back toward the shore. Finally, Angelo does stop, blinking to clear his eyes while the waves continue to smack against his face and chest. Frustration threatens to drag him down, but he pushes on. He's actually gaining on Tasso now. Harder and harder Angelo kicks, violently coursing through the water, the beach just ahead.

Then, without knowing why, he reaches out, his hand seeming to act of its own volition, just as it had on that afternoon with Mihaela. He grabs his father's ankle, pulling him backward, tugging him under the water, but Tasso breaks free to reach the shore.

Angelo wades up onto the beach after Tasso, who says without turning around, "That was fun, *eh*? Just like we used to do in the pool when you were a boy."

Still feeling that rage toward his dad, who left all those years ago before teaching him to be a man, Angelo aims at a spot just below Tasso's shoulder blades. He lunges forward, slamming his forearm into his father's back and sending him face-first onto the sand.

"What the hell are you doing?" Tasso shouts, rolling over to look up at his son.

Before he can stop himself, Angelo is atop his father, struggling to pin him down. Angelo's teeth are bared, his chest heaving. He wants to see something in his father's face, though isn't sure what. Other people on shore are looking now, their expressions puzzled. Then, with seemingly minimal effort, Tasso pushes Angelo aside and gets to his feet. "Come on, *re.* Time to eat."

Angelo says nothing as he follows his father toward the house, angry now at himself.

TWENTY-ONE

AN UNSPOKEN TRADITION seemingly mandates that men in this family are to be shirtless while enjoying the midday meal. However, Angelo has yet to ask how the practice came to be or if it carries any significance beyond offering relief on sweltering summer afternoons. As to whether it's a year-round custom, he is doubtful, but it has been in standing every summer he has visited. Angelo remembers being able to, as a boy, measure the gradual maturation of his body in comparison to those of his male cousins of the same age. From age three years to ten, he used them as models—even if not always conscious of doing so—flexing his muscles or checking for some vague sign of puberty. Here, among blood relations, the fact that Angelo's abdomen is scarred never seems an issue.

While not an official rule, it appears as though only once Angelo has stripped off his tank top can the meal commence. And so he does, folding and draping it over the back of his chair while Uncle Elias gives a subtle nod of approval and Aunt Voula serves the dishes of *astako mai saltsa*. Angelo is hungrier than he had realized after the long car ride and fierce swim. He digs right into the shelled lobster meat, cramming a large forkful into his mouth, dipping his hunk of bread into the sauce.

Uncle Elias slaps a hand—the size of an oar head—against Angelo's back. "You like the food?" he asks.

Angelo nods enthusiastically as he chews.

"I don't think he likes it, Voula," Elias says.

Angelo finally swallows. "I do!"

"He's just being nice. I don't think he likes it."

Voula cuts her eyes at her husband. "Leave the child alone, *re*."

Elias chuckles and gently pinches Angelo on the back of the neck. A game they have played since Angelo was young: Uncle Elias taunting Voula about her cooking, Angelo quickly coming to her defense. To his mind, Voula's skills in the kitchen are potentially unparalleled across the entirety of Greece.

"Isn't Yiayia eating?" Angelo asks.

"She already ate downstairs," Tasso replies. "In bed. She's too weak to have her meal at the table."

Angelo looks at his father, tries to read the man's expression. These are the first words he has spoken since leaving the beach. Angelo is uncertain as to whether or not the man has come to sense the tension... Angelo's tension, anyway. Angelo glances around at this trio of bodies: Uncle Elias' impressive gut pressed against the table's edge, Aunt Voula's breasts threatening to spill out the top of her blouse as she leans toward her plate, and Tasso with elbows on the table, hard chest sparsely coated with dark hair.

Angelo gazes down at his own chest, not nearly as defined as his father's, pale in comparison though he shares the masculine patch of fur. Examining his dad's torso again, Angelo notices reddish marks along his ribs, the places where Angelo's fingers dug into the skin while they wrestled in the sand. Perhaps he had wanted to mar the man just as the surgeons had marred him. *But if so, why?* He considers apologizing but can't make the words come, and it might be awkward here at the table in Voula and Elia's presence. Instead, he stuffs his mouth with more food.

"Which do you like better, Angelo," Elias asks, looking up from his plate, "*Ameriki* or *Ellada*?"

Aunt Voula clicks her tongue and mimes a swipe at Elias with her palm. "Leave the child alone."

The age-old question, Angelo thinks. *Which do you prefer, America or Greece?* He has been asked this same thing every time he's made a trip, various relatives inquiring as to where his patriotism resides. Or maybe his heart. In the past, Angelo has always tried to be diplomatic, reassuring everyone that he loves both countries equally. Faced with the question now, however, he attempts to come up with something unique, an answer that will express how he truly feels.

"It's hard to say, *Thio*," he begins. "When I'm in America, I don't feel like I totally belong. I try to make a place for myself, a place that's both Greece and America, a place that embodies that hyphen between Greek and American where I can truly be myself. But right now I feel like my heart is with you... my family... and that's what counts."

Uncle Elias just blinks, paused with his wine glass at his lips, and Angelo considers that maybe he's made a mistake in his Greek phrasing. But then Elias knocks back the liquid and lifts a hand. "Voula! Get the child some more food. He loves it!"

"That's okay," Angelo tries to protest. "I'm still working on..."

But Voula shovels lobster onto his plate then asks, "How come you waited so many years to visit us?"

Angelo looks up, though he can't meet Voula's gaze for long, as if to do so will leave him exposed, as if his aunt might glimpse a level of cowardice beyond any reluctance to reunite with his father. What if the woman discovers that, in the years following his last visit, in those days of budding adolescence, he had thought little of them at all. What if she notices he had taken his relatives for granted, so wrapped up in his fear of flying that it was the only thing that mattered? Such a fear now seems all the more shameful given that he has flown at last and nothing bad has happened.

He fiddles with his fork, scolding himself for not anticipating such a question. There must be a hundred replies that won't injure anyone's feelings, if only he can find one. And then he just says, "I don't know," surprised and disappointed that a statement so utterly inarticulate should surface. For a moment, he faces his father. "Is it enough to say that life got in the way? That I wanted to come but just couldn't?" He shrugs. "I guess that explains even less, but it's the truth all the same."

Voula looks puzzled, as does Elias. Tasso's face is unreadable, but finally he says, "Angelo stayed away because he's afraid of odysseys and most things unfamiliar."

Angelo starts to speak, but his father holds up a hand.

"I'm not saying it's a bad thing," Tasso continues. "Angelo isn't like me when I was young, and he's not like his cousins. He's had his own battles in life to fight and in his own way. But he's a young man now. And he's here. And he loves us all. And that's that. Now, can someone pass the bread?"

For a moment, Angelo feels angry. His father has simplified, understated, and underrated what should be complicated and very serious issues. Almost dismissed them, in fact, in an old school manly way. A very Greek, manly way.

Voula concedes, "Of course, we could have come to America once or twice. But we didn't..."

"Tickets are expensive," Tasso reminds his sister.

"Still, it's not much of an excuse."

Elias waves his hands. "Forget all this. It is all past like ancient ruins, and we are not archaeologists to dig up and try to explain everything. Angelo is here, and as Tasso has said, that is that. Angelo, how do you plan to spend your time? In *Ellada* there are so many things to see."

Angelo feels relieved, if not entirely satisfied. "I want to be around all of you as much as possible. Swimming and hanging out, making up for the lost time." He wonders how they have imagined him all these years, the long-lost relative in America, their exiled cousin, nephew, grandson. Likely there have been periods when he has rarely crossed their minds.

"I want to take Angelo on a road trip around the Peloponnese," Tasso says. "Surely to Mycenae, Epidavros, and Nafplio. That way he can experience the true Greece in a way he wouldn't have been able to appreciate when he was a boy." He turns to Angelo. "How does that sound?"

Angelo nods, thinking that sounds exciting, though he's unsure how it will be to spend all those hours in the car with his father. For some reason he regrets never having learned to drive.

"And tonight?" Voula asks. "The child's first evening in the village?"

Tasso smiles. "His cousins want to take him out for drinks."

"Ah, good."

* * *

Later, Angelo stands over his grandmother, watching her sleep as she gently puffs air through her lips. He clicks off the TV and then goes into his room. Tasso lies on the other bed reading a book, and Angelo stretches out on his own mattress to gaze at the ceiling while doves coo beyond the window. This is the time of the traditional late afternoon siesta, those hours set aside to digest a huge lunch. Angelo recalls on his previous visits to Greece when he passed this lull in the day while playing with toys he had brought along. And then, when he was older, he had immersed himself in a novel or tried a round of solitaire. But he rarely slept. Too great was the anticipation of the nearing Greek night and its many wonders: lights strung along the wharf and reflecting from the onyx water like many small moons on a necklace as he ran loose with his cousins. They would sneak just far enough beyond sight of their parents to relish a taste of freedom. Upon returning, their virgin lips had savored sips of ouzo or whiskey. Caught up in reminiscing, he doesn't hear Tasso speak until his father repeats himself.

"I said do you have a problem?"

"What do you mean?"

"The way you rammed into me on the beach."

"How come you didn't say anything?"

"I figured you were just tired. Cranky like you would get as a child. But then, during the meal, I could tell that something was wrong."

Angelo says, "Maybe you're right, I was just tired. And maybe I was a little cranky at your turning our swim into a contest."

"I hadn't thought of it that way, but if something is bothering you, let me know."

Angelo wants to tell his father exactly what *is* bothering him, but remembers his childhood when the man demanded that Angelo speak to him only in Greek,

Tasso cutting no slack when Angelo garbled a word or phrase. Now, feeling a little childish, Angelo improvises. "Why does everybody call me 'the child?' *Toh pethee, toh pethee.*"

Tasso raises an eyebrow. "*Toh pethee* is a term of endearment. You should know that. Nobody means it literally or negatively."

"How old do you have to be to earn a new term of endearment?"

"I know sixty-year-old men called *toh pethee*. It's certainly nothing to bitch about."

Again a dove coos outside the window, and Angelo meets its eyes. "I shouldn't have to tell you what's bothering me. You should already know."

"I'm not a god to read your mind. And that is a womanish thing to say."

Anger flares again. Angelo almost remarks that he was raised by a woman—a strong, independent woman—because a man abandoned him. But instead he says, "Speaking of women, where are all your girlfriends?"

"What?" Tasso looks genuinely confused. "If you mean Xandria, I had planned to introduce you." He cocks his head. "I didn't know you were so interested in meeting my girlfriend."

"Only one?" asks Angelo before he can stop himself.

Tasso frowns. "Yes."

Angelo feels a little ashamed, though that brings another twinge of anger. But he asks, "Xandria? Is that short for Alexandria?"

"No, just Xandria."

"Sounds like a pole-dancer's name."

For a moment he thinks he's gone too far, but Tasso tilts his head back and laughs. Then seriously he asks, "Do you go to whores?"

Payback? But this is a manly conversation. Angelo considers a reply, but Tasso goes on, "I know you have girlfriends. You've told me. But what about the times in between? A young man has his urges."

Angelo frowns. "What you call the times in between, I call everyday life."

"You're funny."

"It wasn't a joke, Dad." Angelo forces a shrug. "I thought only *malakas* pay for sex."

"We all end up paying, one way or another," Tasso says.

An hour ago, Angelo wouldn't have imagined having such a conversation with his father. *Isn't this a good thing?* "What about your times in between?"

"Twice, when I was a teenager. Most of the village boys did."

Angelo relaxes. "Because the respectable girls were sheltered at home, right?"

"Yes."

"What about the tourist girls?"

Tasso smiles. "Tourist season arrives only once a year."

"So, this prostitute..." Angelo begins. "She paid you, right?"

Tasso laughs. "My second visit was free."

Angelo's laugh comes easily. He has no problem believing his father. Even if it isn't true.

Tasso adds, "It will be my treat. We'll go after our nap."

"I wasn't really serious, Dad."

Tasso puts his book aside and stretches out to sleep. "There's a place just outside the village."

"Really, it's okay."

"Are you afraid?"

"No!"

"Then we'll go. But now, time to rest." Tasso closes his eyes.

Angelo lies back on his pillow and regards the dove regarding him. Part of him is horrified, ridiculous as that may be. Nonetheless, he is intrigued. What joy to savor a female scent, to run his fingertips over a woman's skin. And it's not like he's never entertained the idea of soliciting a little pleasure. And more than the lap dance in San Francisco with... *what was her name?* There were several nights following his breakup with Tracy when he perused the Internet for escort services, tempted by those that mentioned "Greek," though he'd realized that meant something else in such a context. But things are different here, and perhaps this Greek *is* really Greek?

He ponders this for a while. The dove outside on a tree branch seems totally non-committal, its cooing only a soft lullaby that soon takes effect.

Tasso gently shakes Angelo's shoulder. It is maybe an hour later, and for a moment Angelo wonders if he'd only dreamed their conversation. Well, it is ultimately his decision, and he nods when his father's eyebrows arch a bit to remind him of the question. He follows his dad through the house and they pass Eleni asleep in her bed, her body curved like a question mark, then move across the yard in stealth like two mischievous boys.

Tasso drives slowly through town, and Angelo gazes out at the village, the ocean caressing its toes. The waves seem to be the only things moving, all else sleepily still beneath the late-afternoon heat. As they did upon first arriving, they cruise the narrow cobblestone street that serves as the main drag. To the right are a series of small hotels, bars, eateries, and shops selling everything from bathing suits to fresh baked goods. The buildings are tall and narrow, painted in pale tones and fronted by squat, non-indigenous palm trees. Many are more than one story and have apartments on their top floors. Angelo watches a woman come out on her wrought iron balcony to take laundry off a line.

To the left, facing the ocean under the shade of umbrellas, are the outdoor seating areas belonging to the adjacent tavernas. Currently, only two tables are occupied, both by pairs of Nordic-looking tourists who suspiciously eye a stray cat slinking past their shins.

Angelo absorbs it all, briefly forgetting their ultimate destination as the scenery lulls him into a meditative sense of calm. He already longs for the near future when his jet lag will be over and he can get into the rhythm of life in this place. The veins of this main street branch off into smaller lanes that lead through hills clustered with homes. The majority of them are painted a brilliant white, with roofs of terra-cotta tiles. Angelo yearns to explore those byways, to traverse their narrow, winding courses as pirates of days long past might have done. He wishes there were more people out now, impatient to see his fellow Greeks amid their everyday routine, as if they could impart something valuable to him merely through the act of being observed.

Then they are beyond the village limits, and the car rolls through a stretch of empty countryside. High, golden grass lines the now dirt road, the earth tone palette broken here and there by the silvery leaves of thick-trunked olive trees. Angelo watches a pair of crows soar overhead then glances at his father, the man sitting straight and silent, his eyes never leaving the road. Angelo wishes there was some way to see into the man's head, glimpse the world through his eyes, read his thoughts without having to ask what they are.

Tasso turns onto an even narrower road that seems to be hardly more than a goat trail. Ahead, at the end, is a fairly large house. It's the only dwelling in sight, flat-roofed and unassuming with a pair of black-and-brown mutts prowling the front yard. Tasso pulls up and stops the car.

"Here," he says, offering a roll of euros as if it was a roll of quarters to keep Angelo amused in an old game arcade. "I'll be back to pick you up in about an hour."

Angelo automatically accepts the money as if it *was* only a roll of quarters, then realizes it isn't. "You're leaving?" he asks, his voice squeaking slightly like an adolescent's.

"No sense in sitting in the car in this heat."

"But..."

Tasso smiles with no trace of a smirk or a tongue in cheek. "This place is run by a local doctor, so everything's clean and healthy."

Seeing no way out but out, Angelo exits the car, watching his father make a casual U-turn and then drive away, trailing dust. Absurdly, he feels as if he's been left—perhaps like young David Copperfield—at some very questionable boarding school. It occurs to him that he doesn't have to go in; he could simply walk down the road for a while and then return in about an hour. *And then what? Lie to his father? Say he'd had a headache?* Believable in this case.

But he takes a deep breath and crosses the yard, the pair of dogs coming to sniff at him. At the front door, he's unsure whether to knock; this is, after all, a house—

in at least two senses of the word. He gently taps the door frame three times, almost hoping no one is home.

But an elderly woman appears in a moment, almost seeming to materialize out of the shadows within, looking like a stand-in for everyone's favorite Greek aunt. She's clad in a long cotton dress despite the heat, her head wrapped in a pale blue scarf complimenting the dark intensity of her eyes, which regard Angelo as if he's a beloved nephew paying her a visit.

The point of no return, he thinks, as the woman, smiling, steps aside to usher him in. There is a large front room, mellowly lit by sun-glow through curtains; it looks every bit like someone's home. There's even a little bird in a cage, though what kind he doesn't know, and it meets his gaze for a second. He follows the woman down a short hallway and through a small kitchen friendly with the scents of *macaronia mai kema,* past an even smaller bathroom. Then they stop in the doorway of what appears to be the largest room in the house, though it's sparsely furnished with only a colorful rug and—naturally—a comfortable-looking bed. Beside it is a small table topped with a candle crowned in glass.

Angelo hears another dove cooing in the distance, and through the window, he watches crows gathering in an olive tree, maybe for the oncoming night. At this moment the world seems to be breathing all around him, the earth softly sighing beneath his feet.

He finds the old woman gone, as if she has simply disappeared. But then several much younger emerge from another doorway. They line up facing him, and Angelo swallows hard, feeling like he's the one on display. But his father would have no such thoughts. Puffing his chest just a little, he scans the selection. There are six in all, ranging from plain to passably pretty; none that he would call strikingly beautiful, at least by American standards. He remembers the velvet trap into which he fell during his strip-club visit but somehow knows there is none of that here. Well, he's not a blushing virgin—although he feels a little like one—and decides he will go through with this and enjoy it for what it is.

He makes his choice, reaching for the hand of a tall, dark-haired, bedroom-eyed woman with ample breasts and voluptuous thighs. She smiles at him pleasantly with no hint of fake coyness, and the others—looking neither disappointed nor relieved—file back into the curtain-draped doorway farther up the hall.

"...*Er*, what's your name?" Angelo asks.

The woman smiles again. "Eva."

"*Mai lene* Angelo."

Another pleasant smile. "Hello, Angelo."

Well, he thinks, *maybe she is happy that I'm young, reasonably good-looking, and not some gnarly old fisherman with ouzo on his breath and anchovy scales in his graying hair*.

Eva, still holding his hand, seemingly genuine warmth in her touch, leads him into the room. They sit on the bed, Angelo having to shift a couple times to accommodate a budding new erection. Eva guides his hands along her legs, over her breasts, and then he takes charge, surprising himself with a new level of assertiveness. It's unexpected, and yet it seems born of this country, its salt-tinged air, its natural aromas of honest earth and real life.

The dove coos outside the window.

* * *

Angelo stands on the house's front porch. He leans over the wooden railing, a blade of grass twined around his finger. The dogs stand on hind legs against the rail and nose his hand cheerfully. The crows also seem to approve. He gazes into the distance, the hills glowing golden against the sun, and recalls a passage from *The Iliad*; the one in which Priam mourns the death of Hector and says something about how he expects the very hounds who guard his palace to devour his flesh after he himself is dead, though Angelo's not sure what that means.

It was a good thing, what occurred back in the house, though he finds it hard to believe that he's gone through with it. Most surprising is that he didn't fumble about, his body finding a rhythm faster than expected.

That initial assertiveness he'd felt upon sitting with Eva on the bed only seemed to strengthen as their passion grew, Angelo drinking in her flesh, savoring every touch as though he might never get another opportunity. He entered her slowly, grinding his hips. Gradually, as she writhed with pleasure beneath him, he felt that he was shedding something he'd outgrown, a shell no longer of use.

When the Peugeot pulls up, Angelo climbs in, not having to act casual. Tasso doesn't ask him how it went, doesn't smirk or poke him in the ribs. *And, after all, it had been a natural man-thing.*

TWENTY-TWO

NIGHT'S DESCENT UPON the village occurs seductively, darkness unveiling itself one shadow at a time. From his vantage point at the harbor, Angelo watches this striptease of sorts, the last remnants of dusk pulling away to reveal darkness beneath. Or perhaps it's only his visit to the "house" that shades his perspective. He sits at one of the outdoor taverna tables amid stray cats and boisterous children and smiles at the cousins around him: only five of them; not even half the clan. But it would be overwhelming to greet them all at once. He feels laughter brimming within and sets it free. His cousins laugh, too, as the wharf lights cast a golden glow over their features. In each face, reflected in each pair of eyes, he is somehow able to glimpse fragments of their shared past: playing on the beach, exploring the town corners and alleys, clustering around their *yiayia* in hopes of scoring a *Socofreta* or a string of *komboloi*. He remembers when it first dawned on him, as a young boy, that they were family... that they shared a *yiayia* and aunts and uncles, despite the fact that he lived a world away. It had been one of those small moments that occur in childhood, the ones that shimmer for an instant before passing on to leave a new awareness.

There is Panos, his father's apprentice in their construction business—six feet tall and barrel-chested, with hair as dark and thick as Angelo's, his face beaming as he sits hand in hand with his fiancée, a pleasant woman whose name Angelo is embarrassed to have already forgotten. Angelo does recall that Panos is younger than he by just two weeks, and during his last visit, they had been like twins.

There is Panos's younger brother Yiorgos, dark and intense, eyes like a falcon's, missing nothing. Yiorgos bore the brunt of practical jokes on behalf of the older boys and yet remained stoic through it all; a little tank rumbling with an out-thrust lower lip, scraped elbows and knees, never letting forth a cry.

There is Katerina—also Angelo's age—tall and gorgeous, with rapids of curls flowing down her shoulders, and striking green eyes. Angelo is unable to help blushing at the memory that she was his first patient in games of doctor.

There is her younger sister Marianthe, ever-smiling, face round and boyish. She was always a faithful playmate: climbing trees right along with the male cousins, never to be outdone. From what Angelo gathers now, Marianthe shares his penchant for the arts, busy penning her poems when not working behind the desk of a local hotel.

Lastly, there sits little Stamatis, regarding Angelo with a hint of wariness. Stamatis just turned fourteen and wasn't born at the time of Angelo's last visit, so was raised with only a vague awareness of his cousin in America. Angelo is about to ask him about his interests, chief among them—according to Uncle Leonidas—the study of marine life in the Mediterranean. But Panos speaks before Angelo.

"Cousin, tell us news from America."

"America is just work, work, work..." Angelo pauses, unable to escape the irony of making such a statement while being currently unemployed but then goes on. "Most families aren't close. Not like they are here. And the TV tells you to 'buy this, eat that, look like this,' or you're not part of the cool culture." For some reason, Angelo expects his cousin to rally around this cynicism, decry the capitalist machine, and impart some Greek wisdom, but Panos says, "You are lucky to be able to complain of too much work. Here, there are barely any jobs. We are fortunate in the village, because we support one another, but in the cities, people can hardly make it. I see on the news that Americans think we are spoiled, with our protests over the loss of our pensions, but even with these pensions, we still don't make half of what you earn in the States."

Angelo glances down at his plate, the wax paper translucent with oil, the remnants of his gyro dinner scattered about. Panos's sentiments echo those of Tasso's during the drive from the airport, and Angelo feels slightly embarrassed at having made such a silly, sweeping remark. "Do you think things will get better?" he asks.

"I hope so, cousin, but it will take a long while to turn them around. We have many bad habits to break, and if the country exits the euro, as the news people say we might, then we will be in for an even harder time." Panos looks at his future wife. "We would like to make a trip to America. Maybe after Krisa and I are married."

"In America," Stamatis says, speaking for the first time as his eyes meet Angelo's, "do you live around the bad people with guns? Like we see in these music videos?"

"No. But really, there are very few 'bad people with guns.' Most of the blacks in America are good people, like anyone else."

"Your father tells us that you are almost finished with your studies," says Katerina. "What do you hope to do after?"

"I don't know yet. I want to continue making art. Maybe I'll be a teacher, too."

"In your city," Yiorgos begins, "do you have many Greek-American friends? We saw on TV, after *Ellada* won the Euro 2004 football championship, Greek-Americans going crazy in Chicago, New York. Many places."

Angelo thinks of George, Vassili, and Jimmy. He didn't see them much in the days leading up to his departure. No phone calls to wish him safe travels, but with their social circle being as large as it is, he knows better than to take their lack of keeping in touch as a personal snub. They have busy lives, many people with whom to share their time. Still, Angelo wonders if he was too quick to call them friends.

"Not so many," he says at last. "The Greeks in California are more spread out than in Illinois or New York."

"What about girlfriends?" Marianthe asks, smiling like a cherub.

"Not right now," Angelo says with a helpless shrug, as though sorry to let her down. The cousins all exchange glances then collectively lower their heads ever so slightly. Angelo wonders if rumors of his romantic woes have crossed the Atlantic unbeknownst to him. "I was seeing someone for a while," he adds, "but it didn't last. Maybe I'll meet somebody new when I go back."

"Your father," Panos says, "has a girlfriend. Xandria is her name. She's very nice."

"I'm surprised there's anyone left for my dad to date."

"Sorry?"

"I mean, the village being as small as it is, I'd guess my father has kept company with most of the available women by now."

Panos looks puzzled. "I think Uncle Tasso has been alone for some time."

Katerina adds, "The occasions on which we see your father, he is usually out with his brothers or by himself. Before Xandria, he hadn't brought a woman around the family in quite a while."

"Oh. Have you ever asked him why?"

Panos shrugs. "He doesn't seem lonesome. I assume he enjoys his life as it is."

Angelo feels he should change the subject but says anyway, "Maybe he wants to keep his love life private. What if he's seeing a bunch of women and nobody knows about it?"

Panos smiles. "This is a small town, Angelo. Everyone knows everything."

Angelo doesn't know why it's of such importance for his father to uphold the image to which he seems to be clinging. Certainly Angelo didn't create that image like one of his drawings.

The conversation flows on, and he and his cousins conduct a sort of loose interrogation of one another, digging ever deeper to mine their mutual histories and perhaps stumble upon something that will bring them even closer together. There is a lull, and Angelo becomes aware of all the activity around them as the harbor bustles with nightlife: young couples strolling hand-in-hand; families gathered at wharf's edge to watch large fish pop their heads just above the water's surface. Groups of teenage boys eye groups of teenage girls, neither bold enough to make a move. Young children race around clutching giant ice cream cones, hurrying to devour them before they fall victim to the warm, Mediterranean evening.

Someone orders another round of ouzo. Angelo clinks glasses with his cousins, and they savor slow sips. Angelo wonders where his father is tonight, having left after bringing Angelo home. *Out with Xandria*? But then—perhaps prompted by this last drink—Angelo is suddenly overcome with tremendous fatigue. It is such that one moment he's raising his glass in another utterance of *"Yiamas!"* and the next his eyes are closing, his head drooping.

Then Panos and Katerina are helping him up from the chair, escorting him back home. The last thing Angelo recalls is glancing over at his father's empty bed.

TWENTY-THREE

THE DAYS TAKE SHAPE in near-flawless arcs, as though the hours are carved from marble: smooth, precise, etched with symmetry. Mornings curve into afternoon, afternoon into evening, and before long Angelo is able to sleep through the night until well beyond sunrise, and tension between him and his father seems to have eased. Generally, Angelo doesn't see him until the midday meals in Aunt Voula's kitchen. Tasso rises at first light to hunt for construction work with Uncle Leonidas. By the lunch hour when he returns, both he and Angelo are so rabid with hunger, there's no time for much serious talk. After gorging themselves, they retire to the bedroom where Angelo sketches while Tasso sleeps. By nightfall, they are surrounded by loved ones vying for attention. Angelo remains curious about Xandria, but Tasso hasn't hinted as to when he'll bring the woman around.

The hours spent in his father's absence are at once the most rigid and the most carefree. Angelo wakes between eight-thirty and nine, leisurely getting out of bed to wash and then head upstairs. He takes a chair onto the balcony and gazes at the indigo pulse of the ocean until Aunt Voula brings his breakfast, always the same: a cup of thick, velvety yogurt topped with local honey and chopped walnuts. He eats slowly between sips of orange juice, willing to help Voula with the chores, but his aunt invariably declines.

After breakfast, she allows herself a short break between washing dishes, folding laundry, sweeping floors, and gathering ingredients for lunch to join Angelo on the balcony. They chat until a neighbor arrives with a loaf of fresh-baked bread and some freshly harvested herbs. Then Angelo rises to embark on his daily walk through the village, trekking up the hills to meander among the houses. It almost feels as though the dwellings, most ancient homes to many generations, are likewise studying him, perhaps to satisfy themselves that he is worthy to wander their lanes. Among the houses are small shops: a butcher with lamb carcasses slowly rotating in the window like some carnivore mobile; a *souvlaki* and *gyro* restaurant featuring condiments different than similar eateries along the waterfront. A somewhat shabby boutique offers wedding necessities. In comparison to the harbor, life seems somehow different up here; more mysterious, full of hidden corners, and shadowy alleys.

Retracing his steps back down to the water, he walks along the winding streets, lined in places with colorful flowers of pink, pale blue, and orange. Sometimes, upon reaching the harbor, he sits at one of the tables among the locals and tourists, the former usually looking serene—or maybe simply satisfied—like calm old resident seabirds, compared to the latter's constant chirping.

He watches the clear blue waves, perhaps hoping to catch a glimpse of a Flying Dolphin; not the mammal, but one of the blue-and-yellow passenger ships so named. They remind him of those days as a child when he'd sat in Eleni's lap while she spotted them from the front yard, Angelo clapping with delight upon laying eyes on one.

Other times, when he doesn't feel like pausing, he walks on into the small forest that edges the village and strolls among the tall trees and lush foliage, listening to the cicadas. Below the cliff-hanging trails are small and often deserted beaches where the tourists seldom go, pebbly inlets accessible by only narrow, heart-stopping paths.

On a couple occasions, he has glimpsed a young woman in one of the isolated coves, sitting atop the rocks below. She is olive-toned and slender; he can't be sure of her age from a distance, though she moves with a youthful stride. She is always in a white bathing suit—a rather modest single-piece—with long dark hair and eyes that, even at a distance, appear to shimmer. Upon sighting her, Angelo always has to stop, though it feels slightly wrong to stand gazing at her unseen—he's sure—from his lofty vantage point like a hawk observing a dove.

Once or twice he's considered braving the breathtaking path down to meet her but has always lost his nerve, and not simply because of the dangerous trail. What would be his explanation—or excuse—for disturbing the peaceful solitude she has obviously sought? She looks like a local and surely must be; there is a good possibility he wouldn't be able to keep up with her Greek. What's strange is that she perpetually seems to vanish at one point or another, Angelo looking at her one moment, glimpsing nothing the next, as if she's been swallowed by the ether. He takes this as his cue to leave, even hurrying out of the forest as though witness to something supernatural.

Nevertheless, he thinks it would be charming, perhaps more satisfying somehow, to find romance with a Greek woman—one from Greece and *in* Greece—not a Greek-American. Not another Mihaela. Unfortunately—at least according to his cousins—most local women are wise to the ways of visitors and reluctant to be some foreigner's fling. And, through inquires, he's learned that even the "house" on the hill is not overly welcome to foreign trade.

Gone seem the days he's heard of when tourists had love affairs with naive ladies of the village eager to explore newfound freedoms. Despite the specter of lean economic times, it still seems common to see Greek men—*kamakia*—sweep foreign girls off their feet. Maybe that's expected as part of the Greek experience. Angelo has, more than once, considered this might give him an advantage, assuming he wanted a foreign fling. He's discussed such things with his cousin Thanasis who, at his harborside workshop, preps parts needed for boat building. Angelo makes a habit of arriving mid-mornings while Thanasis takes a frappe break.

"You really like the *gomenes* here. I can tell by how often we talk about them," Thanasis says one morning, sipping his iced coffee through a neon-orange straw.

"But they don't want you. I don't mean you personally, cousin. I mean outsiders in general."

Outsider.

Angelo gets snagged on the word's barbed wire syllables. *Ironic,* he thinks, *that he has flown across an ocean to escape such a label.* But he persists, inquiring as to whether his cousin knows the girl who frequents the little beach. Thanasis considers for a long moment but ultimately says no, although he agrees she must be local to venture along that particular cove. Its path would discourage even a goat.

Today Angelo has brought fresh *bougatsa* from a pastry shop up the hill. He offers one to Thanasis then takes another for himself. They chew in silence, Angelo letting the sugar glaze over his disappointment as he scans his cousin's workplace. Lengths of wood jut from every corner; thicker beams lean against the wall, piles of planking are stacked in abundance. High in a loft at the rear of the shop is the hull of a boat, its wood coated red with a special sealant paint. Angelo imagines this vessel completed, taking to the water for the first time, the entire town gathering to witness its baptism in the sea.

He gazes at his cousin Thanasis: boat-builder, wise man, philosopher. Angelo supposes they share a unique bond, given that Thanasis is one of his few relatives from Despina's side of the family. Most of her kin reside in Athens these days. Angelo studies Thanasis: the young man's wiry build and comfortable, easy smile; his paint-spattered clothes and calloused hands. Angelo tries to calculate how many boats he may have already built in his lifetime. How many ships presently sailing the sea bear the imprint of Thanasis?

Angelo knows by now that Thanasis's empty frappe cup is a signal to set his own sail. Giving his cousin an embrace of farewell, he steps out into the sunlight. The day, despite its small setback in regard to solving the mystery of the solitary girl in the cove, continues on a course as smooth and predictable as most other days.

The time arrives for Angelo to return to Yiayia's house. He stays downstairs to sit with Eleni. They don't say much, Angelo merely holding the old woman's hand. So different is Eleni's temperament in comparison with Yiayia Maria. Of course, the fact that Yiayia Eleni is considerably older could have a lot to do with it. Also, she has the benefit of living in a perfectly serene seaside village, constantly surrounded by her family.

Some days, after enjoying the simple routine, Angelo wishes he could extend his trip for the entire summer. Yet, on other days, he misses his American home. He calls his mother then and gets updates, though finds he isn't missing much. Craig is still in his mother's life—probably a good thing—and Yiayia continues to make her usual mischief.

When he finally checks a calendar, he's surprised that only a week has passed. It seems like much longer if he measures time by the amount of new sketches he's completed. His pad is nearly filled with detailed renderings of The Mythical Greek alongside faithful depictions of real-life village locals. During one of their phone calls, his mother says that Papou, during a visit to Greece, was inspired solely by the precision with which the sun sent shadows etching across the terrain and was compelled to capture such an effect in each piece he created afterward.

One sweltering evening after the siesta, he sits shirtless in Yiayia's yard, the pad in his lap, attempting to capture Uncle Elias. He's gotten the ever-so-unique protrusion of the man's belly down to his satisfaction. Now he just needs to be true to the otherworldly joy present in his uncle's squinty-eyed grin. Somewhere in the trees, a bird sings a song still foreign to Angelo's ears. Then he hears footsteps and turns to see his father emerging from the house clad in only his swimming trunks. He gently squeezes Angelo's shoulder.

"If you want to swim, you should get ready now." Then he adds, "Tonight we are meeting Xandria for dinner."

At last.

A short time later they take to the water. Angelo keeps pace with his father easily now, and they swim in silence that—at least on the surface—feels comfortable. The light shifts above them, purplish at the horizon, and Angelo, gazing into it, finds himself alone. Looking around, he sees his father swim to shore to retrieve a small net buried in the sand. By the time Angelo arrives, his father has collected several sea urchins in it. Then he reveals a small pocket knife like a child's magic trick. He splits the urchins with the blade, and they snack on the briny eggs as the sun descends into the ocean, Angelo almost expecting a hiss as the fiery ball is finally quenched.

"Better with lemon," Tasso remarks.

"And some bread," Angelo adds.

Tasso smiles. "Very Greek."

"You had that stuff stashed here? The net and the knife?"

"I figured we'd come swimming this evening. Thought it might be a nice surprise."

"Like Xandria?"

"Yes, I suppose."

"How come you've waited this long to introduce us?"

"You've only been here a week, Angelo. I wanted to be sure..."

"That I was ready?"

"That she was ready."

Angelo blinks, surprised. "How do you mean?"

Tasso meets Angelo's eyes in the rapidly fading light. For a moment there is only the lapping of waves on the sand and the cry of a gull. "Angelo, you're the most important person in my life. If I'm going to let a woman meet you, I have to be certain that she's worthy."

* * *

The curiosity that first descended upon Angelo after Tasso's last words on the beach only increases as his father guides the Peugeot along the harbor street. Of course he wants to ask questions, but greater is his desire to maneuver like a local with no impatience to greet the future and seemingly few regrets of the past. Instead, he watches a silver-mustachioed grandfather, perfectly picture-postcard Greek in a battered old fisherman's cap. The man sits at a taverna table fiddling with his *komboloi* while checking his modern cell phone. Nearby, a young boy dribbles a soccer ball between his feet.

Angelo eyes his father, trying to read him but failing, as usual. Given that Tasso is the kind of man who can have any woman he wants, Angelo is terribly curious about the one he is soon to meet.

Tasso turns into a side street that winds a short way up a hill past flowers dozing in the dusk. He parks in front of a small home; on the porch, a lounging giant German Shepherd mix lifts its massive head to peer at the car. Its ears stand alert, though its amber eyes look large and friendly.

Tasso steps out wearing starched, cream-colored slacks, polished brown dress shoes, and a white shirt with its sleeves rolled up to the elbows. Though his father has made no sign, Angelo waits in the car. The dog rolls onto its back to invite a belly rub, trustfully offering its vulnerable parts. Tasso complies for a moment then softly knocks on the door. A moment later it opens, Angelo straining to see what must surely be a goddess. Initially, he can only glimpse a shapely leg that seems to meet his expectations.

At last, Xandria reveals herself in full. Angelo's first impression is that she is indeed quite pretty, though not really a Helen. Still, he's not disappointed. She possesses a slender figure. Her chestnut hair reaches mid-back and frames a pleasantly-rounded face. No, not bad at all.

After leaving the car and mounting the porch, the dog of course checks him out as Angelo greets Xandria with the customary double-cheek kiss. "*Hairo polee*," he says.

"*Epesis*," Xandria offers in return. "I have heard so much about you."

"Likewise," Angelo says, lying. "It's great to finally put such a lovely face to the name."

Xandria smiles. "Not only are you handsome as you father, but you're just as charming."

"All right, you two," Tasso says, motioning them toward the car. "Plenty of time to talk on the way to the restaurant."

Angelo gets into the back seat. He's glad for the vantage point, able to watch his father's and Xandria's interactions. But they're really nothing special: they look just like any other couple comfortable with themselves and going out to dinner. Why had he expected something a lot more passionate?

Xandria turns to face him, dappled in shadow and light from windows as they drive along the street. "Your father and I went to school together here in the village. I remember you when you were very small. You wore a cap with silver wings on the sides, like the crown of Hermes."

Angelo recalls the silly hat but not having met Xandria and apologizes for that.

"Who at that age remembers old people?"

She isn't that old.

"Your father tells me that you used to talk of wanting to move to the village, own horses, and earn money by putting on puppet shows for the locals."

Angelo finds himself surprised that his father would remember such things. *But why should that seem a surprise?* He considers what he might do here, as in do for a living, if he actually stayed—not just the whole summer but longer—but then replies with a smile, "I think my plans may have changed a little since I wore that cap."

"But you're still interested in art?"

"Yes."

"What are you working on now?"

"I've seen some of it," Tasso answers before Angelo. "He's almost got enough to make a book. Sort of a..." He, too, pauses to get a grip on translation. "...graphic novel about a character called The Greek." He chuckles. "Sort of looks like me. It's really not bad."

Really not bad? Angelo is tempted to say that The Greek is based on himself, not his father, but that, too, would be childish. Instead he asks, "What do you do, Xandria?" *Assuming my dad doesn't keep you... which I would find hard to believe.*

"I work in Athens."

"You commute all that way every day? Why not just move to the city?" *Though I think I know the answer to that.*

Xandra smiles. "Because then I wouldn't have..."
Right!
"... Mama to make me delicious meals."
"Oh."
"And I only have to be in the office three days a week at most. The rest I can do from home online. My partner and I run a matchmaking service. I'm sure you have similar companies in the States. We do a form of Speed Dating. We're actually responsible for quite a few marriages."

"Interesting," is the only response Angelo can muster. Something feels like it's crumbling inside him; ruins giving way to time. Naive as it is from his present viewpoint, Angelo had imagined that even in the busy cities, Greeks would find romance in traditional ways.

A not uncomfortable silence settles as they leave the village behind, Angelo feeling a twinge of—something—as they pass the road leading to the "house." He half expects Tasso to give him a meaningful glance in the mirror, but the man only swerves to avoid a hedgehog. Angelo catches a glimpse of the animal as it scurries into the tall, dry grass. A little farther on, Tasso leaves the paved road for another narrow, dusty lane. They climb a steep hill, the road growing ever narrower as the Peugeot continues to ascend as if reaching to the now risen moon.

At last, Tasso brings the car to a stop at what seems the summit, though appears to be only an empty field. More tall grass, olive and pine trees. Then Angelo spots a small, wooden A-frame house with four picnic tables out front, glass-shielded candles glowing on them. Only one is occupied by two men sitting across from each other, a ceramic jug of wine between them, glasses half-filled with what may be *krasee*.

"Here we are," Tasso says, stepping from the car. "Angelo, you're going to love this place. They make the best *paithakia* around. Those are my friends, Mihalis and Zacharia... whom you might recognize."

They reach the table. Angelo claims a spot on the bench beside Zacharia, whom he does find familiar though unplaceable. Then it dawns on him: Mr. Skourtis! Upon closer glance, the man looks almost the same as when Angelo last saw him so many years ago. Except now he appears to have more hair on his forearms and bristling from the top of his shirt than on his moonlit head. Tasso and Xandria, meanwhile, take seats on the opposite bench beside Mihalis, a swarthy fellow with rugged features and a piercing gaze. They all clink wine glasses and shout, "*Yiamas!*"

Then, Angelo turns to Mr. Skourtis and asks, "Are you on vacation, too?"

"No, no," Mr. Skourtis says. "I closed the diner and moved back a couple years after your father." He wraps a hefty arm around Angelo's shoulder. "*Ela*, my friend, which do you prefer: *Ellada* or America?"

On the verge of giving his usual diplomatic answer, Angelo takes a breath and thinks, *what the hell*? "Greece. *Ellada* all the way." *At least while I'm here.*

This provokes an uproar of cheers and another clink of wine glasses. After, Mr. Skourtis asks, "Have the ways of the *kamaki* revealed themselves to you yet?"

Angelo clears his throat. "Not exactly."

Mr. Skourtis seems to consider. "Perhaps you should count that as a blessing. Save yourself many a headache."

Angelo frowns, on the verge of asking the man to explain, but then the food arrives: bountiful village salads, warm bread and *tzatziki*, platters heaped with fried potatoes, and the specialty—lamb chops grilled to perfection. Angelo eats slowly, savoring each bite, while everyone else chatters in rapid-fire Greek. He tries to keep pace with the conversation at first but finally gives up. His eyes stay on his father and Xandria. Tasso holds court as usual, speaking as much with his hands as his voice, impersonating people unknown to Angelo, though he feels he knows them after Tasso's caricatures.

More intriguing, though, is how Tasso interacts with Xandria. Not through words but through body language. Every so often, the two of them seem to share a brief private moment, smiling with their heads leaned close like longtime friends—or lovers—who often share each other's thoughts. Angelo is surprised to see his father's hand tremble ever so slightly as it closes over Xandria's, surprised even further when Tasso's cheeks flush a bit in the candlelight while looking into the woman's eyes. Reaching to refill her glass, Tasso knocks it over with very un-Tasso-like clumsiness.

"*Opa!*" Tasso shouts, grabbing a napkin to blot the wine as it drenches the tablecloth. Xandria helps, and four hands work fast to clean up the mess. Again, their eyes meet, Tasso looking almost embarrassed. Finally, they pile a heap of wet napkins off to one side, and Tasso fills Xandria's wine glass with almost childish care.

Angelo realizes that he's never seen this man before. In the moonlight and the candle glow, his father appears boyishly handsome.

Angelo is no longer so hungry but keeps eating because the food is delicious and because it gives him something else on which to focus. And he continues downing more wine, the glasses small—juice glasses for children—so there proves a great discrepancy between how much he assumes he's drinking and how much he's actually consumed.

Soon, the edges of his vision blur, the world glimpsed through a filter of fuzzy candle and moon-lit haze. Then he's smiling for no apparent reason, relishing the carefree laughter emanating from Mihalis. Greek words hover like hummingbirds in the air above his head, a garble of conjugated verbs somehow aiding his buzz.

"You're so quiet over there," Xandria says at last, her words taking a moment to register. "Had enough to eat?"

Angelo leans back, pats his belly, and stifles a burp. "Yes."

Tasso smiles. Then, slipping an arm around Xandria, he lifts his glass with his free hand and offers it across the table. "*Yiamas*, son."

Angelo clinks his glass and echoes his father.

Tasso gazes at him for a time, eyes reflecting the golden candle, then says, "Stay on your flight path, *re*."

Angelo blinks. "Flight path?"

"Like a good pilot. So you will reach your true destination."

Angelo shakes some clouds from his head. "And where is that?"

"Wherever you are yourself."

"Wherever you go, there you are."

Those words seem just nonsense he's read somewhere, but Tasso says seriously, "You make me very proud, Angelo."

Angelo says, "I do?" before he can catch himself.

Tasso cocks his head in mock wonder then laughs. As a much younger Angelo might say, "Duh."

TWENTY-FOUR

THE PELOPONNESE REGION of Greece resembles a hand with three splayed fingers, the grasp of a giant reaching into the ocean; fitting, since this section of land holds such prominence in the scope of world history. Traces of many ancient sites are scattered across its rugged flesh, birthplace to a plethora of Grecian traditions and heroes, both mythical and real. To the east, at the edge of what could be viewed as the pinkie of this hand, lies the village from which Tasso hails. Further up is the site of the ancient theater of Epidavros, still home to some of the best natural acoustics in the world. Further on is the city of Nafplio, the country's first modern capital. A bit to the west is the site of Mycenaea, the ancient city-state once belonging to King Agamemnon.

It seems to Angelo, examining the map spread across his thighs, that the distance separating all these places is too great to traverse in a single day, but his father assures him that's not the case. According to Tasso, a journey around the entire peninsula can be accomplished in a few days. This trip won't even require traveling half that mileage.

Angelo sits on the edge of his bed as morning sun filters through the curtains. He awoke about five minutes before, surprised to see that his father hadn't left for work but instead stood over him with the map in hand. Today is the day, apparently, though Tasso has given no previous hint. *But this is Greece*, Angelo thinks, *land of spontaneous action regardless of any consequences, and let the feathers fall where they may.*

Today is also the day, Angelo seems certain, when he will confront his father about their past troubles and try to reach an understanding, never mind the outcome.

"If you want to eat something before we go, better hurry," Tasso says, entering the room again, gleaming from a shower.

Angelo thinks of a shower, too, but his father looks impatient. To be with him, he wonders—despite what he'd said on that evening with Xandria—or just to get this over with, like a session of quality time prescribed by conscience if not by a court? "It's all right. I can wait."

Soon they are on the road. Pink Floyd's *Dark Side of the Moon* plays on the stereo. Good driving music though it is, the album would enhance the experience more if the traffic flowed as smoothly as the soundtrack; if the drivers sharing the morning highway weren't Greek drivers who stomped their brakes and smashed the gas, swerving among the two lanes like demolition derbyists hungry for collisions—or at least for the thrill of narrowly avoiding them.

Angelo gradually adjusts to the spastic rhythm of the ride. Momentum lurches him forward and then shoves him back against the seat with bobble-head effects. Not that Tasso seems to be having any trouble navigating this chaos.

Trash lines the roadside; odd that Angelo didn't notice it, or at least this much of it, on the way from Athens. The landscape is tarnished by discarded food containers, paper goods, and random plastic. Aluminum cans glare in the sun, scattered in the dry yellow grass and around the bases of byway trees like garish, rotting fruit. Outside the cities, recycling and other methods of trash reduction have been slow to be accepted by people who, for many centuries, had little post-consumer waste.

Tasso pulls off the main road and drives into a small village, no more than a dozen little houses, a church, a *kafenion*, and a bakery. They stop at the bakery, and Tasso buys loaves of olive bread and cold bottles of *lemonada* from the proprietor. Angelo asks him about the economic crisis, expecting the man to cringe or yammer out a panicked rant about some quickly impending doom. But the baker only shrugs and says, "*Ellada* has weathered countless wars, countless catastrophes. This she will also weather in time."

And probably litter, too.

The bread is fresh and warm and immediately staves their hunger, while the lemonades counteract the rapidly increasing heat. Angelo is just finishing his share as they come to their first stop on this tour: Epidavros. At the ancient theater, Angelo stands center stage. It's nothing more than a wide round of earth backdropped by a cluster of trees and facing a towering half circle of thousand-plus-year-old stadium seating. Yet he seems to feel it vibrate with the collective breaths of unseen spirits.

But the living are not absent here: tourists speak a variety of languages, as if reenacting the Tower of Babble, while cameras snap and whir in a chorus of captured moments. Angelo looks around for his father and finally spots him on one of the weathered stone slabs of the bleachers. Angelo breathes deeply and listens, but if there are any birds, their songs are drowned by the chattering tourists. Surely he will recognize, or there will be a sign, when the time has come—as the Walrus said—to talk of many things.

Back in the car, they reach Nafplio to take a walk through the city's Old Town. The Venetian influence is readily apparent in the architecture, which utilizes dramatic archways and beautiful wrought iron balconies. They trek to the harbor with its view of Bourtzi castle as it rises from the middle of the ocean like a relic of Atlantis. Then they move on to the castle of Palamidi, a giant fortress accessible via more than a thousand steps that ascend the steep mountainside.

Angelo puts a hand to his brow, shading his eyes against the sun, and gazes up at the structure high above the city. He's overcome by a sudden urge to be up there, almost as if something waits for him—*the sign he's half expecting? The sign he feels he deserves?*

"Let's give it a shot, Dad," he says, finger pointed skyward.

Tasso thoughtfully eyes the castle. "That's quite a climb, Angelo. I've done it before, but it's not easy."

"I want to, Dad."

"You sure? In this heat?"

"Yes."

"Okay. After you."

They ascend, and despite his need or hope, it isn't long before Angelo feels the burn in his leg muscles. Ropes of fire coil along his calves and up the backs of his thighs. He keeps his gaze on the ancient steps, watching his feet rise again and again. The surface is slippery in places where the stone has been worn as smooth as glass by the tread of centuries' of feet shod in everything from sandals to combat boots and Nikes. He slips a few times, but Tasso is right behind him to prevent a fall. Higher and higher they climb. The reward upon reaching the castle is a mighty view of the entire city and the sparkling ocean beyond. No wonder royalty chose to fortify their kingdom at this particular spot where surroundings can be viewed from all sides, and any attack from even the most formidable foe could be anticipated and promptly thwarted.

"The Venetians built this place. Really something, isn't it?" Tasso says, resting a palm on Angelo's shoulder and, surprisingly, puffing a bit.

Angelo nods, his own chest heaving. The air up here is fresh and sea-scented, feeling clean as if it were new and the first to be breathed by gods. He watches a flock of seagulls collect at the very crest of the castle.

"Dad?"

"Yes?"

But Angelo suddenly feels dizzy, wavers dangerously close to the cliff's sheer edge. His father grabs his arm. "Careful, Angelo, this isn't America where they put rails around everything."

"Yeah, I should've remembered that."

Tasso studies him with concern. "Are you all right?"

"I'm fine. Guess it was just the climb." Angelo smiles a little. "Even being here all this time I'm not in as good a shape as you."

Tasso laughs. "I'm wearier than I may look, Angelo. Let's rest awhile. What were you about to ask me?"

"I... forgot."

They stay for another twenty minutes or so in silence, admiring the view. Finally, they begin the descent. Angelo glances back once, up to that clear quiet place in the sky, the very place he would have imagined choosing to hash things out with his father. But the words just hadn't come, the altitude perhaps rendering the air too thin for serious discussion. Angelo feels little frustration, however. Greece may be a place fit for spontaneity, but it's also a land where all things come together as they are meant to in due time.

Back on human soil again, immersed in twenty-first century air, they stop at a small kiosk to buy sodas and snacks before driving on. A while later, they stand under the Lion Gates at Mycenae. The lions are carved into the rock in hind-legged stances, heads lifted skyward as though in mid-roar; two jungle kings baring savage teeth over a single crown.

Interesting though they are, it's not an especially remarkable place. The air is just air. Not much different from the Oakland breeze on a hot summer day. The only bird in sight is a single scruffy crow pecking at bits of tourist litter. It seems indifferent to Angelo, like a homeless gypsy child who sees no hope in begging. Yet suddenly Angelo asks, "Dad, why did you leave?"

Tasso looks puzzled. "I've been right here the whole time."

"No. I mean why did you leave the country, America, after you and Mom split up?"

The crow gives a caw, which sounds more derisive than encouraging.

Tasso steps back a pace as if trying to size up Angelo, the sun directly behind him so he morphs into a dark silhouette against a backdrop of luminous gold.

Strangely, the crow's mocking croak seems to give Angelo strength or maybe just fires his anger. "Can't you say something? Anything?"

"I didn't *just* leave," Tasso finally responds. "And you know that. Where is this coming from all the sudden?"

"Excuse me, do you speak English?"

It takes a moment for Angelo to realize that he's being asked that question. He turns to see a family of four—Mom, Dad, Buddy and Sis—obviously American in their Old Navy gear and bright fanny packs.

"Yeah," he says a little gruffly, annoyed by this inane interruption.

The father holds out a digital camera. "Would you take our picture in front of the gate?"

Again the crow makes a mocking sound, and Angelo feels another flash of anger. This obviously isn't the right place. Or the right time. And, like everything else in his life, he's seemingly fucked this up, too.

He takes the camera and forces a smile. Feeling like the cynical crow who must have seen this thousands of times, he waits for the family to pose, carefully sights through the viewfinder—this is important to them—and snaps a picture.

"Thank you very much," the mother says, slowly and distinctly, and then they are gone, probably to purchase refrigerator magnets shaped like the Parthenon.

"Can you answer my question?" Tasso asks abruptly.

"What?"

"Why are you asking this now?"

Angelo glances at the crow. *Guess it's as good a time as any.* "We need to talk about this, Dad. *I* need to talk about this. Don't tell me you never think about the way things ended between you and Mom... and between us."

Tasso looks puzzled again, genuinely puzzled and not just stalling to think of an answer. After a time he says, "I thought we'd grown beyond it. Moved on with our lives, and put it behind us."

Angelo frowns. "You obviously have. But that's no surprise. It would've been easy for you."

"Easy? Why would you think...?" Now Tasso looks angry, though just for a moment, then he spreads his palms. "What else could I have done, Angelo? In the States, aside from you and your mother, I was practically alone."

Angelo starts to speak, but Tasso holds up a hand. "The Greek community, you are about to say? Just because there is one, such as there is where we lived, does not mean I felt I belonged to it. And when I moved out of our house, I *was* really alone, so what was I to do?" He eyes the crow as if it might be an eavesdropper, a witness to an admission of something that should have been private. "I waited until you were almost eighteen, until you were on the verge of becoming a man. Then it was time. Not to get away from you, but to get back to myself. To again be the man I really am in a place where I truly belong. In a place where I'm not alone." His earnest eyes hold Angelo's. "I'm sorry if it seems like I abandoned you. Truly I am. I kept in touch as much as I could through the years, right?"

"Yes," Angelo admits.

"And still, I'm sorry. That things didn't work out between me and your mother. That sometimes I took out my anger on you. That I wasn't a better man than I am. What more can I say?"

Angelo studies the scruffy old crow, which now appears to study him back through eyes like molten gold. This suddenly seems very anticlimactic after all these years of building up. Unfair that the truth should be so simple: that his father wasn't a better man. But, no, not simply a better man, but the *perfect* man who Angelo always thought he should be. Who Angelo thought he deserved. *Why? Because his own life wasn't perfect?* Wasn't even average, because of how he'd been born imperfect?

There seems to be a million things he could say— perhaps a million things he *should* say—but he finally just says, "Thanks, Dad."

"You are not disappointed in me? Or angry?"

"No, Dad. Not anymore… Did I ever have any right to be?"

Tasso regards the crow again, who has gone back to scavenging trash. "Of course you did. But it is you who must decide if you want to hold onto that anger, to carry it with you for life. As we grow older, Angelo—or maybe I should say mature—we realize that those who should never let us down probably will, in one way or another. But that does not mean they still don't love you. It only means…"

Angelo nods. "That no one is perfect. And sometimes maybe that's your own fault for expecting perfection. Comic book heroes who have no faults."

Tasso smiles. "Even Greek heroes were never perfect. Nor were their gods."

Angelo smiles now. "Can I ask you another question?"

"That's a question already."

"*Déjà vu*. Is Xandria really the first woman you've been with in a while?"

"Who told you that?"

"My cousins."

"So typically Greek. And yes."

"I guess your *kamaki* days really are behind you then."

Tasso laughs. "The past is behind us all. Besides, I told you that I was never really much of a—"

But Angelo cuts him off with, "You're not disappointed in me anymore?"

"Anymore? Angelo, I was never disappointed in you. If sometimes I was hard on you, it wasn't because I was trying to make you meet my expectations. I only tried to show that you weren't as..." Tasso seems to consider word choices, and Angelo makes it easy for him.

"Handicapped?"

"I suppose that must do," Tasso agrees. "As handicapped as you thought you were."

"As in, be all you can be?"

Tasso does not seem to get the reference, yet he clearly understands the meaning. "Yes, Angelo, all you can be if you want to be it."

The crow takes wing and circles, seeming to perform aerobatics only to show that it can, cawing down at Angelo, who simply ignores it.

His father puts a hand on his shoulder. "Time to go home, son. Are you hungry? We didn't have lunch. And by the time we get home, Voula and Elias will have already eaten. There's a good *souvlaki* place just up the road."

"Oh. I'm okay, Dad. Unless you want to stop?"

"What about something to drink? Are you thirsty?"

Angelo is about to say no; he's tired and just wants to get home. But then he reconsiders. "Sure, Dad. And a *souvlaki* sounds good."

TWENTY-FIVE

THE DAYS PASS. Try as Angelo does to grasp moments and keep them from flying away like birds, they disappear from the cage anyhow. At their essence, these hours are simply intervals shaped around meals: moments spent waiting to eat, those spent eating, and those spent digesting. Angelo comes to realize one afternoon that Tasso did do his best and perhaps a lot better than his father had done for him.

Clad in a floral print dress while seated out in the garden on those early evenings after the siesta time, Yiayia Eleni gazes at Angelo with sad, wet eyes while whispering his name and pointing a finger skyward to trace an arc among the clouds. It's as if Eleni is at once coming to terms with his eventual departure, preparing herself for the inevitable loss, while simultaneously giving Angelo the signal that it's okay to leave; drawing a flight plan on which he will safely fly home. Suspecting he will never see her again, Angelo spends extra time with Yiayia in the mornings after breakfast, sitting by her bed to hold her hand and share a smile, though he hopes she will be here next year.

Similarly, all his cousins come around in the afternoons and often ask about his future plans. He tells them that in all likelihood he will return next summer and doesn't want another extended period to keep them apart. Impossible now, he assures them, since these connections have been re-established. His cousins still want to know more about America, as though such knowledge will feed some part of them long left malnourished. Angelo's advice to cherish their Greece seems mostly dismissed as irrelevant. They seem to find it hard to believe that even by jet airplane it takes over five hours to cross the U.S. from coast to coast when one could fly from Greece and across most of Europe in such a long time.

Tasso is also obviously aware that his and Angelo's time together is quickly approaching an end, though he has an odd, perhaps typically Greek, way of showing it. He makes an ever-growing list of things he wants Angelo to send him: his vintage *Bouzouki*, a box of clothes probably still collecting dust in the back of Despina's closet, an address book, also in the closet, tucked between two pages of which is a copy of his contractor's license, and a framed photograph of him and Angelo in front of the eagle enclosure at the San Francisco Zoo, taken when Angelo was a boy, among other things. Angelo, of course, promises to do so.

It seems the news of his impending departure has also made its rounds through the village. Angelo is unable to take a stroll without being stopped on multiple occasions—sometimes by complete strangers—who want to know how he feels about leaving. Some ask if he wouldn't mind saying hello to a relative of theirs in America, no matter how many times he tries to explain that it's a very big place.

Then there are the dreams that begin the Sunday night of his final week in Greece: vividly detailed depictions of how his return trip might go wrong; methodical scenes of him packing bags, trudging through an airport in search of his gate, navigating security, and finally boarding the plane. The flight itself must be uneventful because he never remembers it. After landing and going through customs, his passport is always gone. Instead, he pulls out a booklet of photos from his Greek vacation, upon which, of course, the agent roars, "Entry denied!" and vague uniformed figures surround him.

One morning, after having breakfast and spending some time with Yiayia, he accompanies Aunt Voula to the home of a friend who lives on the outskirts of the village. The woman, named Stephania, has a stone house on a stretch of land lush with fruit trees—great thick-trunked varieties, their branches heavy with cherries, plums, and peaches. Sunlight filters between the green leaves and dapples the earth with shadow, and birds serenade among the foliage. While Voula and Stephania sit at a marble-topped table and chat over coffee, Angelo is given the task of collecting ripe fruit in a basket. From a shed he extracts a rickety ladder, leans it against a tree, and ascends. He fills the basket with cherries, then climbs down to place it next to Stephania's chair before getting another basket and dragging the ladder to another tree. When this basket is full of plums, he drops off the goods then goes to get more. Gradually, he begins to sweat with the heat and the work, his shirt sticking to his back, clinging to the skin under his arms. Despite this, he savors the sweet scent of the fruit, the different textures against his palms, the fuzzy peach skin, the slickness of plums, the collective weight of cherries by the bunches. When he's finally finished, having combed the entire orchard, he returns the ladder to the shed and joins the women at the table.

Stephania inspects the harvest as if Angelo is being paid by the basket, though always nodding approval. She brings him a glass of water, and just when he thinks it's time to rest, she directs him toward a young apricot tree. With a sigh, he gets up and goes to it, gazing in puzzlement over his shoulder when all he finds are smallish bulbs of fruit still mostly green. Then Stephania joins him, parting the branches so he stands beneath a canopy of leaves that glows with sunlight. At last Angelo sees it. At the back of the tree, almost shimmering like some soft jewel, a single, ripe apricot. He looks over at Stephania as she motions for him to take it. He does so tentatively, almost as if afraid it will burst in his grasp. But it doesn't; it feels firm and heavy for its size. The branch it clings to bends as he pulls, reluctant to surrender its gem. And then it comes free, and Angelo steps back to admire it.

"Eat," Stephania says, her voice as small as a bird's.

Angelo takes a bite, a bit of juice dribbling down his chin, and he knows that this is the best apricot he has ever tasted. This apricot has to be the archetype on which all others are based. Voula smiles. He savors the rest of the apricot, taking small bites and chewing slowly, wanting another when the first is gone too quickly.

Stephania divides up the collected bounty, loading Angelo's arms with a few full bags before sending him and Voula off. They walk back to the village, the sacks over Angelo's shoulders. Finally, as they near their house, he can contain his curiosity no longer.

"Why do we need so much fruit?" he asks.

"How do you say in English, is good for you, no?"

"But so much?"

"Maybe I will make some *pites mai fruta*. Keep you healthy and strong for your journey back to America."

"The time has gone by fast, hasn't it?"

"Yes. We are all so sad that you must leave us soon, but we know you will come back."

"Yes, Thia."

"And when you finish your studies in another year, maybe you will come to live with us for just a little while?"

Angelo looks away. He hadn't considered such a thing, but perhaps it would be nice to try an extended stay, give this land adequate time to continue making him over in its likeness. "Maybe, Thia," he says. "If I'm able."

"I hope so," The woman replies. "Do you know why I had you come along to Stephania's house? It is because I wanted you to do some real work while you are still here. To get a feel for what our days are really like in and around the village. How can you truly experience Greece if all your time is spent on the beach or at the *taverna* or taking pictures of ancient things? How can the land penetrate your soul if its soil never touches your fingers? And besides, a little work will do you good as you prepare to leave. It will help your mind again become disciplined, and the transition won't be so difficult when you arrive in your other home."

Angelo nods. "I hadn't thought about that, but I think you're right. And it's also a way to thank you for all you've done for me while I've been here."

This last statement stops Voula in her tracks. She kicks up dust as she turns sharply to face him, hands to her hips. "You don't need to thank me for any of that, you hear? We are family. It is only what families do."

Angelo thinks he has given offense. "I didn't mean anything by it."

Voula begins walking again. "I know. Now, will you be willing to help Elias when we get to the house?"

"Of course."

"Let's hurry then. I'm sure those bags are growing heavy."

That proves an understatement as, by the time they arrive home, the sacks seem to have doubled in weight. Angelo sets them down on the front steps, Voula going up without him while he hangs back to catch his breath and admire the sea. It's an even deeper blue today, sparkling under the sun and promising cool relief from the heat, sure to revive his tired muscles. *Four days,* he thinks while peering into the horizon on which a sailboat passes, its Greek flag fluttering in the wind. In four days, this will be part of the patchwork from which memories are woven.

"*Pou esouna, re*?" Uncle Elias calls to him from a ladder set against the front of the house. He wears nothing but cut-off jean shorts and a ball cap, a paint bucket hanging beside him, his hand wielding a thick-bristled brush.

"What are you doing?" Angelo asks, shading his eyes against the sun.

"Taking a break," the man replies, beginning a heavy-footed descent that seems to test the old ladder. Once on the ground, he takes a stretch and scratches at his gargantuan belly, then hands Angelo the brush as if it's a relay baton. "Enjoy."

"*Ah*, this I have to see."

Angelo turns to find his father, just emerged from the house in swim trunks and sandals, gazing at him with arms crossed over wiry chest, his expression holding encouragement. Angelo realizes that Tasso would never have expected him to either climb a ladder or paint. Too fragile, maybe, or too clumsy. He ascends the ladder, dunks his brush, and gets to work. He uses long, steady strokes, careful to catch drips, covering the wall with a fresh coat of white. From up here he can see the adjacent rooftops, tile baking in the heat. In the mouth of one chimney there lies a nest which he suspects belongs to a hawk. The eyases stretch and crane their fragile necks toward the sun like flowers moving with the light. He watches them for a long time, transfixed as their tiny beaks open and close in hopes of catching nourishment that has not yet arrived.

Some birds mate for life, he knows. The males of certain types build elaborate dwellings to attract a partner, utilizing twigs and plant debris, even bright scraps of ribbon and bits of aluminum or glass in hopes of winning their objects of admiration. The males of other varieties go so far as to sit on the eggs while the females search for food.

Angelo looks down at his father, the man still watching him from below, and then returns to his task, confident that he is doing a good job, one Tasso can be proud of. It seems Voula was right: the work invigorates him, and he knows a little bit of what Uncle Elias goes through six days a week—when things are steady—and what his cousins experience in helping their fathers with the construction jobs. He paints the entire front of the house. When he's finished, he surprisingly craves another task. Aunt Voula says that in fact she does have something else for him to do, but first they must have the midday meal.

"He's a good boy," Elias says as they sit down to eat, speaking as if Angelo is not in the room.

"A man," Tasso corrects, putting a hand on Angelo's shoulder.

Angelo feels as he did on that morning over a month ago, when Tasso first greeted him at the airport. A man though he is, he can still be made to feel like a boy glowing under his father's approval, but maybe that is natural.

After the meal, Elias and Tasso retire to their rooms for the siesta. Angelo stays upstairs with Voula, resting on the couch while she cleans dishes before joining him on the sofa.

"I would like you to paint something for us."

Angelo smiles. "The rest of the house?"

"A mural on the wall of the front room downstairs."

Angelo cocks his head. "Of what?"

"You are the artist."

"Okay. You have smaller brushes? And more paint? Different colors besides white?"

"Of course."

In the front room downstairs, right as one enters through the wrought iron side entrance, Voula lays old tarp on the floor and furnishes Angelo with supplies then leaves him alone. For a long time he just stares at the wall, but ideas eventually come.

According to his grad-school professors, there are no mistakes in art, only opportunities to consider new possibilities, to turn blemishes into beauty. No way of sticking especially close to notions preconceived. One can't paint or draw successfully from a position of fear, whether it be fear of making a mistake or the criticism of others or even complete failure. This was difficult to accept at first, in the early days of his studies, but such a constriction began to shape his creative process. It steers him along now, a random splash of blue becoming the beginnings of a seascape, another errant stroke of his brush giving birth to the ocean floor. A tremendous task to create something worthy of Yiayia's home, but he paints through doubt and fatigue, through time itself.

Eventually, the shifting of light through the window causes him to look around and see shades of evening tinting the room. His hands are caked with drying pigment, the tarp at his feet a kaleidoscope of multi-hued spatters. He steps back to examine his work, a grand imagining of life below the ocean's surface. Fish large and small are rendered in silver tones, octopi share rock space with anemones and urchins and coral. Above this ocean scene, toward the ceiling, a winged boy is shown soaring near the sun, his appendages withstanding the heat so that he remains airborne despite the risk.

After cleaning up, he goes upstairs to tell everyone that the piece is complete. All together they collect in the front room to see Angelo's creation. Eleni is helped out of bed so she can see it, too, and they all gaze and murmur in evident admiration.

Angelo feels self-conscious, the sensation increasing as the entire family is invited over to view his mural. One by one they arrive, congratulating Angelo on his work. It quickly turns into a party as food is brought over from the *souvlaki* place up the hill, and homemade wine is distributed out of recycled water bottles. Chairs are carried out to the yard, and they sit to eat under the stars. Angelo is hungry, and his stomach soon grows tight and warm with the food and wine. Amongst the talk and the laughter, he feels serene, nearly lulled to sleep. He thinks of an honest day's work for an honest day's pay. *Or is it the other way around?*

At some point, the phone rings inside the house. Voula rises to answer it then hurries back to tell Angelo that the call is for him. He takes it in the front room, away from all the commotion, where he can see his mural while he talks.

"Hi, Angelo."

"Hey, Ma."

"Ready to come home soon?"

"Don't have much of a choice."

"Glad to hear you're enjoying yourself."

"It's great here! Especially now after... well, I'll tell you about it when I get home. Still, I'm kind of looking forward to returning."

A long pause. "Angelo, there's something I have to tell you.

For some reason Angelo looks up at the flying boy, who still seems safely aloft. "What is it?"

"Yiayia had a heart attack a few nights ago."

"Is she okay now?"

"She's doing a lot better. She's even back here in the house. The doctors found that overall she's in good health. But she might be bedridden for a long time. I wanted to give you warning before you came back, that's all, but I don't want you to worry."

"Well, it's natural to worry about something like that." Angelo looks up at the boy again. "Is there anything else? It's okay, Ma, don't worry about me worrying." He wishes she could see his smile. "I've had a lot of practice at it."

Despina seems to hesitate but then says. "I haven't mentioned anything the other times we've talked because, really, I don't want you to worry. But it seems

Yiayia is in the early stages of Alzheimer's. It's progressed fast, but she's still pretty aware."

"Meaning she remembers who you are?"

"Most of the time. But she's quiet these days."

"I'm sorry, Ma. I don't know what to say."

"There isn't much to say, honey. These things are a part of life."

"Yeah, I guess they are."

"I'm sorry I had to let you know like this. Just promise me you'll enjoy these last few days of your trip. And don't worry about things that you can't do anything about. Yiayia wouldn't want that."

Angelo nods before remembering, like his smile, it can't be seen. "Okay."

"I should let you go now. I'm sorry about the bad news."

"Don't be, Ma. I'm glad you told me so I'll be prepared. Give Yiayia my love."

"I will. We'll see you soon. And everything will be fine flying home."

"I know."

"Angelo?"

"Still here, Ma."

"How are things between you and your father?"

"Good, Ma. But the details can wait until I get home."

"Yes."

"Okay. Bye, Ma."

"Goodbye, Angelo."

Angelo gazes at the painting a while after hanging up. It's some of his best work, and those wings, at least, will never fail. He goes back outside where the voices of his relatives are united in song. He sits close to Yiayia Eleni, touching her hand. She turns to him, offering a smile. Then she dabs her eyes with a tissue and points her index finger skyward, indicating the way back home through the night mist and the stars high above.

TWENTY-SIX

AT THE AIRPORT on his final Friday morning, Angelo realizes that he has no idea how to tell his father goodbye. Just saying the word, whether in Greek or English, simply doesn't seem meaningful enough. And yet to say more will feel insincere, words spoken only to fill empty space—a space somehow too vast to leave empty but maybe too intimidating in its very vastness to attempt to fill with words. And so he just stands there, carry-on bag slung over a shoulder. He considers that perhaps their farewells have already been said and in meaningful ways, his family wishing him safe travels and a quick return to their open arms.

"Go now, *re*. Don't miss your plane," Tasso says, finally. "But give me a hug first."

Angelo embraces his father, savoring that trace of aftershave, the stubbled cheek brushing his own. "I love you, Dad."

"I love you, too, Angelo. Remember, stay on your flight plan."

That is all that needs to be said, for the words feel right. Angelo nods then heads for security, allowing himself only one look back to see Tasso still standing there watching him. He almost expects a wave then remembers something he'd read, an old seafaring tradition carried on into the times of flight and followed now by airplane pilots: wave a ship out of sight and you may never see her again.

Aboard the plane, he feels alone but not anxious. From his carry-on he extracts the most recent sketch of The Greek to tinker with it, perhaps to adjust the figure's smile so that it appears more sincere.

"I guess this is me," a young woman says, stowing her luggage overhead before taking the seat next to Angelo. "Did you draw that?"

Angelo's wings only falter a moment, a single missed beat but no altitude lost. "I did."

"It's awesome. Believe it or not, I was an art major in college. Sculpture."

Angelo's smile comes naturally. "Why wouldn't I believe it? You've got an artist's aura."

"Thank you," says the young woman. "But I haven't done anything in years. Seeing a sketch like that makes me want to get back to my own stuff. I'm Phaedra, by the way."

"Angelo," says Angelo before adding, "Plans in London?"

"Actually, I'm going to San Francisco. I'm from the Bay Area."

"Cool. Me, too."

Phaedra smiles, too. "That is cool. I assume you're Greek? You sure look like it. In the best way."

"Greek-American. Headed home after visiting my roots."

"Small world, so am I. My family lives in Athens."

"Mine is still in the *horyo*."

"That must be nice, even with the economy."

"I think so. They have, well, maybe call it a more optimistic perspective."

Phaedra nods. "I can understand how they would, being closer to their past. Maybe with the wisdom of history, if you know what I mean?"

"I think I do."

"We might have a lot to talk about, if you feel like talking."

Angelo smiles again. "I do."

The plane ascends. A different airline, though these skies indeed seem friendly.

"Cocktails?"

Angelo smiles at Phaedra. Then he glances up at the flight attendant and says, "Please. For two."

END

ACKNOWLEDGMENTS

I'd like to express gratitude toward the people instrumental in the creation of this book:

My professors at the Mills College Creative Writing MFA program—Micheline Marcom and Patricia Powell, in particular, whose feedback and insights helped shape the novel's early drafts.

My old friend and fellow author Jess Mowry—also a source of invaluable feedback in regard to my writing.

My entire team—April Gerard, Jessica West, Kathryn Galán, and Shari Ryan. It's a pleasure working with you all, and I can't thank you enough.

Excerpts of this novel were previously published, in slightly different form, in *Sparkle + Blink* 63 (Quiet Lightning 2015) and in *Φωνές (Voices) Vol. 1 & 3* (Voices of Hellenism 2013 & 2015). A special thank you to Annamarie Buonocore, Alexandra Kostoulas, and Evan Karp for igniting a spark.

ABOUT THE AUTHOR

APOLLO PAPAFRANGOU is a writer of novels, short stories, and poems. He is a graduate of the Mills College Creative Writing MFA program and is the author of *Concrete Candy*, a short story collection published when he was just fifteen years old by Anchor Books, with French and Danish editions.

He has since written for HBO Films, which optioned the movie rights to his novel *The Fence*, and his fiction has appeared in the Simon & Schuster anthology *Trapped*, and *Voices*, a collection of works by Greek writers published by Nine Muses Press, among other publications.

He attributes his passion for storytelling to being raised in a Greek-American household where the epics of his ancestors were combined with contemporary family lore. If he wasn't an author, Apollo would be a singer-songwriter under the moniker Greek Lightning, wooing audiences with stormy R&B ballads.

Apollo lives in Oakland, California.

To stay in touch with the author, visit his website at www.apollopapafrangou.com. Sign up for the email newsletter to receive the latest word from Apollo, in addition to exclusive content and giveaways.

If you enjoyed reading Wings of Wax, please consider leaving a review on the website of your purchase and/or Goodreads.

61039323R00151

Made in the USA
Charleston, SC
15 September 2016